Intro

From Famine to Feast by Pame

Once a wealthy socialite, Olivia has lost everything—family, home, position. Starting over as a lowly Harvey Girl isn't exactly her idea of a good time, but God has other plans. Wayne Gregory is a man of determination and grit. He's struggling to unite his family, provide a home, and come to terms with his new position in life. Against the mesmerizing background of Arizona's Grand Canyon, both Olivia and Gregory find that starting over together can take them *From Famine to Feast*.

Armed and Dangerous by Dianne Christner

Harvey Girl Edie Harris gets her wish for adventure when robbers besiege her train. As the only person who can identify one of the robbers, Edie's assistance in sketching a wanted poster is procured by Ranger Wade Sloan of the Arizona Territory. When her life eerily parallels her newly purchased dime novel, Edie imagines the outlaw will seek revenge. Even worse, she fears the ranger and his love.

The Richest Knight by Nancy J. Farrier

Lillian Robinson will do anything to escape her life of poverty. She becomes a Harvey Girl to find a husband who can give her the riches she wants. Coming from a wealthy, powerful family, Franklin Knight desires to escape that lifestyle and find God's will for him. Will Lillian understand the value of a heart for God from *The Richest Knight* before she makes the worst mistake of her life?

Shelter from the Storm by Darlene Mindrup

Fleeing from an abusive and violent husband, Katie O'Neil takes on a new identity as a Harvey Girl and hides out in Arizona. Her past catches up with her when her brother-in-law arrives one day unannounced. Having loved Katie for years, Clay O'Neil struggles with whether his interest is for her benefit or his own. Only God can heal Katie's hurt and bring peace to her battered heart, and only God can give Clay what he's truly searching for.

Grand Canyon Brides

Four Harvey Girls Work to Tame the Old West Along the Rails

Dianne Christner, Nancy J. Farrier,
Darlene Mindrup, Pamela Kaye Tracy

ISBN 1-59789-072-3

Cover image credits: Harvey Girls image © Steve Jacobson
Canyon image © Photodisc

All scripture quotations are taken from the King James Version of the Bible.

Published by Barbour Publishing, Inc., P.O. Box 719, Uhrichsville, Ohio 44683, www.barbourbooks.com

Our mission is to publish and distribute inspirational products offering exceptional value and biblical encouragement to the masses.

Printed in the United States of America.
5 4 3 2 1

Grand Canyon Brides

From Famine to Feast

Pamela Kaye Tracy

Dedication

To the food service workers who worked alongside me when we'd really rather have been someplace else! In so many cases, you were family more than friends!

From Mr. C's Steakhouse in Omaha, Nebraska, during the 70's and high school.

My busgirl buddies: Patty McCoy, Julie Livingston, Robin Martin, and Sammi Lambertson.

From Red Lobster in Abilene, Texas, during the 80's and college.

My waitress and cook buddies: Kelly Musick and Greg Stockard.

From Red Lobster in Lubbock, Texas, still the 80's and yet another college.

My waitress and cook buddies: Monika Rogers, Tom Cryer, plus Jeff, Don, and Candy.

Oh, to be young again!

She had a sister called Mary,
who sat at the Lord's feet listening to what he said.
But Martha was distracted by all the preparations
that had to be made.
LUKE 10: 39-40

Chapter 1

Topeka, Kansas, 1906

"What do you mean Prescott, Kansas, is no more?" Olivia Prescott took a step backward, almost tripping on her satchel. "That's impossible. I live there!"

If she thought it would do any good, she'd stamp her feet. In the last four weeks, she'd been on an ocean liner and two trains and now hoped to board the stage that serviced her hometown—a hometown she hadn't seen in almost a year. All she wanted was a giant hug from her father, a taste of Mrs. Baudouin's cooking, a bath, and a bed. If the phone lines had reached Prescott, she'd demand the agent call her father, but since Prescott wasn't a railroad stop, it was always last to get the latest gadgets. "Call my father's lawyer, Jasper Ennis," she demanded.

The agent disappeared into a back room, and Olivia leaned over the counter. His voice was muted, but she could hear about every other word. The gist of the conversation implied that Ennis was out of town and wouldn't return until Monday.

"Sorry, miss, but Mr. Ennis—"

"I heard," Olivia interrupted. "*You'll* just have to get me to Prescott."

"Factory closed down two months ago. We kept a stage going for a while, but now there ain't no need."

Olivia leaned on the counter again—this time to keep herself from falling from shock. "Look, there must be some mistake. The factory couldn't have closed down."

The agent spat into a jar in the corner. "The schedule's written on the board right behind you. I erased the Prescott route myself."

"Sir, I had a letter postmarked 'Prescott' dated January third, just three months ago!" Anger so tangible she could almost touch it swelled in her bosom. "It existed then!" She brushed at the dusty fabric of her gray traveling dress and reminded herself to keep calm—as the headmistress at Grace School for Ladies insisted—and ladylike. It meant so much to her father—her being a lady. He had some mistaken idea that being raised by an old curmudgeon—his words, not hers—might limit her social graces. He certainly blamed himself for her habit of fidgeting. So she'd gone off to school.

"Stage don't go there no mores," the agent repeated. "I'm sorry, miss."

"That's impossible. I'm Olivia Prescott. The town is named after my father. I've lived there all my life. I'd know—" But *would* she? During the last year, after she graduated high school, she'd been overseas, traveling with a school friend's family. Papa had hated the thought of so much time apart but said the experience would be good for her. Her mother had always dreamed of taking Olivia overseas, but pneumonia had other plans for Grace Prescott. Ten years ago, she'd been the first

Prescott buried in the local cemetery.

Olivia headed for the hard wooden bench and sat down. She hadn't received a letter from Papa in well over. . . How long had it been? She shuddered.

Papa wasn't much of a letter writer. Still, Mrs. Baudouin would have tried—

Oh no! Mrs. Baudouin had the itinerary, but the Fremonts had deviated from their plans during the last few months. Mrs. Baudouin wouldn't have known where to look. If anything, she would have sent correspondence to France, but Olivia had wound up in Spain instead.

Dread pricked Olivia's heart. She slowly headed back to the counter. "I'm sorry I didn't believe you. It's just. . .I live there. And you're telling me everybody left. They couldn't have left *without me*. I've got to get home."

She'd been born with blond curls and blue eyes and had mastered the distraught look at birth. It worked on everyone but Mrs. Baudouin; it worked on the tobacco-spitting agent, too. He disappeared to make another telephone call.

Tapping her foot impatiently, Olivia studied the room. Wanted posters graced the far wall. Another wall boasted a chalkboard with the times and routes of the stagecoach. The final wall had job postings. The biggest advertisement depicted a woman, dressed in black and white, holding a tray of food. The caption read: YOUNG WOMEN 18–30 YEARS OF AGE, OF GOOD CHARACTER, ATTRACTIVE AND INTELLIGENT, NEEDED TO WORK IN THE WEST.

"I found ya some help," the stage agent said, reentering the room.

In a matter of minutes, Olivia hired the agent's acquaintance to drive her and her belongings to her hometown, just fifteen miles from Topeka, and rumored now to be a ghost town.

In a matter of hours, just four, when the outskirts of town came into view, she realized the potential validity of the rumors as the farm wagon bumped to a stop in front of a deserted mercantile. Glancing down Main Street, Olivia felt faint. Nothing, absolutely nothing about this day had gone right.

Businesses had open doors. Open because there was no need to lock empty rooms. Streets once teeming with horses and townspeople now contained blowing dust and more garbage than Olivia had ever seen in one place.

The driver finally asked, "Ma'am, you sure this is where you want to be?"

She'd stopped biting her nails more than two years ago. Today seemed a good time to start again. "Yes. No."

He nodded as if he understood. "You getting down?"

"No."

"You wanting me to take you somewheres else?"

"No."

"Well, ma'am, I'm right confused."

Confused was not a strong enough word to describe what Olivia felt, but she didn't dare step off the farm wagon. She might disappear like the town.

"Olivia, *pourquoi êtes-vous seul?*"

Never had a sound been so appreciated. Olivia hurried down from the wagon, without waiting for the driver's help, and rushed toward her father's housekeeper. "Mrs. Baudouin, oh, I'm so glad to see you!"

Adelande Baudouin traversed carefully past the broken furniture, discarded toys, and rotting food that lined the once-crowded street. Born in France, and still threatening to return, Mrs. Baudouin called Kansas home while she saved up enough money for fare. Olivia's father, John Prescott, claimed Mrs. Baudouin had enough saved to sail to the moon and back—twice. Today she wore her usual dark blue dress and sensible shoes. Even though she seemed to be the last soul in town, her gray hair was pinned in a neat bun. She was a no-nonsense, brisk churchgoer. Olivia's father claimed when the woman got to heaven, she'd whisk it into order the way she had their household.

Mrs. Baudouin broke form today. Hugs had never been a priority, so when she enveloped Olivia in one, Olivia's dread intensified.

"Where is Papa?" Olivia croaked.

"Didn't Mr. Ennis tell you?" Mrs. Baudouin loosened her hold and stepped back.

"No. The only thing I know is that the stage doesn't stop here anymore and that the factory closed. What happened?"

"Oh, that Jasper Ennis. I do not know what's gotten into him this last month. He was supposed to send someone for your belongings. I told him my position in town started Monday and I couldn't stay here any longer. I assumed when I saw you drive into town that you'd come to assist me."

"Assist with what?" Olivia looked around. "What happened to the town, to the people, to Papa?"

"Shall I unload your trunks, miss?" The driver shifted uncomfortably.

"Leave them loaded," Mrs. Baudouin directed. "There's a few more at the big white house at the end of the street."

"I don't want my bags to stay loaded," Olivia began.

"You can't stay here alone," Mrs. Baudouin said gently. "The town is gone, and so is your father." Mrs. Baudouin closed her eyes and moved her mouth in a silent prayer. Finally, she spoke. "Ah, such *un temps triste.* Olivia, your father left for a meeting in Topeka two months ago. He never returned. The sheriff from Topeka came, but he didn't find anything. Then Mr. Ennis came. That's when we discovered what LeRoy Baker had been doing."

"LeRoy Baker? Mr. Baker? You mean Papa's bookkeeper?"

"He embezzled everything. It looks like your father might have been involved."

Olivia didn't remember much about the next few hours, only that the driver agreed to wait while they gathered her belongings. The look he gave the farm wagon implied he hoped she didn't have many and that what she did have didn't weigh much.

Her home, the only one she'd ever known, waited at the end of Main Street. The lawn of the two-story structure was overgrown. The porch lacked its familiar wicker chairs. The swing hanging from the oak in the front yard looked deserted and lonely.

She hadn't appreciated the hustle and bustle of the community enough. Only now that it had disappeared did she realize just what she'd had—what she had lost. There were so many things to tell her papa: stories from school, adventures while in Europe, and her worries about boys and algebra and the latest fashions that always seemed to take so long to make it to Prescott.

Where is Papa?

Olivia swallowed. If she were to fall apart now, maybe she'd never gain control.

Mrs. Baudouin took one look at Olivia's face and said, "Child, I cannot imagine what you're feeling. I've gone over that last day I saw your father, and nothing seemed unusual. I waited all this time in that house expecting him to appear and set things right, but he's gone. I'm sure Mr. Ennis has some holdings for you, and I've secured a position in town. Come to Topeka until you figure out where you want to go."

"Papa had no family left, and Mama never had any. How can there possibly be a place I *want* to go? Besides, Papa will be back. I just know it."

"Then your papa will have to find you in Topeka," Mrs. Baudouin advised. "Mr. Ennis needs to speak with you. I could just thump that man. He was supposed to meet you at the train and tell you everything."

"I can't do this."

"Child, you have no choice," Mrs. Baudouin said. "We don't know where you father is."

Olivia quickly glanced away. The look on the housekeeper's face said more than her few words. John Prescott was either guilty of a crime or *dead*.

❧

April gave way to May while Olivia used the last of her money to pay for a hotel room and mail letters to the sheriffs in distant towns. For all the good it had done, she might as well have saddled a horse and ridden over the plains, shouting John Prescott's name. She'd considered it, but too late. To survive, one needed money and family. Without her father, she was lost; without money, she was helpless—which is why today she was checking out of the Topeka Hotel she and her father had always stayed at.

There was a time when Olivia considered Topeka exciting, but the last month had changed that thought. She'd never again consider Topeka anything but gloomy. There was also a time when Olivia thought the world and everyone in it were her friends; she no longer thought that. The people she'd contacted about her father all seemed to believe him guilty, except Mrs. Baudouin, who traveled with Olivia to nearby towns to look for John Prescott.

The local sheriff seemed to think *nothing* was the worthwhile thing to do in the case of Olivia's father.

Papa always said that when the world changed, one had to change with it. Olivia's world encompassed a nearly empty purse and an acting-out-of-character lawyer—a lawyer she needed to see one last time before redirecting her life.

Mr. Ennis's office was a red brick building that managed to look as square and pretentious as the lawyer himself. The bricks were red; Mr. Ennis had red, splotchy cheeks. The door was tall and wide; Mr. Ennis was tall and wide. Instead of a shingle, Mr. Ennis had an engraved sign, which made it and him stand apart from the neighboring businesses. Mr. Ennis had few friends. Olivia had come to this conclusion during the last month while she stayed at the hotel and tried to figure out her holdings.

Clutching the suitcase as it started to slip, Olivia hoped this appointment would go better than her last appointment. That one, just three days ago, had been a disaster. Ennis could only go over the details of a useless will. Useless because until it was "proved" that her father was deceased, nothing could be done. And even if something could be done, she'd been left a home she neither knew how to run nor could afford to keep. One she had no hope of selling. She'd been left a business with no stock, no employees, and no reputation. It, too, was not marketable. She'd been left a bank account ravaged by her father's bookkeeper—and some claimed ravaged by her father.

The suitcase grew heavier as she lugged it into Mr. Ennis's foyer. She wanted to go over her father's will one last time before making a life-changing decision. There had to be some way she could obtain enough funds to survive until her father returned. Some way to continue searching for her father since the sheriff claimed he'd done all he could.

Olivia refused to believe she'd done all *she* could.

In a matter of an hour, she sat across from Mr. Ennis and studied her father's will while Mr. Ennis rambled about how much he'd admired her father, admired *her*.

"You have no one else," Mr. Ennis said loudly.

"What?" Olivia clutched the will as if it were a shield.

"I said you have no one else."

"So what are my options?"

"Weren't you listening to me, Olivia?"

"I'm sorry. I guess I was not."

"I asked you to marry me. I'll take care of you the way you are accustomed. It's what your father would have wanted."

"But—" Olivia blustered. "But—" Words—indeed, whole sentences—of protest came to mind: *I'm not ready; you are twice my age; I do not love you.* Battling for equal consideration was her common sense: *You've always had servants; his money will help look for Papa; love can come later.* She spoke none of her thoughts aloud because his offer had done one thing. Up to now, she'd felt alone, but at least she had been feeling something. Mr. Ennis's proposal was like a knife peeling away the last remnants of her secure childhood and leaving her an empty shell.

"I appreciate your offer, Mr. Ennis, but I decline." She was surprised at the steadiness of her voice. She should be stuttering, crying, encouraging him to look for money that apparently didn't exist, and begging him to start looking for her father again.

She stood, and he stood with her. "Olivia, I have a house the size of your father's. I have a bank account the size of your father's. Nothing in your world would change except your name."

"Everything in my world has changed," she said calmly, "including you."

Chapter 2

"Used ta be, ya could shoot buffalo right from the train window. Yup, I made a lot of money on them beasts. Sure hated it when there weren't but a few of them left. Ya could eat just about every part of them. Tongue was the best."

Wayne Gregory looked at the sparse desert scenery and tried to imagine the creatures his talkative seatmate described. Nodding at the man, Wayne bent and took his Bible from the small bag he'd carried on board. During his two years in Auburn, God and Esther were the only things that kept him going.

"And," continued the man who'd identified himself as Daniel Applegate a good ten hours ago, "I hear some guy up near the canyon has him a buffalo farm."

With a sigh, Wayne closed his Bible. Delving into the scriptures and listening to his seatmate were incompatible. Glancing around, he pretended a great interest in the other passengers, anything to tune out Mr. Applegate. The man claimed to have held every occupation from railroad engineer to mountain man to shoe salesman. He changed his stories every time the train whistle blew.

Four young ladies were seated near the back of the car. Judging by their looks and the study material in their hands, Wayne guessed they were headed to the same place he was: the El Tovar Restaurant at the Grand Canyon. They would be Harvey Girls; he would be their boss. They were looking forward to adventure; he had nothing to look forward to—except for his daughter's arrival in two weeks.

"Yup, he's mixing cows with buffalo. He calls 'em cattalo. I hear they're good eatin'. If you're managing that Harvey House, ya might want to add that to your menu."

"I don't make the menus. They're set."

Now that he'd gotten a response, Mr. Applegate's ramblings intensified. Wayne continued looking at what he figured were future employees. At his last real job, the law firm of Conn and Williams, he'd been in charge of secretaries, clerks, and students—all men. They were up and coming, modern society—as was New York City, his hometown. If the El Tovar was anything like Dearborn Station, the Harvey House in Illinois he'd trained at, he'd be in charge of more than fifty employees: waitresses, yardmen, and maids—a real mixture of jobs and cultures.

The El Tovar had been open only a year, and Wayne was grateful for the job. He'd left Auburn with four other men. Save for him, none of them knew what tomorrow would bring. None of them cared. None of them knew God. Wayne figured if Job could bounce back after all he lost, then self-pity didn't belong in Wayne Gregory's life, either. But he had Esther, eight years old and dependent on her father. And he had God.

"Yup," Mr. Applegate continued, "Old Fred Harvey had him a good idea. Wish I'd have thought it. 'Course, I wasn't but a youngster when he put it all in place."

Fred Harvey was a topic Wayne knew all too well. The five weeks he'd trained in Chicago had been harder than prepping for a court date. Wayne hadn't even been alive when Fred Harvey opened his first restaurant. And if he had been alive, he wouldn't have cared except from a customer standpoint. All Wayne's life he'd known what he wanted to do. He would ape his father. He'd study law, marry, have a family, and die knowing that on Judgment Day he'd hear "Well done, thou good and faithful servant."

His father, Matthew Gregory, had simply hung out a shingle and worked *for* and *with* the common people. He'd made enough money to provide for his family. Wayne had wanted the same—except going into partnership with Conn and Williams meant he'd make enough money to provide for his family *and* have a lot left over.

Father would have figured out the partners were skimming off the top. Father would have figured it out before the partners skipped town and left him to answer for their sins.

The four young ladies—a blond, a redhead, and two brunettes—wouldn't know their boss had gone from feast to famine; wouldn't know he was a Harvey House manager only because his college roommate had been a Harvey cousin; wouldn't know he hated the very idea of being what amounted to an innkeeper. But he'd do it because he no longer had the heart to practice law, and he owed his daughter the example of a father who took care of his own.

The redhead laughed, and most of the men in the car watched appreciatively. Even his seatmate took notice. "They employees of yours?"

"I assume so."

The old man, who asked to be called Daniel, nodded. "Fred Harvey stipulated his girls be attractive, and whoever hired this lot was right on the mark."

Wayne had to agree. The two brunettes looked to be sisters. They were animated and rosy-cheeked—farm-bred, he figured. The redhead had quite a presence. She seemed to be keeping the other three in line. The blond was the only mystery. She bit a nail while staring out the window and fidgeted in a way that made him know she wanted to run. Like him, though, she nodded every once in a while to give the illusion she was listening. Even from a distance he could see the unhappiness in her eyes.

"Everyone has a story," his seatmate said.

Hours later, Wayne rubbed sleep from his eyes and stared past a gathering of Native Americans selling their wares beside the train station. Up a small incline sat the rustic four-story log-and-boulder building that would be home for who knew how many years. Hope spiraled in his chest as he waited for the passengers in front of him to board the touring car that would take them from the train depot to the magnificent hotel. Unlike the Harvey House in Chicago, the El Tovar was not a bustling restaurant that catered to a hurried crowd. No doubt guests were inside enjoying a leisurely breakfast while the staff saw to their whims and readied for lunch. Travelers often stayed for weeks at the Grand Canyon.

The newcomers who exited the touring car fit mostly into three categories. Some were here on a day trip from Williams and might want breakfast but even more likely carried their own and would prefer to get an early start on one of the trails—either on foot or by mule. Others would check in to the hotel first and decide on a meal later. The final few were employees of either Fred Harvey or the Santa Fe Railroad.

A dark-haired woman, dressed in the Harvey black-and-white uniform, her hair upswept in a neat bun, stood at the front door. "You must be Mr. Gregory. I'll take a moment to seat our guests, and then I'll alert Mr. Niles that you are here."

Wayne knew about Albert Niles. For the next three months, Wayne would work alongside the experienced Mr. Niles during the canyon's busy season.

"Good to see you, Mr. Gregory. I have been looking forward to having help." A dark-haired man with a full mustache and deep voice stepped out onto the porch. Niles was much younger than Wayne expected and looked as though he'd be as comfortable in buckskin as he was in his black suit.

"Nice to meet you, too," Wayne said.

A few minutes later, the tour began. First, Niles introduced Wayne to the hotel's manager, Charley Brant. He, along with Niles, had been at the El Tovar from day one. Charley's wife, Niles explained, took a keen interest in the Harvey Girls and often had the girls help with charity events. Wayne continued to follow Niles through the gift shop, several art galleries, the dining room—truthfully more rooms than Wayne could begin to remember. The El Tovar, with its Swiss chalet architecture, was the most luxurious hotel between the Rocky Mountains and San Francisco. As they went in and out of rooms, Niles addressed every employee by name.

The breakfast rush was ending as Niles led Wayne back into the El Tovar's lobby. The Harvey Girls hustled to attention. The four girls from the train hurried in, followed by the woman who had first greeted Wayne. She stood beside Mr. Niles.

"Ah, Mary, perfect timing as always." Niles turned to Wayne. "This is Mary O'Dell, our head waitress. As fine an assistant as you could hope for." Turning back to Mary, he asked, "Are these the new girls?"

"Introduce yourselves," Mary ordered.

Wayne wasn't surprised when the redhead went first. "I'm Constance Gibson. I'm here to work the summer. I have six years of experience with the company."

The brunettes spoke at the same time. "I'm Sar—"

"I'm Mab—"

They looked at each other and laughed. Finally, one said, "I'm Sarah Jane Miller. This is my sister Mabel. We're from Oklahoma. Our family owns a farm there, and we're hoping to help out a bit by sending money home."

The blond didn't step forward like the other three. She had changed from her elaborate gray traveling dress into a frilly pink dress—one completely inappropriate for the canyon or any type of labor.

Constance nudged her.

"I'm Olivia Prescott from Prescott, Kansas."

"Ohhh," came a low murmur from an employee Wayne couldn't distinguish.

"Ah, my father, er"—she glanced at the twins—"My family is having some hard times, and I need work."

"You mean your father ran out and left his employees without jobs or paychecks."

"Michelle!" Mary O'Dell looked daggers at one of the waitresses—the same one who'd said, "Ohhh," earlier. "Come with me."

"That's not true," Olivia's soft voice raised, and Wayne, for the first time, thought she might have some spunk after all. "My father is missing. His bookkeeper stole all the money. That's why the factory closed down."

"Your father's missing?" Constance asked. "Oh, I'm so sorry."

Watching as Mary marched a hostile Michelle out of the room, Wayne felt sorry for both of them, but especially Olivia. What were the chances of stepping off a train hundreds of miles from home and finding that bad luck had preceded you?

"Wayne? Wayne Gregory?"

Every head turned to stare at the man standing just a few tables away.

A few years ago Robert Thatcher had been a clerk at Conn and Williams. Robert had been a friend of the Conns, hired by family connections and later fired by their orders by Wayne. He'd never figured out what the young man had done to deserve his partners' wrath, but he'd written a nice reference and arranged for a job interview at a nearby factory. Thatcher hadn't appreciated either effort.

"Wayne Gregory." Thatcher nodded, clearly liking that he had everyone's attention. "When did you get out of Auburn Prison?"

Twenty-one pairs of eyes switched from Thatcher to Wayne. He cleared his throat and said, "It's my turn to introduce myself. "I'm Wayne Gregory, from New York City. I hired on with the Harvey organization five months ago, just two days after I was released from prison. I served two years and four days for embezzlement. My term was actually longer, but the men who were really guilty of the crime were apprehended and confessed. I received a full pardon from the governor."

"Whom did you embezzle?" someone asked.

"I didn't embezzle; my partners did."

At first Wayne thought Constance had aired the question, but judging from the way the girls and Niles were staring at Olivia, it must have been her.

"Were you a bookkeeper?" she asked.

"No, a lawyer."

The expression on Olivia's face turned from curiosity to speculation.

Before the jury of waitresses started asking personal questions, Wayne decided it was time to move on. "Dinah, would you please show Mr. Thatcher to a table?"

Later, in the small room Niles used as an office, Wayne watched as one of the girls cleared Thatcher's plate. The man was talking a mile a minute and waving his coffee cup around—apparently not noticing the amount of spillage.

"I'm impressed with how you handled that outburst," Niles said.

"Truthfully, I'm glad Thatcher arrived when he did. I wasn't going to mention my prison term, but not sharing the information felt underhanded. Puts me in mind of Matthew 10:26: 'Fear them not therefore: for there is nothing covered, that shall not be revealed; and hid, that shall not be known.' Almost since the Harvey Company hired me on, I've wondered whether to make my past known, and now that I have, I'm not afraid. It's like a burden has been lifted."

Niles glanced at his watch and handed a stack of papers to Wayne. "These girls have some interesting pasts. Take a moment to get acquainted with your staff, then we'll get ready for the lunch hour."

There were fourteen waitresses in all. The one with the

longest employment was Mary O'Dell, whom Niles had identified as the head waitress. She was a widow with ten years of experience. Constance Gibson, who'd impressed him both on the train and during introductions, was a six-year employee. She was a floater more than anything else and couldn't really call any Harvey House her home. Dinah Weston, whose face Wayne couldn't recall, had been with the Harvey Company five years. Her record was spotless.

He finished looking over thirteen files. He'd purposely left number fourteen, Olivia Prescott's, for last. She intrigued him. Why didn't she like bookkeepers, and why did his being a lawyer—an ex-lawyer—affect her so? Her file was a bit thicker than the others. Along with the sheet documenting her personal information, he perused what he called the Harvey Girl report card. Olivia's evaluation was quite dismal. He opened an envelope and found newspaper clippings and a personal note from the head waitress who'd trained Olivia.

Dear Sir:

No doubt you've looked over Olivia Prescott's evaluation and are wondering why she was allowed to proceed in the Harvey establishment. I believe that if given opportunity, Olivia can be an asset. She is meticulous and knowledgeable. The local customers took a shine to her in a very short time. This is why I encouraged management to send her to the El Tovar. I believe the slower pace will allow her to find her place in the Harvey establishment. Please give her every opportunity.

Sincerely,
Ruth Owens

A prima donna. He should have guessed from the way she dressed. Best he send her back from where she came before she caused any more trouble. He fingered Olivia's file—on the job for just a few hours and already a thorn in his side. She admitted to having family problems. Well, he had family problems, too. He needed to get Esther away from his in-laws before they spoiled her as thoroughly as they'd spoiled her mother.

Wayne closed his eyes. He could almost see Analise, smell Analise. If he were thankful about any aspect of his jail time, it was that Analise had died well before his sentencing. She probably would have wound up in jail herself for protesting. He pushed the thought of his wife away. It still hurt too much.

Yes, he certainly understood family problems.

"Mr. Gregory?" A Harvey Girl stood at the door. He recognized her as the one who'd diverted the discussion away from embezzlement and onto his daughter.

"Yes, and you are?"

"I'm Dinah Weston."

Ah, his third most experienced Harvey Girl. He remembered her from this morning. She'd stood out because she was the lone female of average looks. Her mouth was a little too big, as were her teeth. Maybe in a different scenario her homeliness wouldn't be so obvious, but here, with thirteen other waitresses who looked as if they belonged on the cover of one of his wife's ladies magazines, she was a lone wolf.

Except for her eyes. Those equaled Olivia's. And they were just as sad. He tossed down Olivia's folder. She was taking up too much of his time and thoughts.

"Yes, Miss Weston, do you need something?"

"I'm waiting on your acquaintance Mr. Thatcher."

Wayne kept his face impassive, although he wanted to grimace. "And?"

"He claims that you'll be taking care of his luncheon bill. I thought I'd better check with you first."

Chapter 3

"This is not going to work!" Michelle Harrison stood in the middle of the dormitory bedroom and glared at Olivia.

"I agree." Olivia felt her face flame as she realized that not only her acquaintances from the train were witnessing her discomfort but also Mr. Niles.

"Ladies, one of the prerequisites of being a Harvey Girl is the ability to work in harmony with others." Mary O'Dell might have been talking to herself for all the attention Michelle gave. Her glare never wavered.

"I didn't know, when I unpacked, that this was your room." Olivia sat on the bed she'd claimed only this afternoon.

"There are no empty rooms," Mary said. "And it's not fair to change room assignments simply because you two cannot get along. You haven't even tried."

"Oh, we've tried. I've known Her Highness since first grade. Her father cheated my father. We lost everything!" Michelle's face turned a splotchy red.

"My father is missing. He's as much a victim as—"

"Your father's a thief!" Michelle insisted.

Olivia closed her eyes and tried to remember what it felt like to be happy and secure. She and Michelle had been in the same class during school. They'd shared desks, books, and a love for chocolate. They'd been best friends. But sometime after sixth grade, when it became apparent that Olivia would be going off to high school and Michelle would be going to work at the factory, their friendship had changed—ended.

"Miss O'Dell, Olivia can share a room with us," Mabel said. "We're used to sharing a bedroom with our little sister. Olivia probably doesn't snore like she does."

Mr. Niles looked disgusted with the whole scene. Olivia half-expected him to fire her. Instead, he said, "Pack your things, Olivia. You may move into Mary's room."

"Head waitresses are not supposed to share," Michelle muttered.

"Head waitresses can do whatever they want," Mary said curtly, looking curiously at Mr. Niles. He nodded and left.

Olivia pulled her trunk from under the bed. "I'm so sorry. This is not how I wanted to begin. Michelle, I assure you—"

"I don't want to hear it."

"I will do three to a room," Olivia offered.

"Nonsense. It's only for a few months," Mary said. "Once the busy season ends, we'll reassess the roommate situation."

Constance, Sarah Jane, and Mabel all pitched in, and soon the girls were carrying Olivia's belongings to Mary's room. The head waitress hurried ahead and moved a half-completed dress from what would be Olivia's bed.

"Oh, it's beautiful," Sarah Jane exclaimed. "I've always wanted to own a dress like this."

"But when we did quilting bees back home," Mabel said,

"the ladies always put her on a corner. Later they pulled out her stitches."

"Did not!"

"Did!"

To Olivia's surprise, instead of squaring off, both girls burst into peels of laughter. Constance joined in, and even Mary forced a smile.

"I wish my sister and I got along like you two do," Constance said.

"We're twins," Mabel explained. "Mama says we have a special bond."

Sitting on her newly acquired bed, Olivia listened to the spirited banter and perused the room. Located at the end of the dormitory, it was directly across the road from the El Tovar and was twice the size of the other waitresses' rooms.

Mary wasn't just bunking in her room; *nesting* was a better word. The wooden walls were adorned with photos. Most were scenic views of different locations. There were a few Harvey group pictures. Mary had also put up her own curtains, white and frilly, now fluttering in a warm breeze that couldn't be equaled in Olivia's Kansas. A phonograph occupied one corner. A stack of records, more than Olivia had ever seen before, sat on a small table.

"I need to get back to work." Mary looked at Olivia, who had just started to unpack. "I hope your other clothes are a bit more serviceable. You'll find the canyon a pretty rough-and-tumble place."

"These are all of my clothes," she whispered. She'd owned a closetful just two months ago. She'd sold all but her gray traveling suit and two dresses. All to pay for the lawyer fees Mr.

Ennis charged after she turned down his marriage proposal.

"Then I suggest you use your first paycheck to buy a simpler wardrobe. If you want to fit in with the girls..." Her words trailed off, and she walked away.

"I know!" Sarah Jane practically jumped up and down. "I'll trade you one of my everyday dresses for one of yours. We're about the same size."

Mabel's mouth opened, and it seemed to take her a moment to gather her thoughts. "That's not fair. I want—"

"I have more than one dress to trade," Olivia offered. In a blink, all three girls were out of the room.

Mabel, Sarah Jane, and Constance skidded back into the room, each clutching a dress and waiting expectantly with this-is-Christmas expressions on their faces. Olivia obediently handed over her dresses and without hesitating took off the one she wore.

A few minutes later, Mabel, Sarah Jane, and Constance were preening in what they considered high fashion. Olivia felt almost matronly as she watched them prance up and down the hall pretending to be waiting for handsome men and on their way to the social event of the century.

Had she ever felt so flamboyant in one of her dresses?

No, she'd taken them for granted.

The dresses she'd traded were not her best, yet these three women acted as though she'd given them gold. The dresses that now hung in her own closet were... She searched for a suitable word: sturdy. Two were dirt brown, and the other was the same severe dark blue that Mrs. Baudouin favored. They were a bit heavier and coarser than Olivia liked, but they all fit, although Constance's would need to be hemmed. She reached out tentatively and fingered a patched sleeve. Oh, she wanted her old life back. She wanted Papa and Mrs. Baudouin to take care of her. She'd know not to take things for granted now.

"We're changing back into our regular clothes," Sarah Jane called from her room two doors down. "Then we're going exploring. Get ready, Olivia!"

She'd been standing in her underclothes, too amazed by the turn of events to even be embarrassed. Slowly she pulled a dress off its hanger. Which twin this dress had belonged to, she couldn't say. A moment later, looking in the mirror, Olivia tried to smile. She felt as drab as she looked.

"Are you ready?" Mabel asked, stepping into the room. "Sarah Jane takes forever." She glanced around the room. "I've never seen so many records. She must spend all her earnings on them."

Constance joined them. "Mary O'Dell is well-known among the Harvey Girls. She used to be married to a banker. When he died, she didn't have the money to keep her home. The phonograph is the only thing Mary kept. It's her prized possession."

"Must be difficult to keep moving it."

"Are you coming?" Sarah Jane yelled from her room.

Grabbing her hat and gloves, Olivia followed her friends out the door. They skirted the restaurant's front porch and hurried to a group of people admiring the most marvelous view Olivia had ever seen. The walls of the canyon jutted out in various formations, reminding Olivia of stair steps, which changed from white to brown with rust and tan interspersed. A mule and rider traveled along what looked to be a tiny trail.

"The Colorado River has to be somewhere down there," Sarah Jane whispered.

Olivia understood the whisper. The canyon demanded reverence.

"My, my," Constance breathed. "No wonder all the girls want to transfer here."

Olivia's papa had always claimed that the best view was in one's own backyard. If he were here, she could tell him he was wrong. But if he were *here*, she wouldn't tell him he was wrong; she'd tell him she loved him.

"This is nothing like our farm," Sarah Jane said.

"Our farm's beautiful," Mabel defended. "It's just a bit flat."

"My hometown is flat, too," Olivia said.

"Did your father really own a factory?" Sarah Jane asked.

Constance put a hand on Olivia's shoulder. "Maybe this isn't the best time."

If she didn't tell the girls what had happened, they'd hear only Michelle's side, so she swallowed hard and said, "There never will be a best time. My father did own a factory. He employed most of the town. And Michelle is telling the truth; her family is owed a last paycheck. Nobody seems to know where Papa is. He disappeared."

"I wondered why you didn't share your life history on the train like the rest of us," Mabel said. "What did you do?"

"I wasn't even home when all this happened. I was in Europe. My whole world collapsed while I was away, and I didn't even know it."

"That had to be rough," Mabel said. "We never had to worry about Ma and Pa. They never go anywhere. I don't think Ma's even been outside of our hometown. One of us is supposed to write every night without fail, or she's sending Pa after us."

"Europe," Sarah Jane repeated. "You really were rich. Did

you get to go to high school?"

"Yes, and I was set on going to college."

"Is that why you're here? So you can earn enough money to finish school?"

"No," Olivia said. She felt flustered because she was about to share an idea that hadn't been shared with anyone—not Mr. Ennis, not Mrs. Baudouin. She'd been too afraid they'd laugh.

"I'm going to save my money and hire a private detective to find my father."

Nobody laughed. Instead, together, they strolled down the walkway in silence for a few minutes. Olivia took a breath. This moment, at the Grand Canyon, certainly felt right: taking in the sights, watching the people, and feeling a part of something, well, permanent.

"What did you do when you got home and found out about your father and the factory?" Constance asked.

"The housekeeper and I packed what we could and sold most of it, and then I joined the Harvey establishment. Like I said, I intend to hire a detective, and that costs money."

The girls nodded. Olivia's from-riches-to-rags descent seemed to somewhat erase the barrier that her travels to Europe and education might have imposed.

"You have no family to help?" Mabel asked.

"None," Olivia admitted.

The girls stopped to enjoy the view one more time. A gray-haired man joined them. "The Colorado River carved this canyon. Probably took a couple of million years."

"Really?" Sarah Jane asked.

"Yup, what you're looking at is sedimentary rock and—" He stopped. "Aw, you young ladies aren't interested in a history lesson. I'll bet you have some young men—"

"No, we're interested," Sarah Jane insisted.

The man identified himself as Daniel Applegate. He knew enough about the canyon to write a book and was quite willing to share. Olivia liked the sound of the man's voice. After what seemed like only minutes but was actually more than an hour, he excused himself, and the girls made their way past the El Tovar, across the road, and up the steps into the dormitory. A few of their peers had returned from work, and laughter came from the entertainment room.

"I can hardly wait until I feel comfortable in there," Mabel said.

"It's easy." Constance veered to the left, dragging them with her. "Let's pop in now and introduce ourselves."

Olivia pulled away. She'd never considered herself easily intimidated, but the thought of facing Michelle was more than she could handle right now. "I'm going upstairs. It's been a long day."

"I'll go write Mama," Sarah Jane told Mabel. "You can do it tomorrow."

Lanterns hung on pegs every few feet. The dormitory had appeared of average size when they'd moved their belongings in during the late afternoon. Now that the sun had given way to the moon, the place seemed expanded somehow. The wooden planks on the floor creaked under their feet. Outside, crickets chirped and an owl hooted. Sarah Jane said good night and turned into her room. Olivia entered her quarters. Standing in the middle of the room, she waited for exhaustion to overtake her.

Since returning from Europe, sleep had been the one

avenue she could take for escape. During her Harvey Girl training, she'd fallen into bed so tired she'd barely had time to adjust the pillow. But today, her first as a full-time employee at the Grand Canyon's El Tovar, she felt wide-awake. She lit the lantern and finished unpacking. After a few minutes, with nothing else to do, she sat on the bed, folded her hands, unfolded them, tried to still the fidgeting of her thumbs, and listened to the night noise.

Alone. She felt so alone.

Maybe she should have tried the entertainment room. Sparring with Michelle might ease some of the loneliness. But, no, tonight was not the night to start trying to win back Michelle's friendship or, at least, defend her father's honor. Tonight was for reflection and maybe even, as Mrs. Baudouin suggested, prayer. Olivia stood and walked over to Mary's side of the room to take a closer look at the photos. Mary, along with Mr. Niles, had been part of the opening crew at quite a few Harvey Houses.

Her perusal over, Olivia pulled off her dress and went to hang it up. The closet door was partially open. Funny, she remembered closing it, but maybe Mary had returned to the room. Reaching for a hanger, Olivia pushed one of the other dresses aside. The skirt flared out a bit, and Olivia looked down. She knew before she even grasped the material. Her "new" dress—dull, brown, and serviceable—was ruined. Someone had taken a knife, or a pair of scissors, and slashed the skirt into ribbons. A quick look proved the second dress butchered even more than the first.

Olivia Prescott now owned only one "serviceable" dress. The one she had on.

Chapter 4

Wayne set down his favorite fountain pen and studied the three women in front of him. This was not the type of morning he'd envisioned. For the past week, he'd noticed how slow Olivia worked and planned to take her aside and discuss the note Ruth Owens had penned. He'd intended to urge her to work harder at both dealing with customers and dealing with her contemporaries. Instead, there were "issues" to deal with.

"I tell you, I didn't do it." Michelle Harrison sputtered. Strawberry blond and freckled, with a hot temper, the woman fairly trembled with indignity. Her whole demeanor screamed innocence. On the other hand, Olivia displayed what he'd always identified in court as bottled anger. She was silent except for her eyes. Simmering rage threatened to erupt. Her demeanor screamed injustice.

Mary O'Dell had marched the two girls in at first light. The destroyed dresses were flung over a chair by his office door. Olivia's lips were pressed together so tightly only a straight line showed. Michelle's lips were much the same.

Wayne held up his hand, motioning Michelle to stop, and

addressed Olivia. "When do you think it happened?"

"A week ago," Mary said indignantly. "And I just found out about it."

"It happened my first night here while I was out looking at the canyon."

Wayne picked up a pencil and some paper and jotted down the hours Olivia claimed to be at the canyon's edge and Michelle's response. He needed to keep a record. His eyes fell on Olivia's file, still on top of his desk. Already the thickest of his crew, it was about to expand a bit more.

"And did anyone see you cleaning your station?" Wayne asked Michelle.

"Mary did!"

Mary nodded. "I remember that night. I checked her station after nine and watched her leave."

"Anyone see you enter the dorm?"

"Why am I getting all the questions?" Michelle argued. "Ask her some. Maybe she did it herself. Her Highness doesn't want to face me every day and—"

"Enough." Wayne stood. "I'll do a bit more checking. Michelle, I'd better not find even one person who remembers you disappearing from the restaurant floor."

"If I were to even think about destroying Olivia's property, which is not something I'd do, I'd never have guessed those dresses were hers."

A distant whistle sounded, reminding Wayne the morning train was on its way. "Thank you for your time, Michelle."

She blinked, as if surprised to find him considerate.

"Olivia, I'd like to speak with you for a few more minutes."

Michelle smirked and left the office followed by Mary.

Olivia glared at him. He was tempted to stare her down. It was what he would have done in court. Could she be guilty of what Michelle charged? Had she ruined her clothes purposely?

"What do you think happened?" He made his words gentle, soothing, hoping to gain her trust. If she thought him an ally, she might confess.

"I think someone took a pair of scissors to my clothes."

"Who?"

She rolled her eyes skyward. "Michelle *is* the obvious choice. She hates me."

"Michelle seems to have a decent alibi."

Olivia stood and said calmly, "Often criminals escape while the innocent pay."

He'd felt that same way for two years, but the lawyer in him—*the Christian in him*—knew she was wrong. "Your world is now the Harvey world, and you're not getting off to a very agreeable beginning."

"You think this is my fault!" Her checks went red with indignity.

Although Wayne tried not to notice, the blush only heightened her beauty. Her Elsie collar topped a neat black bow. The white ribbon in her hair made her innocent yet alluring. She'd look just fine sitting on the couch of a lavish New York apartment. *His* New York apartment.

He shook his head of the ridiculous thought. She was a hothouse flower who probably didn't travel well—amazing she'd made it this far. And thinking of New York and spacious apartments only made him long for a lifestyle no longer his. "Miss Prescott, your presence is causing dissension among my employees. My head waitress now has a roommate she doesn't need. Michelle, who hasn't had any problems, is accused of vandalism. Furthermore, the train is about to arrive and instead of filling saltshakers, I know half my employees are speculating about what's happening in here."

"I didn't want to report the incident in the first place." Olivia's chin jutted out. "Mary made me. *I* can take care of my own problems."

She snatched up the dresses and stomped out of his office.

Watching her go, Wayne tried to keep his smile at bay. She'd ruined a perfectly good morning, but she'd done it with style.

Unfortunately, even as he smiled at the woman's spunk, he realized his favorite fountain pen was missing.

The dining room took up half of the hotel's main floor. White tablecloths covered more than twenty round tables. Fresh flowers stood proudly as centerpieces. Shining silverware, fine chinaware, and sparkling crystal were set up for the morning arrivals.

The clang of dishes, rumble of ice buckets, and murmur of conversation meant all was in place. Wayne walked through the dining room noting which girls were acting in leisure and which in haste. Most were standing at attention by their stations. Michelle wasn't rushing, but agitation was obvious as she arranged cups and saucers on her tables. Sarah Jane looked poised for flight, and Wayne checked to see why.

Olivia.

Her station consisted of four tables, and only two were set up. Oblivious to her peers' readiness, Olivia had the centerpiece pulled forward and was busy rearranging the flowers.

"Miss Prescott!" The words came out harsher than he'd intended. They echoed through the dining room.

Mary O'Dell looked up, let out a little screech, and hurried over. "We open in ten minutes," she hissed as she guided the centerpiece back to the middle of the table.

"But the flowers—" Olivia clearly wanted to continue rearranging as she pulled the flowers back toward her.

Mary interrupted, "Were arranged by an expert."

"Then the expert is underqualified and overpaid."

"Look around you." Sarah Jane joined them. She took the flowers, guided them back in the center, and hurried to Olivia's third table. Her sister joined her, and soon the two had the table almost set up. Constance and Dinah finished the fourth table.

Olivia looked up and blinked, and chagrin took over her features.

Wayne thought about pulling Olivia into his office again. He could lecture her about time management and question her about his pen, but customers arrived, and Mary began seating them. First came a family of five. In Dearborn Station, where Wayne had trained, no men had been allowed in a Harvey dining room without a coat. The coat rule obviously didn't apply here, or maybe it just wasn't enforced. But then again, Arizona wasn't even a state!

Next came two young men who grinned foolishly at Michelle and made Wayne curious as to their relationship. Harvey Girls signed a contract stipulating they would not marry during their contract. In many locations they were the only decent women. Keeping them as waitresses and not wives was a nearly impossible task.

An elderly couple took their seats. The husband chose where

the wife would sit and then inspected the silverware. They reminded Wayne of his in-laws—who had been in charge of Esther for the last two years. One more week to go and he'd be off to New York to retrieve his daughter. He lived for that day.

Daniel took the last seat at the table and glanced around the room as if searching for someone. Michelle took their orders while discreetly arranging their cups. Daniel's, the father's, and the elderly man's cups faced up and soon were filled with coffee. The elderly woman's cup faced down and received hot tea. The mother and two teenagers had cups left tilted against the saucer, which meant iced tea. The two children fiddled with their cups and moved them from their position, but Dinah, serving as "drink girl," knew to give them milk.

Constance entered the dining room carrying plates of thick steaks; some had also ordered eggs. Mabel placed a platter of hash browns on the table, and Sarah Jane followed with pan-sized wheat cakes, their aroma decrying the need for maple syrup.

Other customers entered. Trailing after a party of seven, Robert Thatcher stared pointedly at Wayne. Dinah always tried to make sure she served the man, and if he didn't pay his bill, she saw that the amount was added to his hotel costs. Some of the other girls weren't so savvy. Mary O'Dell fed the man for free. Olivia, on the other hand, took a somewhat perverse joy in handing Wayne the bill.

Niles came from the kitchen and began working the room. He shook the elderly man's hand. Next, he refilled two glasses of tea before he took over the seating of customers and filled up three more tables. Finally, he took note of Robert, winked at Wayne, and with a flourish personally handed Robert his bill.

As of yet, Robert hadn't tried to pawn off his bill in Niles's view.

Wayne checked his watch. The train was due any minute. In Dearborn Station, the train meant business. At the El Tovar, the train just meant *more* business. One more sweep of the restaurant assured Wayne that everything was at the ready.

The perusal had also netted him two more items of interest.

Mary O'Dell stood immobile, staring across the room. The tea pitcher tipped slightly and dripped as she stared across the room at Niles and Olivia.

Niles had his hand on Olivia's shoulder and was complimenting the flower arrangements on her first two tables.

Chapter 5

Crossing the road from the El Tovar toward the dormitory, Olivia figured there were two things she wanted in celebration of completing her second week of waitressing.

First, she wanted Wayne Gregory to crawl back under a rock. The ex-lawyer took every opportunity to make her feel useless. She didn't move fast enough, she didn't keep the food hot enough, and she didn't give equal attention to everyone.

He'd basically called her both inept and a snob.

She was grateful he was leaving in the morning to get his daughter. She needed a break from his scrutiny. His face softened every time he mentioned Esther's name. If not for witnessing the slight vulnerability, she'd believe Mr. Gregory wasn't capable of love or kindness. He didn't even know how to smile. Thank goodness for Mr. Niles. He smiled often, and he knew how to make a girl feel important. He had her come in early and rearrange the flowers. He sought her opinion on the layout of the gift shop. Moreover, he was impressed by the fact that certain customers already requested her station.

The second thing she wanted was a different roommate—

one who was willing to share and one who might even be inclined toward friendship. For the last week, Mary seemed to take some sort of joy in scolding Olivia while in the privacy of their room—where Olivia truly believed she should have some peace.

Not that peace seemed obtainable. Tonight was yet another failing. She'd been the last one out of the dining room again. For some reason, she never finished at the same time as the rest of the waitresses, even though her customers usually cashed out early. Mr. Niles said it was because she was meticulous. Mr. Gregory muttered the dreaded word *inept* then added *slow*. At least her *supposed* snobbery couldn't be blamed!

Thankfully, Mrs. Brant, the hotel manager's wife, had been in the mood for conversation and had helped finish up washing the ashtrays and sugar bowls, enabling Olivia to get to her room at a decent hour. Tonight the light was on. Most evenings, when they wound up together, Mary played show tunes on the phonograph—ruling out conversation—and sewed. Watching her tonight, Olivia again bit back the offer to help. Mary wouldn't appreciate suggestions—not from Olivia, not from anyone.

Laughter rippled outside. Olivia went to the window. Shadowy figures waltzed across the porch of the El Tovar. Pushing the curtain aside, she took a deep breath of pine, fireplace, and dust. A longing for something, someone, she couldn't identify, plagued her.

The phonograph whirred to a halt. Mary put down her sewing, walked over, and closed it down. Silence settled like a tight, restricting blanket. Olivia looked around for something, *anything*, to do. She'd already combined the two ruined dresses into one. It was serviceable and actually had a bit more flounce.

Maybe she should reread the letter Mrs. Baudouin had sent, but she could recite it by heart: The housekeeper liked her new job but missed Olivia, liked Topeka more than Prescott but wanted to return to France, and was still pressing the sheriff and Mr. Ennis to keep looking for Olivia's father.

In the whole world, the only person who missed Olivia was Mrs. Baudouin and maybe Mr. Ennis. But after her last meeting with him, he didn't count.

Mary cleared her throat and said accusingly, "You do realize you've been taking up quite a bit of Niles's attention."

This wasn't the first time Mary had brought up Mr. Niles or had referred to him as simply "Niles." Olivia treaded carefully. "I know. I think he's trying to save me from being fired. Mr. Gregory is not impressed with my performance."

Mary sniffed, as if Mr. Gregory's opinion didn't matter, or maybe the sniff was an agreement of Mr. Gregory's assessment. "If you need assistance, I'm the one you should seek out—not Niles."

Not a chance, thought Olivia. She remembered the brisk manner with which Mary had taken over the tables that first day. Mary's whole demeanor shouted that Harvey Girls were supposed to be all-knowing and not need supervision from anyone—not the head waitress and certainly not the manager.

The silence in the room deepened. The window let in plenty of air, but the stuffiness of the room didn't abate. Desperation, more than interest, inspired her to break the room's silence. She had to succeed at this job—to survive and to locate her father. Getting along with her roommate would be a big step toward some semblance of normalcy. "Looks like you're almost finished with that dress."

"I should finish tonight," Mary said stiffly. "Did you know Mr. Gregory is holding church services starting the Sunday after this one?"

The news came as no surprise. She'd heard the manager spout more than a few Bible verses. His knowledge of the scriptures didn't impress her. LeRoy Baker owned a Bible and occupied pew space at the Prescott church. Attending the Lord's house hadn't stopped her father's bookkeeper from embezzlement and possibly murder.

"I hope Niles attends the services," Mary whispered.

Had Olivia heard correctly? Had Mary just shared a personal desire?

"Probably," Olivia ventured. No doubt Mary already knew church attendance was encouraged by the Harvey organization, and from what Olivia saw, Mr. Niles was a company man. "You know," Olivia continued, very much wanting to understand her roommate, maybe draw close to her for once, "I've always wondered what Mr. Niles's first name is. Do you know?"

"It's Albert." Mary didn't look up from her sewing. No doubt Mary regretted her words about Mr. Niles already, because Mary O'Dell—tall, thin, and with dark hair pulled so tightly in a bun that one could count the strands—obviously wanted more than praise from the man.

She wanted him.

❧

It took only fifteen minutes for the patch of grass under Wayne's feet to flatten. What had he been thinking? He'd done a Sunday school class here and there, but never a full-fledged sermon—and never a sermon given outdoors *to a crowd*!

Niles had insisted on carrying chairs from the dining room outside. Mary was right at his side. Esther sat on one now, looking uncomfortable and alone. Wayne's reunion with his daughter hadn't gone as planned. First, she hadn't wanted to leave her grandparents—two years had allowed for roots to dig deep. Then she'd looked at him as if he were a stranger and called him Mr. Gregory instead of Papa. Next, the long train ride demonstrated to Wayne the true meaning of the word *fidgety*—squirming was an art form mastered by his daughter. As a final insult, last night, her first at the El Tovar, she'd cried herself to sleep.

Wayne felt like a failure. He wasn't warming to the job or to his daughter, nor did he hold out much hope that this sermon would light a fire under the feet of his audience gathered on the El Tovar's porch and spread over the front lawn. All Wayne felt was dry mouth as he noted how many nonemployees were gathering in the audience. "I meant for this to be an intimate service for employees. Who told all these people?"

Niles chuckled. "They have eyes. The Harvey employees are dressed in their best, most are carrying Bibles, and you certainly have the minister pace down pat."

"The minister pace?"

"Every minister I've ever seen usually spent a good deal of preparation time with his head bowed as he paced while mouthing his lesson."

"I'm not only mouthing my lesson," Wayne said dryly, "but also trying to think which hymn I know by heart."

"Surely you know plenty. You've certainly got a scripture for every occasion."

"Can't remember a single tune. I put together this lesson during the train ride home. Between here and Kansas I must have hummed a hundred. Now I can only remember 'Jesus Loves Me.' How about you lead a song or two?"

Niles snorted. "My voice would scatter the masses."

Glancing at his watch, Wayne stepped to his podium and gripped the sides. In forty-five minutes, the staff would need to get to their stations and hurriedly set up for lunch. The restaurant business didn't rest on Sundays but did observe shortened hours. A light breakfast of coffee and donuts had been served this morning, but a full lunch was anticipated by the guests—all of whom seemed gathered before him.

"Thank you for coming." His words carried—after all, he was a lawyer and knew how to project his voice—and the crowd hushed. He took a moment, smiled, and tried to calm himself. What a perfect place for a sermon. Trees, swaying in a gentle breeze, flanked the audience. A few squirrels were in attendance. And the crowd smiled expectantly—save for his daughter, Olivia Prescott, and Robert Thatcher.

Olivia was as fidgety as his daughter.

Robert Thatcher sat near the back, arms crossed, with a look that dared Wayne to attempt redemption.

Deciding that redemption would be a good sermon for next week, Wayne welcomed the audience with what he hoped was a very inspiring prayer and then cleared his throat. "Hopefully, soon," he began, "we'll be organized enough to have different song and prayer leaders. After service today, anyone who'll be around next Sunday is welcome to volunteer. In the meantime, I think 'Amazing Grace' is fairly well-known."

Wayne's first foray as a song leader demonstrated why he was a public speaker and not a singer. Luckily, two women sitting on the porch kept the pace, and of all people, Robert Thatcher, an exuberant alto, kept the song on key.

Wayne had titled his sermon "New Beginnings." He hit on creation, wisdom, and the Word. He realized halfway through that he was trying to cover too much. He should have done creation today, wisdom next Sunday, and then gone on to the Word. Still, the audience willingly flipped their Bibles from Genesis to Proverbs to John.

One of Wayne's strong points while defending a case was giving the jury time to mull over details. He knew how to use silence to increase comprehension. He used this technique during his sermon, pausing often to let the saints ponder his points. While they were turning pages, he studied those in attendance.

He first turned to where Robert Thatcher sat. Robert's judgmental look had been replaced by joy while he'd been singing, but now the man wore a bored frown. Maybe if he had a Bible in front of him, he'd have something to do with his hands and not be so displaced.

Mary O'Dell looked to be the first to find her place. She managed the pages of her Bible as efficiently as she lined up plates of food for her customers. Constance, Dinah, Mabel, and Sarah Jane were a few moments behind her, but judging by the look on their faces, he could tell they were thinking about his lesson and taking it in, while Mary probably felt it more important to keep her place.

Michelle was sitting by the two teenage boys. Wayne now knew they were here with their surveyor parents. The boys seemed very self-sufficient and weren't a bit shy. They looked over Michelle's shoulders as she found the proper scriptures.

Judging by the look on her face, she was more aware of their attention than the sermon.

Olivia obviously didn't handle her Bible much. By the time she found one scripture, he was providing the next.

Sitting just to the left of Olivia was Daniel. The man was like a sore tooth. He was usually the first customer to arrive in the morning and the last to leave. He'd bombarded both Niles and Wayne with questions about the Harvey business, the travel, and the girls. He seemed especially keen on Olivia's background—not that Wayne shared the contents of her file. Daniel had also picked up on the feud between Olivia and Michelle. The man was nosy and apparently didn't own a Bible.

His daughter's Bible remained unopened. Analise's parents had promised to take her to church—something they hadn't done with Analise. He'd believed they kept their promise because they'd made it to Analise as she lay dying. Obviously during the last two years Esther had been in the keeping of pew-warmers—people who attended church but weren't sure why. Wayne could develop a sermon about pew-warmers. He'd parallel them to the people who ordered lavish meals but didn't appreciate the taste.

He had so much to make up to his daughter.

Anger swelled, at an inopportune time. He stumbled through an analogy and forced himself to focus on the faces of strangers instead of friends so he wouldn't get distracted again. One thing was for sure: He needed a lesson on anger, because he felt a real hatred toward his ex-partners. Not so much because of what they'd done to him—although the memory of being set up was the main culprit—but because of what they'd done to his daughter's spiritual welfare.

"I want to close with a scripture. Please turn to John 1:1." He waited a moment then recited from memory. " 'Dearly beloved, avenge not yourselves, but rather give place unto wrath: for it is written, Vengeance is mine; I will repay, saith the Lord.' "

Most had been scurrying to keep up and find the verse, but as he said the words, they looked up.

"Son," Daniel said, "I believe you just quoted Romans 12:19. That verse might be more fitting with a different lesson. One I'm sure you could preach."

Wayne managed a weak smile. He'd just messed up. Instead of finishing with his intended verse, highlighting "beginnings," he'd uttered the verse on his heart—the one he was using while trying to forgive his ex-partners, his in-laws, and truthfully, himself.

Chapter 6

Olivia had really never spent any time with small children. Not that Esther Gregory considered herself small. "I'm eight," she'd announced after she left the table where her father had placed her and started following Olivia.

Mr. Gregory had provided Esther with a Bible, two picture books, pencils, and some old menus. Olivia remembered those early days after her mother died. Before hiring Mrs. Baudouin, John Prescott had taken Olivia into the factory with him. He'd sat her at a table with a giant dictionary and some blank order forms and pencils. She'd done pretty much the same thing Esther did now—pushed the books away and explored.

Esther looked disdainfully at the books. "Mr. Gregory thought I'd like these, but they were too easy. Besides, someone scribbled in them."

"I don't have any books," Olivia said before glancing around to see if any other, more matronly, more *motherly*, waitresses looked inclined to step in.

"I didn't expect you to," Esther said matter-of-factly. Clearly the little girl knew she'd picked the one Harvey Girl who knew nothing about children and therefore wouldn't know how to get rid of one. "Can I help with the flowers?"

"I don't think your father would approve, and why do you call him Mr. Gregory?"

"That's what my grandparents call him. I'll go ask if it's okay for me to help."

Before Olivia could protest, the little girl was gone.

"That's one way to get out of work," Michelle remarked as she held up a saltshaker to make sure it was full. "Get close to the boss's daughter. Soon you'll be back to doing what you do best: nothing."

Dinah Weston spoke up: "I think it's great Esther took a shine to you. She looked so lost yesterday during the sermon."

She wasn't the only one lost, Olivia thought. Mr. Gregory's sermon was unlike any she'd ever heard. Not only was it interesting, but she'd also understood most of it, even the out-of-place scripture at the end. The minister back in Prescott used to yell and pound on his Bible. When she was little, Olivia would burrow her head behind her father's arm. She'd been afraid to look at the preacher for fear he'd look at her.

She didn't mind looking at Mr. Gregory. Funny how at first she'd thought Mr. Niles the more handsome of the two. She'd been wrong, she realized now as she watched him enter the dining room a few steps behind his daughter. This morning his tie was crooked, and his hair looked a bit damp.

Olivia felt her breath quicken. The girls were right about his good looks. Sarah Jane had been the first to notice that Mr. Gregory's hair was the color of dark chocolate. Constance noted his eyes were the same color as his hair. Mabel was especially drawn to what she called his rugged chin.

"You want my daughter to help you?" He sounded amazed.

"I used to help Mama arrange flowers," Esther said.

Olivia watched as emotions played across Mr. Gregory's face. Once again she saw the man he *could* be instead of the man he *was*—the man who seemed intent on convincing her to hang her head and return to Kansas in shame.

"I'd appreciate the help." Olivia touched Esther's shoulder, half-expecting the little girl to shy away. While Esther didn't move any closer, she didn't bolt, either. Mr. Gregory looked from one to the other. "Thank you," he finally said. Olivia caught a glimpse of something she hadn't seen in a long time. It was the look of love, given from a father to his daughter.

Esther was too young to notice or fully appreciate it.

Olivia's knees threatened to buckle as she thought with longing of her own father. Swallowing back tears, she watched Mr. Gregory head back to the kitchen, then she pulled a centerpiece toward her and showed Esther how to contrast different colors and textures to enhance the arrangement. Then she explained how to vary the size and placement of the flowers. Finally, Olivia set Esther to fluffing leaves. Esther's slender hands started at the top of the stem and slowly moved downward, guiding the leaves outward. She managed to deleaf quite a few flowers, but the rest took on a nice perky look.

"My grandparents have a garden," Esther announced loudly, "and a gardener."

"So did Olivia," Michelle added snidely.

"Was your gardener Chinese?" Esther asked. "Was his name Pang?"

"No, his name was—" Michelle stopped.

Olivia waited. Esther had such a look of expectation on her

face. Would Michelle say something ugly?

"His name *is* Herb," Michelle finished. "He's my uncle."

"Is your uncle Chinese?"

It was clear Esther didn't understand the laughter that erupted from the waitresses who'd been listening to the exchange. Michelle laughed, too. The gesture made her look years younger. "No, he's not Chinese. He just likes working the land."

"Then why isn't he a farmer?" Esther asked.

"Because ye have ta own yer own land ta farm, and I don't want ta anymore," Michelle and Olivia chanted in unison, aping the old man's Irish brogue.

"Doesn't want to what?" Esther looked confused. "Farm or own land?"

"Either one," Michelle admitted. "He bought and lost three farms."

"Married and buried three wives," Olivia continued.

"Then decided the land and women just plain didn't like him," Michelle finished.

"I didn't know land can like people."

"I think land only had opinions about my uncle." Michelle graced Olivia with the tiniest of smiles before adding for Esther's sake, "You don't need to worry."

After the flowers were arranged, Esther took a shine to Sarah Jane and helped fold napkins. Once that task was finished, she sat at her original table and fidgeted until Dinah sat down and drew a very realistic likeness of Mr. Niles on the back of an old menu.

"I didn't know you could draw," Constance said, leaning over to watch as Dinah deftly darkened Mr. Niles's whiskers and with her finger smudged in his five o'clock shadow.

"There was an artist in my hometown," Dinah admitted. "She really helped me."

"Will you show me how to get the different shades using the one pencil?"

"Me, too," Esther inserted. "I want to learn."

A moment later, both Constance and Esther were working on drawings of Mr. Niles. Constance unwittingly added about fifty pounds to her boss. Esther looked to have a future as a cartoonist. All the girls gathered around to admire the Mr. Niles replicas. When the man himself entered the dining room, he raised his eyebrows at the giggles and frowned good-naturedly as two of his employees hid papers behind their backs. Esther wasn't quick enough. A moment later, Mr. Niles complimented her artistic talent. Clearly he didn't recognize himself.

After he checked every girl's station, he pulled Olivia aside. "Why are the flowers so bare looking? Half of them look to be missing their leaves."

Wayne found that the Harvey House's laundry was a great place for musing. He checked towels and thought to himself, *One month, two weeks, and three days.* That's how long it would be before the Grand Canyon school resumed, and Wayne would have a place where Esther would hopefully stay put for hours. It would be so much easier for him to manage the restaurant if he could manage his daughter. She was busier than he remembered. But then, he'd never had full-time responsibility. After Analise died, his in-laws had helped. They'd taken over full-time after the constable showed up at his door. Once Wayne made bail, he'd taken Esther back home and prepared his own case.

Only a fool represents himself, more than one of Wayne's contemporaries had advised. Wayne hadn't listened, and to this day, he couldn't fathom how anyone might have convinced the jury of his innocence. His partners had left a trail of damning evidence leading right to Wayne's door.

His first year in jail, he'd been like a man in a trance. He was Job. Everything, *everyone*, he loved had been snatched from him. While incarcerated, his exposure to Esther was limited; his exposure to God was limitless. His second year had been an awakening. He'd relied on his Bible. It had become his best friend and saved him.

"Mr. Gregory," Dinah said, catching up to him as he refolded a stack of linens. "There's a customer complaining about his breakfast. He's being quite abusive."

Entering the dining room, he first noticed Mary O'Dell, as red as a woman could get, with bits of potatoes and eggs smeared on the front of her frock. This had to be the unfortunate breakfast.

"Vous la femme incompétente, j'aurai votre travail!" the customer ranted.

Wayne didn't understand a word.

"Monsieur, calme vers le bas. Nous vous ferons cuire un autre petit déjeuner. J'assurerai personnellement il répond à vos normes." Olivia stepped in front of Mary.

Wayne doubted Olivia understood how unreasonable the inebriated could be. He'd served his time beside remorseful men who'd committed heinous crimes they couldn't recall after they sobered. He quickened his pace, stood in front of his waitresses, and said almost nonchalantly, "What's going on here?"

"Des employés de Youâre, elles m'insultent," the man sputtered.

"He wanted Olivia's station, but she was in the gift shop," Mary explained. "She came and took his order and then went back. When I served him, he looked unhappy. Before I could fetch her to find out why, he grabbed my arm and threw his food at me."

"Que j'aurai tous vos travaux. Le défi vous écouten—!"

"Enough." Wayne motioned for the man to cease talking. "Olivia, ask him what was wrong with the food."

"It doesn't matter what is wrong with the food," Olivia sputtered. "He threw his meal on Mary. There's no excuse for that!"

"Trust me, Olivia."

She clenched her teeth so tightly Wayne could feel the tension, yet she gave a tiny nod before asking, *"Monsieur, ce qui avait tort avec votre nourriture?"*

The man raved for a few moments, and then Olivia translated, "He said he found a hair."

"Tell him to produce the hair," Wayne said.

"What!" Olivia and Mary asked in unison.

"Tell him to produce the hair. Tell him!"

"Monsieur, néanmoins avez-vous les cheveux?"

It took a few minutes before the blustering Frenchman admitted he no longer had the hair. Wayne pretended to look at the wooden floor.

"What are you doing?" Olivia asked.

"Why, I'm looking for the evidence. Ask him what color the hair was."

Olivia obeyed, and the Frenchman shrugged, claiming all hair looked alike.

"Esther, help me look," Wayne ordered.

Esther hit the ground with an ease only an eight-year-old could manage. After a moment, she held up a short brown strand. "Here, Papa!" She slipped her hand in his.

"Is this it?" Wayne patted his daughter's head appreciatively as he held the piece of hair close to the Frenchman's face.

The Frenchman pushed Wayne's hand away and started to sputter in a loud, obnoxious voice, which Wayne quickly dispelled. "Tell him he lacks evidence and that unless he'd like to spend the night in jail for assault, he should leave the restaurant and find some other establishment for his meals."

Olivia repeated the words, and when the Frenchman started to respond, Wayne interrupted and said, "Tell him I will be the one to personally press charges."

"Hah, les cheveux a goûté mieux que les oeufs!" With that, the Frenchman stomped out.

Wayne almost felt exuberant. Not only had he successfully, and peacefully, dispelled an explosive situation, but he'd also managed to win his daughter's admiration—she called him Papa!—while looking like a hero in front of Olivia.

He looked around to see if Niles had wandered in, as he was prone to do on his day off. But, no, Wayne was solely in charge. Already the staff worked together to clear the restaurant of any evidence of the altercation. Esther picked bits of egg off the floor. Olivia knelt next to her and dabbed at splashes of coffee with a napkin. Mary sat at a chair in a corner, staring at Olivia and wearing a stricken expression on her face.

Wayne had just proven to himself that he could manage a restaurant—but kneeling before him was the woman who made it possible. Olivia Prescott, blue blood, speaker of French, one-time owner of overpriced and frilly clothes, meticulous, and his daughter's favorite person and caregiver.

Niles intended to take one employee with him to Belen, New Mexico to open a new Harvey House: Olivia.

Maybe Wayne could survive without Niles, but with Olivia gone. . . He shook his head as he watched Esther following behind Olivia. His little girl aped the waitress's style of walking and insisted on wearing her hair tied back in the same loose bun.

As a lawyer, he should have noticed that Olivia and Esther had a lot in common. They both required plenty of attention. They both hated getting dirty and liked pretty, frilly things. They both had a tendency to do what *they* wanted to do instead of what *he* wanted them to do.

"Mr. Gregory." Dinah Weston appeared at his side again.

Wayne glanced around the restaurant and breathed a sigh of relief—no irate Frenchman.

"Mr. Thatcher has asked to speak with you."

"About his breakfast tab?"

Dinah shook her head. "I don't think so."

Robert Thatcher occupied a bench on the El Tovar's porch. He leaned forward, elbows on his knees, his hands covering his face. He looked like he was praying.

Just as Olivia had taken Wayne by surprise by caring for his daughter, Thatcher had also surprised Wayne. He'd lost his belligerent expression and attended every church service, finally even taking over the song leading.

"You need something?" Wayne asked.

Thatcher stood, and Wayne thought of that long-ago day when he'd dismissed the man from the law firm of Conn and Williams. "I need a job," Thatcher said.

The conversation lasted maybe five minutes before Thatcher headed back to wherever he was boarding. Wayne shook his head for the second time that day. Life was full of surprises, and it seemed he was constantly on the receiving end.

"Strangest conversation I ever heard." Daniel leaned in the doorway, chewing on a toothpick. "You've just given a job to a man you despise."

" 'Love your enemies. . .do good to them that hate you.' " The scripture rolled off Wayne's tongue. As he said the words, he realized that Thatcher wasn't an enemy.

Daniel joined Wayne. "I almost believe you mean what you say."

Wayne smiled. "Truthfully, hiring the man made me feel like I was finally doing my part for the Harvey organization."

"Don't care for your job much?" Daniel asked.

"I didn't say that." Wayne suddenly felt interrogated. "Is there something you need, Daniel?"

"I was interested in your threat to press charges against Mr. Laperouse. Did you know the closest lawyer is fifty miles away in Flagstaff?"

"No, I didn't know that."

"Miss being a lawyer, do you?"

Wayne took a step back. "What else do you know? Did you know I was exonerated? This is the start of a new life for me. Did you follow me here to the El Tovar? Why are you quizzing my employees and even my daughter?"

"You surely are a lawyer at heart. You ask more questions than a widow at a potluck." Taking out his wallet, Daniel showed a badge. "I'm a private detective—"

Annoyed, Wayne interrupted, "You're on the wrong trail.

I shared everything I knew—which wasn't much—with the district attorney. If anyone else was involved—"

"Slow down, Mr. Prosecutor, I'm not here investigating you, although I know more about your case than you do."

"You're not investigating me?"

"No, I'm actually interested in—"

"Olivia Prescott," Wayne finished. It all made sense now: Daniel's questions on the train, his requesting Olivia's station, his meeting the girls for nightly walks. Had Wayne not been so focused on his own problems, he would have noticed.

Daniel grinned. "How did you know?"

"I watch her as much as you do," Wayne admitted. "So if you're really investigating Olivia Prescott, why is it you know so much about my case?"

"A good detective doesn't believe in coincidences. I overheard young Thatcher that first day. Two people with ties to embezzlers seemed quite an unlikely occurrence, so I asked my friend William to find out about you."

"Who is William?"

"Not important," Daniel said, brushing him off. "What is important is your Olivia."

"She's not my Olivia."

Daniel walked to the edge of the porch. After a moment, Wayne followed. Together they watched Olivia—with Esther in tow—picking flowers.

"She's too young for me," Wayne murmured. "She can't be my Olivia."

"A few months ago I'd have agreed with you, but the girl's got more grit than you'd expect. What do you know about her situation?"

"The one newspaper clipping I read stated that her father ran off with the town's money and left everyone, including her, destitute."

Daniel reached in his wallet again and pulled out a telegraph. "Arrived this morning. Seems Miss Prescott has saved enough to hire herself a private detective. Of all things, she contacted the agency I work for. She's willing to pay more than twenty dollars a month just to hire someone to look for her father. That's just about all her earnings, isn't it? Seems she doesn't believe her old man was an embezzler."

"Is he?" Wayne asked.

"*Was* he, you mean? His body was located a week ago. Single gunshot wound."

"You going to tell her?" Wayne watched Olivia and Esther head back their way.

"No," Daniel said.

"Why not?" Wayne demanded. "Isn't that what she hired you for? To find out?"

"Yes, but I think she still has something the men who killed her father want."

"Is she in danger?"

"Not while I'm here."

"Is this putting any of my employees or my daughter in danger?" Wayne thought of his daughter, who now willingly traipsed to church each Sunday morning. She had her favorite spot, right next to Olivia Prescott.

"If I thought that, I'd be the first to tell you. Killing Olivia won't get the killers what they want."

"Which is?"

"Her property. I'm thinking any day someone is going to

turn up looking for Olivia. With Niles, you, and I watching out for her, we should be able to keep her safe."

"Niles? You mean Niles already knows?"

"I told him the day I arrived. He's been keeping an eye on her ever since. It's why he's thinking of taking her to Belen with him."

It all made sense. No wonder Niles put up with Olivia's eccentricities. Wayne slowly shook his head. "Why did you tell Niles and not me?"

"Because I saw the way you were looking at her on the train. I was afraid your attraction to her might interfere with my case."

"And you're only telling me now because the stakes are higher."

Daniel nodded. "That and with your daughter spending so much time with her, seems you more than deserve to know."

Wayne closed his eyes, surprised by a sudden attack of fear. He hadn't felt this way since hearing the foreman of the jury say, "Guilty as charged." Taking a deep breath, he managed to say, "I'm not comfortable keeping her father's death a secret from her."

"I understand," Daniel said. "But she hired me to find the truth, and not telling her is the quickest, easiest, and safest way to arrest those involved."

"This feels dishonest. It feels like a lie, and I—"

"Son, you need to remember I'm not the only one following Olivia. Telling her the truth will put her in danger." Daniel put his wallet away and headed for the door. "You know your Bible. Think of Peter in Matthew 26. He lied to save himself. You're lying to save someone else—someone you love." Daniel certainly had a way of making a point. Not that the man had convinced Wayne that lying could be a virtue. Peter, after he denied Christ, wept bitterly.

Following into the El Tovar's lobby, Wayne cleared his throat loudly enough to get the private investigator's attention.

"Yes?" Daniel turned around.

"You said you knew more about my case than I did," Wayne reminded him. "Just what do you know?"

"I know that young Thatcher knew Conn and Williams were embezzling, and that's why they had you fire him."

Chapter 7

The office looked the same as it had the last time Mr. Gregory dragged her in here, except that her torn dresses were gone. She'd be wondering what she'd done wrong now, except the other waitresses had already been called in for their evaluation. Why did she have to do hers with Mr. Gregory instead of Mr. Niles? Mr. Niles made her feel needed; Mr. Gregory just made her feel out of breath.

The door to the office opened, and Mr. Gregory stepped in—smiling.

Olivia looked behind her. He never smiled at *her*!

"Thanks for waiting, Olivia." He sat down, for some reason smiled at the sight of his fountain pen, and picked up a folder. Opening it, he set aside a few pieces of paper. "Ruth Owens thought highly of you. Tell me why."

"Tell you why she thought highly of me?"

"Yes," Wayne said, nodding. "I want to know what it is that made her see beyond your"—he cleared his throat—"mistakes."

"You mean ineptness."

"I may have judged you too harshly, Olivia. So tell me your strong points."

Olivia sat a bit straighter. She knew her strong points and none of them advanced her waitressing skills. "I can't, sir. Telling you my strong points would feel too much like boasting. Didn't you preach against that last week?"

"I'm glad you were listening." He smiled again.

Olivia looked behind her again.

He shuffled some of the papers and then set them down. "How about I go over your strong points? First of all, you like order and correctness."

"Correctness?" She frowned. Her strong points sounded dull.

"Beauty," he elaborated. "That's evident in the way you hold yourself, the way you took over the centerpieces, and the way you rearranged the gift shop." He leaned forward. "What would you think about managing the gift shop?"

She blinked, almost afraid she'd misunderstood. She would love to spend her days handling the Indian jewelry, pottery, and blankets, plus other memorabilia, as opposed to handling food, but. . . "Will I make the same amount of money?"

"I'll personally see to it."

"How?"

"Since the gift shop closes early, you can wait tables at the end of the day. I believe that's when your regulars come in anyway. Am I right?"

Olivia nodded.

"The loyalty your customers feel to you demonstrates another of your strong points: an inclination to pay attention to customer details. I've watched you. During a rush, you'll help a child cut his meat or redo a little girl's hair ribbons. Some customers are annoyed because all they see is their unfilled coffee cups. But the locals, and those who request you, just seem to sit back and enjoy. I've never seen anything like it."

"That's not saying much, Mr. Gregory. You've only been a manager for about as long as I've been a waitress."

If her bluntness surprised him, he didn't let it show. "That's true, Olivia, but I've dined in the finest restaurants throughout the East. You tend to get more personal with your customers than the typical waitress. It's why Ruth Owens wanted you here. You need to be in a locale where your customers are not in a hurry to catch a train."

Olivia finally smiled back. Every time she cleaned up and walked out of the restaurant last, she wondered if anyone had noticed that her customers seldom seemed to hurry. Daniel liked to talk, and he introduced her to rugged men who told stories while eating *and* chewing on a cigar. Men like the Kolb brothers who photographed the tourists taking mule rides into the Grand Canyon. Men like President Roosevelt who came to dinner in muddy boots and dusty riding clothes and had Mr. Niles talking about the El Tovar building a private dining room for the man.

As much as she thought she'd like working in the gift shop, knowing that she could continue waiting on the customers she counted as friends was a nice incentive.

"And," Mr. Gregory said, his voice changing from brisk to gentle, "there's the matter of your attention to my daughter. From the day she arrived, you've freely given your time to her. I'd like to pay you what I would pay a governess."

"The other girls watch her, too. I'm not quite sure paying just me would be fair."

"Then how about I pay you for watching her on your day off?"

Olivia started to refuse. Surely Mr. Gregory realized she never took a day off. She tried to fill every moment with work, because if she made more money, she might be able to hire a second agency—she wished she would hear back from the first agency—or pay the detective more—anything to find out where her father was or, at least, clear his name.

"How much money?" she asked.

Her new schedule started the following Tuesday. As she dressed, Olivia could barely contain her exuberance. Mary sniffed at the change but didn't comment. Since the encounter with the Frenchman, the head waitress had been decidedly withdrawn. Instead of the usual show tunes and ragtime records she favored, Mary played the few winsome ballads she owned—over and over. Rumors among the girls had Mary counting on going to Belen with Mr. Niles and helping to open the new restaurant. She obviously considered the unfortunate encounter with the customer as detrimental to her career.

"Morning," Olivia called as she entered the restaurant.

A chorus of "Mornings" greeted her. What a wonderful feeling: acceptance.

Esther—wearing the little Harvey uniform Olivia had finally finished—sat in the corner beside Dinah and copied her every pencil stroke. Esther liked drawing scenery best but still enjoyed the hoopla her accidental caricatures incited.

About the time Olivia finished filling the last ice bin, the train arrived. Taking Esther by the hand, Olivia headed for the outdoors.

"Where are we going?" Esther asked. "Will I get dirty? I don't have another dress." The last was uttered accusingly. Esther knew if a Harvey Girl dirtied her uniform, she immediately changed. With only one uniform, Esther dared not get dirty.

"Don't worry. I'm *your* head waitress, and I get to decide when you're too dirty to be seen," Olivia assured.

Esther, who had no intention of getting dirty, nodded. "Now will you tell me where we're going?"

"I thought we'd see what the Indian women are selling." Ever since Olivia had stepped off the train and noted the Native Americans with their wares spread out on blankets, she'd wanted to investigate.

"Papa said I'm not supposed to go near the Indians."

"Yes, but you're also supposed to stay near me. Correct?"

"Correct," Esther agreed.

"And that's where I'm going, so you—"

"And I think I'll go, too." Mr. Gregory stepped up and took Esther's hand.

Esther took a step back and then grinned at her father. Outside of the end-of-day proddings out of the dining room—Esther hated to go to bed—it was the first time Olivia noticed Mr. Gregory touching his daughter. He looked at Olivia, and she thought for a moment that he'd reach for her hand also. Uncomfortable because she actually *wanted* him to, she stepped off the porch and hurried down the path to the train depot, where at almost any time of the day, Native Americans spread out blankets and sold everything from jewelry to pottery to the blanket they used for display.

Olivia held on to her money; she'd just inquired at the detective agency of Baldwin-Felts. Mr. Gregory wasn't so tight-fisted. He purchased a few trinkets for Esther and also fingered, but decided against, a few items for himself.

Then, thirty minutes later, he walked them back to the hotel and into the gift shop. On the register counter lay Esther's drawing of Sarah Jane folding napkins. Mr. Gregory set it aside and proceeded to instruct Olivia on how to use the cash register.

It was the closest she had stood to her manager. She could smell his pepperminty aftershave. For a moment, she wished Mary were training her, because then Olivia's attention would be completely on task instead of on the proximity of Mr. Gregory.

When she finally satisfied him that she could add two plus two and even remember to write it in the book, he left. Olivia took a deep breath and looked around, trying to decide her first duty. Taking the drawing of Sarah Jane, Olivia tacked it to the wall next to the famous print by Thomas Moran. For the rest of the morning, Esther memorized the plaques that accompanied the artwork on display. When customers came in, sometimes she'd read them the history. Daniel wandered in, supplied some additional information about a few of the paintings, and then took off. By the end of the day, Esther had sold two paintings and her drawing of Sarah Jane.

Earning a penny turned the already-too-serious little girl into an instant entrepreneur. Esther immediately took off for her lodgings to gather up all the drawings she had. She returned with a good-sized handful along with two glasses of iced tea and, of all people, Michelle—who carried a tray of food.

"Mr. Gregory said it was time for you to eat lunch." Michelle sat down to eat with them and commented, "I've often wished I could work in here. I really like how you've arranged it. Remember when we used to decorate your mother's parlor?"

"Do I." Olivia laughed. "I remember when we moved Papa's favorite chair."

"And he came in, didn't bother to look, and sat down."

"Well, the light wasn't on."

"And you took the blame," Michelle said gently. "Although it was my idea."

"I remember."

Esther laughed. "Did your papa hurt himself?"

"No, but he broke a vase my mama really liked."

"And he bought her a new one she liked even better so she couldn't stay mad. I've been thinking," Michelle said, "your father wouldn't steal his factory's money and take off. And he certainly wouldn't leave you behind. You must be worried sick."

"Every day," Olivia admitted.

"I'm sorry I called him a criminal that first day. I guess I've been jealous and mad for a long time. Truthfully, I never wanted to go to high school. I wanted to get married and have babies. And guess what? I'm going to marry Benjamin Mason."

He wasn't the cuter of the two young men who so often followed Michelle around, but Olivia thought him friendlier. "When?"

"I need to finish my contract, so not for another six months. Ben's going back to Philadelphia to work in his grandfather's store. We'll both save our money and maybe even buy a house."

"I'm happy for you, Michelle."

"You need to get married and have babies, too. You're really good with Esther. I've been watching and wondering why she didn't choose someone like me to follow. After all"—Michelle grinned—"I'm nicer."

"I picked Miss Olivia because her favorite color is pink," Esther said.

"How did you know?" Olivia asked.

"Papa told me about the pretty dresses you traded away."

Michelle kept grinning. "So the stern Mr. Gregory isn't blind."

"No," Esther said seriously. "He likes pink dresses. He told me so. All my dresses are pink." She stopped and looked down. "Except this one."

"And I don't have a pink dress anymore—just my uniform and then two others." Olivia looked at Michelle and said ruefully, "But you know that."

"I do know that," Michelle said. "But the loss of your clothes is not because of me. I didn't destroy your dresses."

Chapter 8

One of the best things about being the manager of the El Tovar Harvey House was the office. Its view included trees, wildlife, and a vast chasm of canyon highlights. Wayne stared out the window thinking about his daughter and Olivia, his current management job and Olivia, and his old law practice and Olivia.

He was spending entirely too much time thinking about Olivia. He could blame Daniel, but the truth was, even before he knew her history, Olivia demanded his attention.

Spread out before him was all the information Daniel had gleaned so far. LeRoy Baker—not his real name, although no one knew for sure what that was—wasn't just an embezzler. He was also a bigamist and murderer.

Wayne had chuckled the first time he'd seen Olivia's school history. Grace School for Ladies sounded like the sort of place his in-laws would have sent Esther. Now Wayne knew Olivia had been fortunate to be away. LeRoy had married five other girls before relieving their fathers of a lifetime of hard work and earnings.

Daniel had included the obituaries of two of the fathers—

one murdered, the other dead by his own hand.

Wayne said a quick prayer. Suicide wasn't a solution he understood. Plus, it left a bereaved daughter facing a double sorrow: a runaway husband and a deceased father. Of the other three fathers, one had rebuilt his empire, another had become an employee of a business he'd previously owned, and the last had made it his personal vendetta to find Frank Warren, aka Jack Tate, aka William Smith, aka Albert Tucker, aka LeRoy Baker.

Wayne headed toward the dining room; he figured father number five had some explaining to do.

Daniel sat at a corner table drinking coffee. He'd made himself so constant a visitor that the girls were used to working around him. Wayne helped himself to a cup. "LeRoy, or should I call him Frank, got unlucky, didn't he?"

"He hadn't figured on Olivia going to Europe for almost a year," Daniel agreed. "And didn't want to wait that long to get his hands on the money. What else did you get from the papers I gave you?"

"Enough to know that LeRoy won't be showing up here. He's too careful. He's had an accomplice each and every time—someone on the inside."

"In my case," Daniel said ruefully, "it was my oldest daughter's husband. Seems I wasn't turning over enough control and money to him fast enough."

"So you have two heartbroken daughters. No wonder you have a vendetta."

"Interesting word: *vendetta*. I'm not sure that's what I still have. Oh, at first I'd have gladly taken the law into my own hands and strung Frank up, but that's not the way our Lord calls us to act. Yeah"—Daniel shook his head—"that's right, I know the Savior. I lost Him for a while, but I'm slowly getting Him back. Your first sermon really made me think. Do you remember the scripture you accidentally quoted?"

Wayne managed a tight smile. " 'Dearly beloved, avenge not yourselves, but rather give place unto wrath: for it is written, Vengeance is mine; I will repay, saith the Lord.' " That one little mistake had garnished him more compliments than all the scriptures he'd since quoted correctly.

"That's the one. You stumbled all over yourself trying to recover, but that scripture was just what I needed. I saw you up there, just a young pup, and like me you'd watched as much of what you loved was taken. No doubt revenge was something you wanted." Daniel shook his head. "I've spent two years hunting Frank. I'm ready to go home. But first I have to see to it that Frank Warren doesn't hurt anyone else's daughter."

Speaking of keeping an eye on a daughter, Wayne realized that if he didn't hurry, he'd miss out on the morning excursion. A quick look showed Esther and Olivia already heading out the door. Wayne needed to get moving, but he had one last question: "If you're not *really* a private detective and if you had all your money taken from you, how are you financing your time here?"

"I am a private detective for the Baldwin-Felts Detective Agency. I know William Baldwin personally—have ever since we were children. Being on his payroll, although he's not paying me a dime, gives me access to information I'd have trouble finding on my own. How do you think I found out about you? I have an assignment, self-assigned: Find Frank Warren. Oh, Frank got us good, but we'll bounce back. He shut down my business, managed to sell my home and the homes of my daughters, and I hold him responsible for my wife's breakdown, but I've always understood the parable of the talents. I don't keep my eggs all in one basket. I had holdings neither Frank nor my other son-in-law knew about."

"If he'd known about them, would he have gone after them?"

"You betcha."

"And Frank, er, LeRoy must know about Olivia's property, but isn't it useless?"

"That's what she's been told, but now that her father's body has been found, she's potentially a wealthy woman. By the way, when you were nosing around in all that paperwork, did you happen to notice my previous occupation?"

"No," Wayne admitted.

"I owned a factory. As a matter of fact, I've recently inquired about purchasing another one. I'm thinking Prescott, Kansas, might be just the sort of place for me to move my family and start again."

"And today we're. . . ?" Mr. Gregory wasn't a student of the outdoors.

"Looking for arrowheads," Olivia finished for him.

Esther carried a sock, which she was convinced she could fill. So far two pretty rocks and one eagle feather took up space, probably the only items they would find today.

Changing the subject, Mr. Gregory asked, "If Michelle didn't cut those dresses, who did?"

"I was convinced she did it," Olivia admitted. "I never considered anyone else. I mean, *why* would someone destroy my belongings?"

Mr. Gregory helped Esther over a log and guided her away from what he must have considered too close to the edge. A shout came from just below. "Who's up there?"

Olivia leaned over the edge. "Mr. Kolb, what are you doing down there?"

"Stay put," Emery Kolb yelled.

A moment later, Mr. Kolb crawled over the ledge and, muttering something about light, had them arranged too close to the canyon's edge and was shooting a photo. Olivia tried to protest that the picture should be of just Mr. Gregory and his daughter, but Mr. Kolb had something in mind and was in no mood to listen. After more than a few minutes of lens adjustments and more than one repositioning of a fidgeting little girl, Mr. Kolb had what he wanted and ran toward his studio.

Mr. Gregory took up where he left off. "And you absolutely believe Michelle."

"I do."

"When you arrived here, did you know anyone besides Michelle? Someone who might carry a grudge?"

"No, everyone else was a stranger."

"I think you're right about Michelle. Nothing in her file indicates a woman who would jeopardize her career just for a little revenge. Who all knew that you'd exchanged your finery for the other girls' dresses?"

"Well, the other girls."

"Constance, Sarah Jane, and Mabel."

"And Mary O'Dell," Olivia remembered. "But she'd have no reason except that she wasn't enthralled with the idea of having a roommate."

"And she knows it's only temporary," Wayne agreed.

Olivia considered her roommate. She didn't smile much. Constance thought Mary was still grieving her late husband. Both Sarah Jane and Mabel grumbled about Mary's habit of guiding the wealthy to her own tables so that her tips were probably a bit higher than others. Dinah generously claimed it was the head waitress's right to handpick her customers since she spent much of her time training.

Olivia didn't see much training going on. Most of the girls were as efficient as Mary, and those who needed help gravitated toward Constance.

In companionable silence, Olivia and Mr. Gregory followed Esther along the rim. Although Olivia hated to admit it, she was starting to enjoy his company. Last night, when Mr. Gregory noticed that she was the last out of the dining room, he'd waited around to walk her to the dormitory. He didn't talk business like Mr. Niles. Instead, he talked about his former law practice.

Not that she'd spent much time with Mr. Ennis, but it soon became clear to Olivia that Mr. Gregory had what her father called vast knowledge of the law, while Mr. Ennis had only limited knowledge. If John Prescott had been able to retain a lawyer as gifted as Mr. Gregory, LeRoy Baker would have been discovered, and both she and Michelle would still call Prescott home.

And for all his gruffness, his high expectations, and his earlier lack of compassion—at least toward her—Mr. Gregory actually was starting to make Olivia want to spent time with him. The man needed to have some fun.

"Esther, run ahead and wash up before you help Olivia," Mr. Gregory ordered.

"But I didn't find a single arrowhead."

"We'll look again," Olivia promised. "And for today, you can draw one."

And for four days, Esther refused to draw anything but arrowheads. Customers oohed and aahed and purchased quite a few. Esther charged a penny. Her proud papa, who meandered in more times than Olivia was comfortable with, listened to his daughter issue a spiel that resulted in a sale. Mr. Gregory promptly located a table and chair and set up an area behind the register where Esther kept meticulous track of her pennies.

Olivia, of course, had to teach Esther how to curb her enthusiasm.

That Sunday Mr. Gregory preached on tithing. He compared and contrasted the Old and New Testaments and finished with Second Chronicles 24:10: "All the princes and all the people rejoiced, and brought in, and cast into the chest, until they had made an end."

Esther put a penny in the chest Mr. Gregory had used as an example and smiled smugly at Olivia.

Olivia squirmed. She hadn't put money in the plate—ever. She put all her money aside for necessities and Baldwin-Felts.

From his stance on the porch, Mr. Gregory said, " 'Give, and it shall be given unto you; good measure, pressed down, and shaken together, and running over, shall men give into your bosom. For with the same measure that ye mete withal it shall be measured to you again.' "

Olivia didn't understand it all, but she was starting to understand enough, thanks to the example of Mr. Gregory and his daughter. She reached inside her purse.

That night, after the lights went out and all sane people laid their heads on their pillows, the men got together. Between the three of them, they were keeping Olivia under close guard. Niles took breakfast setup, spot checks in the gift shop, and evening shutdown. Daniel seemed to be everywhere, but his assigned duty was watching the arriving train in the morning and inspecting it as it left in the evening. Wayne continued with the hour walk and spot checks in the gift shop and also added Mondays—Olivia's day off. Since she had no family, so far she'd neglected to take a day off—something Niles wasn't aware of. "Mary should have made me aware," he grumbled.

"There's a lot about Mary you don't know." Daniel's words were nonchalant, but his look was steely.

"What do you mean?" Niles asked.

"Never meant to be a private detective and don't intend to stay one, but you boys missed the obvious."

"You going to tell us, or do we have to guess?" Niles asked.

"I know she's one of your favorites. . ." Daniel began.

"She's a good employee. We've opened five Harvey Houses together."

"And while you were busy building your career, she was building a fantasy about your future together."

"Nonsense," Niles said. "Most women tend to think what's there is more than what's really there. Mary's sensible. She knows I'm not the marrying kind."

"Then why did she cut up Olivia's clothes when she thought you might be acting a bit too friendly with our girl?"

"She didn't!"

"She did," Daniel said. "From early on Mary noticed that

Olivia seemed to capture your interest. And consider this. Mary's the seamstress among the waitresses. She knew about the dresses; she owned the scissors. She moves quickly and has so many responsibilities that no one expects her to be in one place."

"But Mary's the one who made Olivia notify me about the dresses," Wayne said.

"Sure she did. When Olivia didn't report the destruction, Mary knew no action would be taken. Mary wanted Olivia transferred. She's also the one who took the fountain pen while you were out of the office. You blamed Olivia, didn't you?"

Wayne felt sheepish. He'd blamed Olivia, harbored a grudge even. As a lawyer, he should have remembered that one was innocent until proven guilty.

"Then you fell in love and didn't give another thought to that fountain pen."

Wayne shook his head. If enough people mentioned his attraction to Olivia, he'd have to do something about it.

"It's a good match," Daniel said gruffly. "If I didn't like Olivia so much, I'd drag you home to meet up with one of my girls." He turned his attention to Niles.

"Don't even think it," Niles said.

For the next half hour, the men did what they'd originally met to do. They pored over the hotel register, looking for someone connected to Olivia. So far no one appeared suspicious. Daniel shook his head. "I'm surprised it's taking this long. Her signature is all that's needed before the necessary paperwork can be filed."

"What if someone legitimate shows up, like her father's lawyer or the French maid she's always writing to?" Wayne started pacing.

"Hopefully, if that happens," Daniel said, "the accomplice won't be far behind. After all, Olivia's still single."

Wayne wasn't surprised when both men smirked at him.

Chapter 9

Wayne left the meeting and detoured to the women's dormitory. Inside, Olivia slept, not knowing her father was dead, not knowing she might be in danger, not knowing Wayne loved her. Spending so much time with Olivia was proving to be as much a curse as a blessing. She made him *miss* his wife. She made him *want* a wife.

Once he satisfied himself that no one lurked about, he headed for his room. Esther snored softly. The sound soothed him. His little girl was starting to thrive. She gained weight and had a healthy glow, and she hadn't cried for her grandparents in more than two weeks. Wayne was about ready to write them and invite them to visit.

Sitting down, he thumbed through some of the documents Daniel had provided. Who could be LeRoy Baker's accomplice? In two of the cases, it had been greedy relatives. In another two, it had been disgruntled employees. In yet another case, it had been a competitor. Maybe Daniel should visit Kansas, speak with that housekeeper, Mrs. Baudouin, and speak with John Prescott's lawyer. Wayne rubbed the bridge of his nose and decided to turn in. He needed to be alert in case Olivia needed him.

❧

The next morning, sitting in the office with Niles, Mary, and Olivia, Wayne remembered Daniel's words: *"The girl's got more grit than you'd expect."* He'd led the group in a quick prayer, and then Niles started the meeting. Throughout Mary's confession, Olivia hadn't winced or gotten angry. Other emotions played across her face: hurt, speculation, pity. The only time she'd acted surprised was when she heard about the fountain pen incident.

Niles had demonstrated more indignity than Olivia had. First, he'd confessed to being blind to Mary's attraction. Then he'd expressed his disgust with the method Mary used to try to get Olivia transferred. "We're transferring Mary to another Harvey House, and she's losing her head waitress status," Niles said. "Unless you'd like a more severe punishment," he added.

"She can stay here and stay head waitress," Olivia offered. "I don't care. I know what it's like to want something so badly you'd try just about anything."

"No," Niles said. "It's time for her to move on."

For a moment, Mary's eyes held hope. Wayne knew she was thinking Belen, but Belen was not a possibility, and Mary had to know there was no way Niles would take her with him now.

"I'll go wherever you say, Mr. Niles," Mary said. She stood slowly then started for the door. She'd gone just a few yards when she stopped and turned around. "I truly am sorry, Olivia. I liked you from the moment you moved in. And when you helped me with that irate customer, I wanted to apologize, but I was ashamed."

She closed the door behind her. Niles rubbed a hand over his eyes. "I'll see that she's taken care of."

"Good," Olivia said softly, "then the prayer worked."

Seated across from a woman who'd just shown mercy when mercy wasn't called for was humbling. And in that moment, for some reason Wayne thought of the photo Kolb had taken and wished it truly could be called a family photo.

❧

Olivia took over for Mary and worked the evening shift even though it was her day off. The other girls knew something was amiss and desperately wanted the gossip, but picking up on Mr. Niles's difficult mood, they wisely left the matter alone. Olivia was grateful. She didn't think she could take any more excitement today.

Of course, she was wrong.

The restaurant closed at nine. Ten minutes before Mr. Niles was set to lock the door, Jasper Ennis walked in.

"Olivia," he said.

A coldness crept up her spine. "Mr. Ennis, what are you doing here?" Then hope surged, and she rushed toward him. "Did you find my father? Do you have news?"

He looked distastefully at her uniform. "I have answers for all your questions. Do you need to go change?"

"No, it will be at least two hours before I've cleaned my station and prepped for tomorrow."

"My dear, you don't need to worry about shifts ever again." He glanced around and frowned. "Surely, after working here, you realize that my offer was generous."

"You mean your offer of marriage?"

Behind her, she heard Michelle gasp and whisper to someone, "Go get Mr. Gregory."

Dinah hustled over. "Sir, may I seat you?"

"You may seat both of us."

"I'm working," Olivia said.

"Oh, sit down with him." Daniel called from a corner table as he took a drink of his coffee. "You girls work too hard. It's the end of the day."

Niles, who Olivia hadn't even realized was nearby, spoke up. "It's your day off anyway, Olivia. If this is an old friend, please feel free to visit."

"Don't make her," Michelle whispered.

Mr. Ennis chose his own table, away from the lingering customers and near a window. Olivia followed, each step feeling heavier. She suddenly understood the old adage "No news is good news."

Michelle brought two glasses of tea.

Olivia tried to keep her hand from shaking as she reached for hers.

"Olivia, you are even lovelier than I remember." Mr. Ennis didn't smile. Nothing in his manner gave credence to his words.

"Thank you, Mr. Ennis, for the compliment, but surely that's not what you came to say."

"No, and I'm not sure this is the appropriate setting."

The tea glass slipped, but Olivia caught it. No doubt Mr. Ennis thought an appropriate setting would be somewhere private. "Do you have any news about my father?"

His hand, cold and white, snaked across the table and settled on top of hers. She flinched but didn't move. She didn't want to give him any excuse not to talk.

"Your father is dead. I've already seen to the burial. I wanted to save you that distress and—"

"Oh!"

Michelle's outburst saved Olivia. She removed her hand and sat up straight. It was the only way she could breathe. She would not let this man see her cry. He'd use this weakness to encourage her to marry him, and she would rather waitress forever. She'd rather wash a million sugar bowls. She'd rather live the rest of her days owning only one dress!

"You're taking this well," Mr. Ennis observed.

"It's not exactly a surprise. If my father were alive, he'd have come for me." She carefully set down the tea glass. Michelle was over by the small breakfast nook in deep discussion with Mr. Gregory. Her hands were moving a mile a minute.

Oh, Michelle, Olivia thought, *my papa's dead. He's dead.*

"Very mature, Olivia. This little stint as a waitress has given you a woman's insight. Hopefully your time here has encouraged you to think about my marriage proposal. Surely you miss the way of life your father provided." Mr. Ennis started removing papers from his briefcase.

"I miss my father. He was my life. You cannot replace that, Mr. Ennis. Again, I must decline your offer." She wanted him to leave, now. She wanted to run to the edge of the canyon and scream her anguish into the unknown.

"Young lady, you are being foolish." Mr. Ennis placed two pieces of paper in front of her. "I know what your father would want, and he'd want you to be well cared for. I can amply provide for you. I understand there's a minister working for the Harvey Company. He can perform the service tonight."

"But he won't," Mr. Gregory said, pulling up a chair and joining them.

"I don't believe I know you—" Mr. Ennis began.

"I'm the minister you're talking about. I'm also Olivia's manager." He picked up the first piece of paper and glanced at it. "Ah, a marriage license, very forward thinking of you."

"I must insist—" Mr. Ennis began.

"And what's this?" Mr. Gregory did the same to the second piece of paper. "Ah, the deed to Olivia's property. You do need her signature on this and soon, since you have an offer for her father's factory."

"There's been an offer on my father's factory?" Olivia sputtered.

"I hardly think you're qualified—"

"Oh, I'm more than qualified. I'm also a lawyer. I wear many hats."

Daniel slid his chair over. Between him and Mr. Gregory, they had Mr. Ennis outnumbered and hemmed in. Niles leaned against a distant wall as if ready to join them at the first sign of trouble.

Daniel picked up the two papers. "You look at them?" he asked Mr. Gregory.

Mr. Gregory nodded.

"Wait a minute," Olivia said. "What's going on here?"

"I've been expecting you to have a visitor," Daniel said. "And I'm not surprised to find it's your father's lawyer."

"Who are you?" Mr. Ennis asked dryly.

"Daniel Applegate. I work for Baldwin-Felts. Ah, I see by your frown that you've heard of them. Olivia's hired me to look into her father's disappearance. I assume you're here to tell her of his demise."

"I hired *you*?" Olivia downed the last of her tea.

"You did," Daniel nodded. Then he turned back to Mr.

Ennis. "Oh, by the way, I'm also an acquaintance of your friend Frank Warren, I mean LeRoy Baker. He relieved me of some money quite a few years ago."

Olivia stood, too fast, and had to sit as dizziness embraced her. Daniel Applegate, the harmless man who knew more about the Grand Canyon than the rangers, who always sat in her station, who spent a lot of time and money in the gift shop, was a detective? And had also been taken in by LeRoy Baker?

Even more unbelievable was Jasper Ennis—her father's lawyer. He was turning red and trying to stand up and gather his papers.

"Daniel, what are you trying to tell me?" Olivia thought she knew, but surely she was mistaken. She'd known Mr. Ennis since childhood. He'd eaten at their table. He'd helped carry her mother's casket. He'd asked Olivia to marry him!

"Unless I miss my guess, this man"—Daniel motioned to Mr. Ennis—"helped LeRoy Baker rob your father. I'm not sure how involved he was in the murder, but I'm guessing he knew, and that makes him an accessory. And now that I've made an offer on your factory, he needs your signature so he can get his hands on the last of your father's assets."

According to Grace School for Ladies, a real lady never slapped; she fainted. Olivia's father had wanted her to be a lady, but today she didn't care. Slapping Mr. Ennis wouldn't bring her father back. Slapping Mr. Ennis probably gave Mr. Gregory an idea for his next sermon. Slapping Mr. Ennis allowed Olivia to do what she'd needed to do for so long: cry.

Mr. Niles started to move toward their table, but Mr. Gregory stood, handing Olivia a tissue and positioning himself behind her while putting his hand gently on her shoulder. Michelle collapsed in a chair at the next table. The rest of the Harvey staff started escorting the customers out of the restaurant.

Mr. Ennis tried to take his papers back. "I—I—this is ludicrous. LeRoy Baker is no friend of mine. I am trying to help Olivia. I will resume my efforts at a later time."

"Now seems a good time," Daniel remarked. "As a matter of fact, Niles and I will escort you to the train depot and then to Williams where the sheriff will be glad to hear about your efforts from the comfort of a cell."

"He was my father's friend. We trusted him," Olivia said softly.

" 'For the love of money is the root of all evil,' " Daniel said, quoting First Timothy. Niles came over, and the two of them escorted an unwilling Mr. Ennis from the room.

Within moments, a passel of Harvey Girls surrounded both Olivia and Mr. Gregory. Olivia was pushed back down into her chair and given a fresh glass of tea to hold. Not that she could drink it. For a moment, the shock of the news had diminished the truth. Her father was dead. When the noise finally died down, she looked up at Mr. Gregory.

"Olivia," he said, "I want to help you."

Not one person in the dining room could mistake his offer as being anything but a proclamation of commitment, and not just in helping her get over the sorrow of her father's death.

Olivia recognized it, too, and wanted so much to embrace the offer, but instead she said, "None of this surprised you."

"No," Mr. Gregory admitted. "Daniel's had us watching out for you for quite a while now."

"And how long have you known my father was dead?" She watched the eyes of this man, this preacher, this person who preached honesty so effortlessly. "You've known for a while, haven't you?"

"Yes," he answered.

Olivia knew he had a reason and that it was probably a good one, but for the moment, the only thing she wanted was the solitude to grieve her father and to grieve the loss of trust.

Two lawyers had vied for her hand—both were dishonest.

It took a week to sort out all the papers in Mr. Ennis's briefcase. Olivia asked Wayne to help, and he did. He made his first foray back into the world of legal documents because he was willing to do anything to appease the woman he loved. The woman he'd lied to. While sitting in the dining room, at the same table Olivia and Jasper Ennis had occupied, Wayne said a silent prayer and waited while Daniel and Olivia read the property bill of sale.

"I've been following Frank Warren for more than a year." Daniel stood and wandered over to one of the restaurant's windows. He stared at the blackness engulfing the Grand Canyon. "It's time to settle down again, spend some time with my family."

Somehow the night fit the mood. Ennis and his crimes represented the blackness, and Olivia and Daniel were the defiant stars who would, and could, rise above the evil done to them. Daniel's handing over the reins of his search for Baker to another Baldwin-Felts agent was a start.

"You're a wealthy woman," Wayne remarked.

"I'd rather have my papa back than all this money."

"I understand," Daniel said. "Do you have any plans?"

"First, I'm heading for Topeka. I want to see Mr. Ennis's

trial through to the end. Then if you'll allow it, I'll come to Prescott and assist you with starting the business. There are plenty of my father's employees who deserve that final paycheck." She looked at Daniel. "I'm hoping you'll hire most of them back, and then I'll handle giving them each an endowment. It's what my papa would have wanted."

"What about after that?" Wayne asked carefully. He hated that he had to tread carefully around Olivia.

"For now, Prescott is my only plan."

A few moments of silence followed.

Wayne watched Olivia, wanting so much to reach for her hands, to offer to travel to Prescott to help sort through the paperwork, to ask for forgiveness again. This woman had forgiven Mary. Why couldn't she forgive him?

"I'm going to leave you youngsters alone," Daniel said. "But, Olivia, first, are you acquainted with the book of Luke?"

"Not as much as I should be," Olivia admitted.

"Luke's the healer. He mentioned forgiveness quite a bit in his book. Everyone"—Daniel looked at Wayne—"makes mistakes. Sometimes the mistake really belongs to someone else." With that, he pointed to himself as he left the room.

Olivia was back to owning three dresses: the one she'd been wearing when Mary slashed the others, the one she created from the two that had been slashed, and one Mary made her during the week she waited for her transfer to come through. Still, packing to leave the El Tovar took about as long as the unpacking had taken. And Olivia felt much the same way: unhappy and alone.

Unhappy because she'd grown to love the place, the people,

and, yes, mostly Mr. Gregory and his daughter, Esther.

Esther carried the photo of the three of them everywhere and showed it to everyone. Ever since hearing that Olivia would be leaving, the little girl had drawn picture after picture of Olivia. To Olivia's embarrassment, they were the number one seller in the gift shop. Just when Olivia thought she couldn't bear her own likeness anymore, Esther deviated. She drew herself in hundreds of different poses, all with tears in her eyes. Even Olivia's untrained eye recognized the child was saying, *Don't leave me. Stay. I love you.* The very words Olivia had seen in Mr. Gregory's expression for the last week.

On Sunday Mr. Gregory had preached a sermon about forgiveness that had the employees wiping their eyes. They finished wiping their eyes and then looked at Olivia in disbelief. The need for forgiveness settled like a lump in Olivia's stomach and wouldn't budge.

Michelle appeared in the doorway of the dormitory room. "I hate that you're leaving right when we got our friendship back. Forgiveness is a wonderful thing, don't you think? Tell me you'll write."

"I'll write."

"Better yet, forgive Mr. Gregory and stay here."

It didn't surprise Olivia that every Harvey Girl knew the whole story, but it did surprise her that down to a one, they all thought she should give Mr. Gregory another chance. Even Mary, before she left to go east, quoted a scripture about forgiveness and mentioned how much Olivia's forgiveness meant.

The Bible was full of scriptures about forgiveness, and everyone at the Grand Canyon was willing to share their favorite. Daniel had about a hundred. He shared them every time he came in the gift shop during Olivia's final week.

Esther and Mrs. Brant stepped up behind Michelle. "We baked cookies," Esther announced.

Olivia almost cried. Her trip to the Grand Canyon had been one of little to eat and a race toward the unknown. Her trip away from the Grand Canyon would be one of plenty to eat—every Harvey Girl had stopped by the night before to donate some type of food item—and a race toward the known.

Olivia was beginning to think she was foolish to leave all this.

"Papa told me to give you this." Esther looked down at her shoes instead of meeting Olivia's eyes. Clearly she was about to do something she didn't want to do. From behind her back she took a piece of paper. At first Olivia thought it was another drawing, but it wasn't.

It was the photo of the three of them.

"Thank you." Olivia meant to give it back. Esther adored the photo. But Olivia decided to take one last look.

Funny, she figured she'd had a shocked expression when Kolb's bulb had flashed, but instead she looked content.

"Honey, you keep the photo," Olivia said.

Esther put her hands behind her back and shook her head.

The train would be leaving in just thirty minutes. Olivia decided to slip the photo to one of the waitresses to return. After all, about ten Harvey Girls were standing at the door and watching the exchange. Even Constance, promoted to head waitress, stood waiting to say good-bye.

Leaning against the wall across from her door was Mr. Gregory.

Olivia had made a rash decision once before. With no

money, experience, or inclination, she'd signed on with the Harvey Company.

No, Olivia didn't want to be a waitress. She really didn't want to work in the gift shop. But if she left, Mr. Gregory might take nature walks or arrow-hunting forays with someone besides her!

"Are you going to preach forgiveness again?" She put down her suitcase.

The small crowd divided so Mr. Gregory could move closer. "If I do, will you call me Wayne instead of Mr. Gregory?"

"I kind of like the sound of Mr. Gregory."

He grinned. "And I kind of like the sound of *Mrs.* Gregory."

Everyone looked at Olivia. There was really only one thing to say.

"I do, too."

PAMELA KAYE TRACY

Pamela Kaye Tracy is a writer and teacher in Scottsdale, Arizona, where she lives with a newly acquired husband (yes, Pamela is somewhat a newlywed) and two confused cats ("Hey, we had her all to ourselves for thirteen years. Where'd this guy come from? But maybe it's okay. He's pretty good about feeding us and petting us"). She was raised in Omaha, Nebraska, and started writing (a very bad science-fiction novel) while earning a BA in journalism at Texas Tech University in Lubbock, Texas.

Her first novel *It Only Takes a Spark* was published in 1999. Since then she has published eight more writings in both romantic comedy and Christian inspiration romance. *Promises and Prayers for Teachers* (Barbour Publishing) was her first nonfiction book and went to number two on the Christian Booksellers Association's best-seller list. Pamela is an English professor at Paradise Valley Community College. Besides writing, teaching, and taking care of her family, she is often asked to speak at various writers' organizations in the Phoenix area. She belongs to Romance Writers of America, the Society of Southwestern Writers, the Arizona Authors Association, and the American Christian Writers Association. In February 2005 her newlywed status changed to that of "newly mom."

Armed and Dangerous

Dianne Christner

Dedication

To my sister, Kathy Flack, who bravely read my first unedited manuscript, who shared a room with me growing up, and whose e-mails always brighten my day.

Chapter 1

El Tovar Hotel at the Grand Canyon, 1908

Armed and Dangerous. Edie Harris mouthed the title as she traced a smooth white finger across the crisp cover of the dime novel, savoring its promise of Wild West adventure even though her father had claimed such stories were highly exaggerated. Her stomach gave a queasy lurch. After two thousand miles of fascinating scenery, the Santa Fe passenger locomotive known as the California Limited pushed westward through the rugged terrain of the desolate Arizona Territory, bringing Edie closer to her own adventure, her new Harvey Girl assignment at the Grand Canyon. She hoped this job would satisfy her longing for that unidentifiable something.

The closer she got to her destination, the El Tovar Hotel, the more nervous she felt. Having anticipated this reaction, Edie had saved *Armed and Dangerous* for this particular segment of her trip. She tried to relax against the plush green velvet seat, adjusted the round-rimmed spectacles on the bridge of her slender nose, and opened the book.

A beautiful señorita resided with her father on a Texas ranch thirty miles from the Mexican border. She made the best tortillas in fifty miles, and all her neighbors loved her, which is why they were so outraged at the ruthless gang of desperados who camped one night on the fringes of the little ranch. The night before the outlaws' terrible deed, they made campfire jokes about the way they always evaded the law.

At that very time, a Texas Ranger determinedly rode a tall dark steed. He rode all through the night, hoping to overtake the outlaws before they escaped across the border.

Soon after daylight, the pretty and unsuspecting señorita left the adobe house and started to the well to draw water. . . .

Forgetting El Tovar and her new job, Edie quickly turned the page, hoping the heartless renegades didn't murder the sweet señorita or worse. But before she could read another page, a squeal of metal brought Edie back to her surroundings inside the Pullman car. She frowned at the train's creaky sounds and loud, choppy clacking. Surely they hadn't arrived at the station already. Marking her page with her finger, she looked out the window.

Edie froze.

A gleaming pair of gray eyes stared at her through the glass. Beneath the man's black hat was a thatch of tumbleweed hair, which blew away from his face by the force of the train's moving air. A faded red kerchief covered the lower portion of his face. The skin around the stranger's eyes crinkled as if he found her horror amusing. But when his kerchief fell down, exposing his face, his amusement vanished. His eyes hardened, and his face looked cruel. A disfigured hand jerked the kerchief back into place.

Edie gasped. A train robbery!

She bellowed out a bloodcurdling scream that would have made her father proud, at the same time accidentally hurling her book. It hit the prim gentleman seated directly in front of her on the back of his ear and bounced off onto the floor by her feet. He jerked his head around in displeasure.

She leaned forward, clutching his shoulder. "Robbers!" she exclaimed, her voice squeaking like a rusty gate. She pointed emphatically at the window. The horrible face had vanished.

"Look, miss—" The train jerked and belched, and Edie fell back against her seat, causing her head to bang the train's wall and her spectacles to set sail. She let out another healthy scream, her voice fully recovered.

The train stopped and hissed. Silence.

"Robbers!" she yelled again. A toddler wailed. Even without her glasses, she could see the mother turn and snap, "You're frightening my children!"

From behind her, the conductor came at a full run, disappearing through the opposite end of the car. "I saw a horrible man in my window!" Edie cried out to the confused passengers. Chaos followed. A shrill female voice rose above the others, "We're going to fall off the bridge! Please, don't anybody move! Don't rock the train!"

Bridge? *Oh bother.* Edie groped the floor for her spectacles, placed them on, and pressed her face to the window again. What she saw turned her skin to gooseflesh. They were perched on a steel bridge that spanned a canyon appearing to be hundreds of feet deep. The Grand Canyon?

"Canyon Diablo," someone murmured.

"What if the robbers try to make us jump?" a child asked hysterically.

"Nobody's going to have to jump, son." The deep, reassuring voice brought Edie's gaze away from the window. A formidable man owned the aisle. The top of his dusty white Stetson measured at least six feet from the train's floor. The man could have walked straight out of *Armed and Dangerous*: sweeping black mustache, broad shoulders under a white shirt. A badge glittered on his chest, peeking through the opening of his tan leather vest. His long legs were tucked into tall leather boots. What impressed her most was the six-inch wide ammunition belt slung at an angle across his slim waist and hip. His stance was ready, legs braced for action; one hand clasped a revolver, and the other gripped a rifle. His gaze left the boy and swept across the other passengers.

This man presented a proper opponent for the face she had observed, the man she had envisioned boarding the train, shooting men, ripping bodices, stealing, mauling. This lawman would surely save them.

His gaze lingered on her face. She felt her cheeks heat.

Shots rang out. The conductor stomped back into the car. "Ranger, they're getting away!"

The lawman wheeled and ran, his boots pounding the train's floor.

Edie leaned far into the aisle and watched them depart, her pulse racing.

Ranger Wade Sloan detested heights. Ever since he was a boy and witnessed his parents' wagon plummet off a sixty-foot cliff to their death, he could not squelch the suffocating reaction that hindered him in situations like this.

He could shoot a rattlesnake without flinching, sleep soundly in a bedroll on the desert floor with no thoughts of scorpions, and track down the deadliest foe, but he could not stand on the edge of a precipice without experiencing constriction of breath and anxiety. He probably never would have taken this job had he known headquarters would send him to, of all places, the Grand Canyon.

Wade saw a bit of himself in the young passenger. That's why he stopped to comfort the lad. "Nobody's going to have to jump, son." The young boy nodded and sank against his mother. The other passengers quieted, too, except for one quoting something from the Bible: "For he shall give his angels charge over thee, to keep thee in all thy ways. They shall bear thee up in their hands, lest thou dash thy foot against a stone." Peace gently hugged Wade's heart, and he turned away from the boy and his mother.

He glanced around the car of passengers, his lawman's brain automatically collecting and classifying information: no one shot, no outlaws present in this car. He started toward the buffet and smoking car when his gaze caught a pretty face displaying open admiration. He saw the glitter of hope in her eyes, and he was glad to see such trust and respect. His gaze lingered. He had never seen a woman who wore spectacles as becomingly as she did.

Wade was used to taking in a heap of facts in a few seconds' time. Neat, well-dressed, traveling alone. His inquisitive mind never rested. Was she meeting someone? Going on to California? Was she one of those Harvey Girls? Since he'd been riding the trains in hopes of apprehending the gang that had been terrorizing the Santa Fe, he was becoming accustomed to the occasional splurge of a good classy meal at the El Tovar Hotel. He'd bet his badge she was headed there herself.

A round of shots grabbed his attention. Thundering footsteps followed. The conductor shouted, "Ranger, they're getting away!"

Wade jerked around and bolted down the aisle. Energy coursed through his limbs, enabling him.

They raced through the connecting cars and out onto an outside platform. The engineer shot off rounds into the blue expanse. Wade lifted his Winchester.

"They disappeared over the side of the trestle," the conductor said.

Wade put his sight on the place he thought they might reappear. They didn't. He scanned the valley below with his field glasses.

"Going after them?" the engineer asked.

Wade had no intention of hanging off the bridge like a circus performer.

"No. They're gone," he said, his voice gruff. "Without a horse, I can't track them. If they had boarded the train, it would've been a different matter. I'd say we get this train off the bridge. We make too big of a target. I'll ride back later and look for clues."

"Seems they always know when you're aboard," the conductor said.

Wade sighed. "They'll slip up sooner or later." Nothing worked with this gang. If he rode along the tracks, he missed the robberies, always at the wrong place at the wrong time.

They seemed to sense when he was aboard. Hopefully someone got a look at one of the robbers this time. "I'm going to question the passengers. Let's get this train back on schedule."

"Yes, sir!" the engineer said.

Wade worked his way through the cars, reassuring the passengers and asking the same question. "We scared the robbers off. Anyone happen to get a look at 'em?"

He'd given up hope when a soft voice beckoned, "I did."

The lady with the spectacles. He strode toward the dark-haired beauty and squatted down in the aisle beside her. "You saw them?" he gently urged.

Her blue eyes widened. "One of them." Her face brightened with animation. "He pressed his face up to my window. I saw him very clearly."

Wade noticed a vacant seat next to hers and nodded toward it. "May I?"

"Of course."

He slid into the seat and removed his Stetson, placing it on his knee. "Will you tell me what you saw?"

She nervously clutched something. He was disappointed to see it was a dime novel. Next her imagination would conjure up the description of some character out of her book. He'd seen it happen before.

"He wore a red kerchief."

He nodded indulgently. "Do you remember the color of his hair? His eyes?"

"Oh yes. His eyes were grayish blue. His hair was light brown."

That could be any man in the territory. "Were there any identifying marks or mannerisms?"

She bit her lip a moment.

As enchanting as he found her, his frustration was building. "Miss, I—"

"Edie Harris." She smiled and blushed.

"Wade Sloan, ma'am. I don't mean to be disrespectful, but I happened to notice what you're reading. Are you sure you're not imagining what you saw?"

Her blush deepened. "I most certainly am not."

"But you are the only one who saw anything. None of the others—"

"Then why did you ask if you didn't want the truth? Just ask that man." She leaned forward and tapped the shoulder of the passenger in front her. "Sir, excuse me. Can you kindly tell the ranger that I saw the bandit?"

The man turned and shrugged. "I honestly think she did. Before the train even stopped, she screamed, saying a robber was in her window. I didn't see anyone, but"—he shrugged again—"I think maybe she did."

Wade cringed. "I'm sorry, ma'am. Terribly sorry I doubted your word. It's just the book, and—"

"It's all right. I understand." She placed her hand on his arm. "I just remembered something. The robber had a deformed hand!"

"Now that is something." More than anything he had been able to glean to date on any member of this gang. He wondered how to handle the situation. "May I ask where you're headed?"

She looked up at him through her thick dark lashes. "El Tovar. I'm a Harvey Girl."

He couldn't contain his knowing smile. "Is that a fact? Would you mind if I stopped by the hotel to question you further?"

"I don't mind, but I don't know what my boss will say. I'm just starting at this location."

"Don't worry. I'll handle everything. Thank you again, Miss Harris."

"You're welcome, Ranger Sloan."

Wade replaced his hat and rose, starting toward the car in which he'd been riding. Maybe his luck was changing after all.

Chapter 2

Edie scurried about the dining room's rustic yet elegant boulder-and-log interior, though not as briskly as she had during the noon crowd. Her first day at El Tovar would have been trying enough even without all the fuss and bother she had attracted over the attempted train robbery. There probably wasn't a Harvey employee around who hadn't heard of Edie Harris by now. Since an early morning customer recognized her from the train, everyone had bombarded her with questions, customers and fellow employees alike.

At first it felt comforting to share her frightening experience, but Constance Gibson, the red-haired, lively, spirited head waitress, soon took her aside and requested she not scare the customers, who no doubt needed to board the train again. Edie tried to quit discussing the incident, but that was about as easy as swatting a pesky fly away; the questions just kept returning.

"Miss!" An attractive, middle-aged customer motioned to Edie.

Hurrying to the woman's table, Edie smiled, and even though she had been trained never to do so, she wiped her sweaty palms on her starched white apron. "Yes, ma'am?"

"Look what happened! My dinner is ruined!" The customer gave her red cloth napkin several hard shakes.

"Oh!" Edie gasped. She was responsible for the small Mount Everest on the customer's roast ribs of prime beef au jus. "I am so sorry. I will replace your meal at once." She deftly snatched the offending plate and the empty glass saltshaker—its missing top now adorned the asparagus vinaigrette—and with two quick strokes brushed most of the stray granules from the white tablecloth onto the plate.

The woman continued to shake her napkin, and Edie hurried toward the kitchen.

Miss Gibson took one look at the plate, and her slightly freckled face paled. "Which table?"

Caught with the evidence in one hand, Edie adjusted her spectacles with the other. "Table ten."

"Place another order! Quickly!" Miss Gibson hurried off toward the distraught customer, muttering something about a free meal.

Edie picked the goopy shaker top out of the food and handed the ruined dinner to a busboy. After she placed the new order, she cleaned and refilled the saltshaker. She was not used to making mistakes. Following her training in Chicago, she'd spent one year at a Kansas Harvey House where she started as badge number fifteen and was quickly promoted to badge number six. Her fine working record allowed her to transfer to the more sought-after Grand Canyon location. She certainly did not wish to get off to a bad start.

Her new roommate, Dinah, appeared and gave her arm a squeeze. "It will get better. The first day at a new location is always the hardest. I probably wouldn't have kept this job at all if I hadn't been a friend of the Harveys."

Edie smiled gratefully. Dinah wasn't as attractive as most of the Harvey Girls with her not-quite-blond, not-quite-brown hair and prominent overbite, but she certainly was one of the kindest.

When the meal replacement was ready, Edie started back to table ten.

"My apologies again," she said, placing the perfectly garnished plate in front of the woman and the saltshaker in the center of the table.

"Miss," the woman said, smiling tentatively, "I hope I wasn't rude before. I'm sure I overreacted."

Edie looked from the woman to her male companion. "Not at all. Thank you for your kindness." Edie leaned forward, confiding, "It's my first day." She would have added, *And yesterday my train was nearly robbed,* except she happened to see Miss Gibson watching them. "Is there anything else I can get for you?"

"No, thank you," the woman said. "I hope tomorrow goes better."

Edie smiled and stepped away, catching a glimpse of the head waitress, who gave her an approving nod. The gesture set her world right again, other than her increasing fatigue from an exhausting day.

Always Edie pushed herself to be a woman who would have made her father proud, one who hailed new experiences, enjoyed challenges, sought adventure—her reason for relocating to the Grand Canyon in the first place. Only, since her papa's death, she was more emotional. She'd had to hold back tears when she'd made the mistake in the dining room. Her father, a true adventurer at heart, would not be pleased to see her like this. If, indeed, he could happen to see her, she would want him to know that she was carrying on well enough on her own, just like he had prepared her to do.

As the evening crowd thinned out, Edie picked up a pitcher of milk, grateful that soon she could get off her feet and relax. Maybe she'd take up *Armed and Dangerous* again and see what happened to the señorita.

She lifted a man's empty glass.

He held up his hand. "Whoa! That's not what I was drinking, miss."

"Oh. I'm sorry." Edie realized she had been daydreaming. "I'll be right back with another pitcher." She wheeled around and nearly ran into head waitress Gibson.

"Miss Harris, Ranger Sloan would like to speak with you about the *you know.*"

"He's here now?" Edie scanned the room.

"Yes, see—over by the door. I told him your shift was nearly over and it was fine. Only, please take him to the Rotunda so that you may speak more discreetly. I'll take the pitcher and see that your customer gets his drink."

"Yes, ma'am." Edie looked toward the door again, and when the tall ranger gave her a friendly wave, her heart gave a little stir. "Thank you, Miss Gibson," Edie said, drawing in a deep breath for calmness.

❧

Wade watched his witness approach. Strands of hair had worked free from her pinned-up style, her face flushed with first-day fatigue.

"Hello, Mr. Sloan." She smiled. "If you will please come with me."

"Ma'am," Wade said, sweeping off his Stetson and falling into step beside her. "How was your first day on the job?"

She shook her head. "Hectic. With the robbery and everything. I'm thankful for a reprieve."

He held the door open. "I'll not keep you long."

They walked to the registration lobby in silence. He had to keep from chuckling when Miss Harris sank into a plush chair and gave an unfeminine sigh of contentment. She motioned for him to sit in the neighboring chair. "Now then," she said as if she were the one in charge. She folded her hands in her lap and looked up at him with that revered expression that had captured his attention on the train, the one that pleased him so.

Wade leaned close and said confidentially, "Since we spoke yesterday, I've telegraphed headquarters with the information you gave me. Seems we have more than one bandit in the Arizona Territory with a disfigured hand. It's a common malady for a gunfighter. They often take a bullet to the hand."

Her eyes widened. "That's fascinating!" Her gaze shifted to the ranger's hands.

He laughed and turned his palms up. "I happen to have all ten fingers."

"Congratulations." Her blue eyes twinkled with mischief then softened. "I'm glad."

She was delightful. Even though he had told her he would keep it short, he found himself desiring to stretch out the interview. "Miss Harris, may I ask you a few questions about the man you saw?"

"Most certainly."

"You said his eyes were grayish blue, hair light brown?"

"His eyes were a dull blue. And that's correct, light brown hair."

"How old do you think he was?"

"Hmm." She tapped her finger. "Old for someone in such a dangerous occupation, I'm sure, but not old enough to be, say, my father. Perhaps thirty, forty?"

Wade glanced sideways. Was she teasing? No, she seemed serious. He reasoned she was the sort of woman who processed her thoughts aloud as she spoke. Often he found her type annoying, but Miss Harris was entertaining. "I see. Thirty or forty."

"But his hair wasn't gray, was it?" she reconsidered.

"You said it was brown, light brown," he encouraged.

"Yes. So I'll guess thirty, then."

"How tall was our adversary?"

"His head clearly filled my window, but I didn't see his, um—legs."

"I understand. His face was covered with a red kerchief?"

"Wait! Did I tell you it fell, and he reached to pull it up? I remember his arm was long. So he must be tall!" She became more animated as she reasoned. "There you have it. Yes, he was tall."

"Good deduction." Wade could not fault her roundabout methods, for she provided a far better description than the average witness. "You saw his entire face?"

"I did." She bobbed her head emphatically.

"If I brought a sketcher to the hotel, do you think you could help us create an accurate portrait?"

She straightened. "I do. His awful face is vividly ingrained in my memory."

"Good. I mean, I'm sorry. It's just that I've been pursuing this gang for a long while. This is the best lead I've had. Sometimes if we apprehend one member, we can get names of his companions. I'll ask around and find someone to do the sketching."

Her hand rested on his arm like it had on the train, and it felt comforting.

"You won't have to do that, Mr. Sloan. My roommate is an artist. She has lined the walls of our room with wonderful drawings and paintings."

Another pleasant surprise. Wade beamed and patted Miss Harris's hand where it rested on his arm. "You have been such a help. Could I meet you both here tomorrow evening?"

"I'll have to ask Dinah. And could we make it later, after our shift?"

"Of course. Thank you." Wade helped her to her feet and bid her good evening. Totally enchanted, he watched her leave then started toward his own hotel room. Often he camped under the stars. On occasion, however, he took a room and enjoyed the luxury of a good meal and bath. Tonight he would sleep in a soft bed, and maybe he would dream about how he would capture the long-elusive criminals, maybe even dream about one fascinating Harvey Girl.

Edie left the ranger and went to the dormitory-style room she shared with Dinah. *Working at the Grand Canyon is turning into the perfect adventure,* she mused happily while washing her face at the basin. She slipped off her black shoes, plopped on the bed, and closed her eyes, letting her body relax from her shoulders to her toes. The image of the handsome ranger filled her thoughts. She hoped Dinah wouldn't mind that she had volunteered her. As if responding to her thoughts, the door opened, and her roommate entered the room.

When Dinah saw Edie on the bed, she gave her a sympathetic smile.

"I'm exhausted," Edie replied. "I'm not sure why. I worked this hard at my last location, too."

"Probably just the stress of having everything new. But if you're exhausted, you won't be happy to hear Miss Gibson is looking for you."

Edie sat up and swung her legs off the bed. "Why? What's wrong?"

Dinah joined Edie on the narrow bed. "She wants you to return to close out your station."

"Oh bother. I thought I was dismissed for the evening." Edie eased off the bed and reached for her shoes. "I should have known better. I've never made so many mistakes in my entire life. I don't know what's wrong with me."

"I'm sure she understands it's been an unusual day for you."

"I'm about to find out," Edie said, giving Dinah a lopsided grin.

"I started to do it for you, but Miss Gibson wouldn't allow it. She said she wanted to talk to you anyway. I'm sorry."

"Not your fault. Thanks." Edie turned to go, wondering what Constance Gibson wished to talk about. The robbery again? When she entered the restaurant, Miss Gibson was by the cash register talking to the Harvey manager, Mr. Niles. Trying not to draw their attention, she quietly slipped to her station and started wiping down a working surface.

Miss Gibson saw her at once. She crossed the room and

inquired with a low voice, "How was your interview with the ranger, Miss Harris?"

"I was able to give him a description of one of the robbers."

"I hope you can put the dreadful experience behind you."

"I'm afraid that won't be possible. He wants me to help him sketch the outlaw."

Miss Gibson clearly disapproved. "How awful. I don't suppose there's any way you can decline?"

"Why would I wish to do that? Do you object?"

"Since you are under my care, I'm only concerned for your safety."

Edie frowned. She had been so fascinated by Ranger Sloan and so proud of being able to identify the outlaw, she had not considered the danger. She returned to her scrubbing. If Ranger Sloan apprehended the outlaw and he was sent to jail or sentenced to be hanged, what if he escaped? Would he take his revenge out on her? She scrubbed harder. He knew she had gotten a good look at his face. What if he came after her, even now, anticipating her involvement?

"Miss Harris? Are you all right? I didn't mean to frighten you. I am only concerned for your welfare."

Edie stopped scrubbing. "Sorry. I was just thinking of that man's evil face and wondering if he will come looking for me."

"You're perfectly safe here. There's always a crowd in the restaurant and even in the dormitory. But perhaps you shouldn't wander off alone for a while. Of course, it's never wise to do so anyway. I think what you need most is rest. Let me finish cleaning this for you."

"Oh no. I couldn't possibly let you do that. I've already made too many mistakes for one day."

"I saw your file, Miss Harris. Your record is impeccable. You're just experiencing a rough start. Thank you for returning, but run along now, dear. My orders."

"That's kind of you. Thank you." Edie gratefully returned to her room and prepared to relax for the second time that evening.

Dinah looked up from sketching at her desk. "That didn't take long."

"Miss Gibson asked me a few questions then ordered me back to my room."

"She really is a good boss."

"I'll say. She's been more than fair with me today." Edie gave a little wave. "Don't let me keep you from your work."

Dinah smiled. "It's not really work. It's how I relax." She took up her pencil again.

"You've been in the West awhile, right?"

"I've been here seven years. I've seen a lot of Harvey Girls come and go." Her voice turned regretful. "Many get married."

"Well, I didn't come here to get married."

Dinah looked surprised. "Why are you here?"

"For the adventure. Speaking of which, do you think that outlaw is going to come looking for me since I saw his face?"

Dinah's hand stilled. She turned. "How would he know where to find you? He doesn't even know your name, right?"

Edie relaxed. "He doesn't know my name, but he can assume I'm at the hotel."

"Does the ranger have any idea who he is?"

"Not yet. He wants to use my identification for a sketch."

Dinah's interest was piqued. "Who's going to do the sketching?"

Edie gave her a crooked grin. "You, I hope. I told him you were an artist. He asked if we could meet him in the Rotunda tomorrow evening after our shift. I hope you're not mad."

Dinah laid down her pencil, crossed the room, and hugged Edie. "I can tell that having you for a roommate is going to be the most exciting thing that has happened to me. Of course I'll help you. If that robber gets any crazy notions about finding you, he'll have two women to deal with."

"Thanks, Dinah. I couldn't have asked for a better roommate. And don't worry," Edie said with more courage than she felt. "That outlaw won't stand a chance against the two of us."

Once Dinah returned to her sketching, Edie prepared for bed and took out *Armed and Dangerous.*

> *Soon after daylight, the pretty and unsuspecting señorita left the adobe house and started to the well to draw water. She hooked a bucket to a long rope and slowly lowered it. A rustle sounded behind her, and a hand clamped across her mouth. Another clasped her waist. The señorita struggled, but she was no match for the man who dragged her across the desert soil to a band of groping men who tied her hands and threw her across a saddle.*

Edie snapped the book closed and placed it on her nightstand. Tonight was not the time to read about kidnapping outlaws. She could feel the señorita's shock and horror as if they were her own, as they very well could be, she reasoned. She rolled over and tried to dispel the image, the interloping fear that clutched her heart. Suddenly a memory from her childhood came to mind. Mother always prayed with her before bed. After mother died, she and papa never prayed. She wondered if it would help now.

Chapter 3

The following evening Edie felt lighthearted, almost giddy. It had been a good day at the restaurant, and rooming with Dinah was fun. They bantered back and forth as they changed out of their drab black skirts, plain high-collared shirts, and black stockings and shoes. Edie pulled on a colorful skirt and added a wide, ornately buckled belt. Her white blouse had soft, wide pleats. She stepped into comfortable kid slippers, and they started to the Rotunda for their appointment with Ranger Sloan.

"I heard the ranger is tall, dark, and handsome," Dinah teased.

"How the gossip flies."

"He ate in the restaurant today."

"I know. Honestly, he is like a storybook character. Tall, fearless, white hat, big guns." Edie put both thumbs in the air and used her hands to illustrate.

"Like the ranger in *Armed and Dangerous*?"

Edie giggled. "How did you know?"

"The cover," Dinah said. "I'm always interested in book covers."

"Shush! There he is," Edie whispered. "Behave yourself."

❧

Wade waited at a table in the corner of the Rotunda, hopefully out of the way of the hotel's customers. The last thing he wanted to do was draw a crowd. After a good night's rest and plenty of time to clear his brain from Miss Harris's charms, he was eager to get the sketch and hit the trail before he let his heart trick him into something different than the free lifestyle he was used to. He was grateful to see Miss Harris appear down the hall and noted that the woman with her carried a sketch pad.

Extending a cheerful greeting, Miss Harris asked, "Been waiting long?"

He felt his resistance slipping already. He could get accustomed to her rosy cheeks. "No, not long."

The woman accompanying her was introduced as Dinah Weston. She seated herself and prepared her sketch pad and pencil. Wade explained the procedure. He would ask questions, and Dinah would use her own ingenuity to sketch according to Miss Harris's responses. Afterward, they would work together to make any necessary changes.

Starting the questioning, Wade asked Edie, "Did the man in the window have a thin face, round face, square face?"

"Lean, rugged."

Dinah's hands made quick, fluent strokes.

Wade pointed at Dinah's sketch. "Like that?"

"Yes, that's good."

"Okay, what can you tell us about his eyes?"

Edie closed her own to recall the image from memory. "They were evil, squinting as if he were laughing at me. Deep lines, here." She pointed to her brow then straightened her spectacles.

A few strokes later, Wade asked, "Better?"

"Yes."

"Once the other facial features are added, we'll come back to the eyes and see if they need to be spaced closer or farther apart."

Both women nodded.

As the portrait fleshed out, Wade was disappointed he didn't recognize the face, but he figured somebody at headquarters might. When they were nearly finished, Dinah broke her pencil and left them to get a different one.

While they waited, Wade couldn't resist a flirtation. "There's a saying we have in the territory, Miss Harris, that any woman can come west on a wagon train, but only a lady can become a Harvey Girl."

"I'm glad the territory speaks so highly of us. Kansas also has a saying about the Harvey Girls. They say the Harvey Girls are civilizing the West. But now I see the truth. It's the rangers doing that job."

"Civilizing the West takes a concerted effort. May I ask what made you decide to become a Harvey Girl?"

"My father."

"He found you the job?"

"No, he was my inspiration."

"Sounds like you love him."

"I did. My father loved adventure. Mother died when I was young, and he gave up that lifestyle to raise me. He always told me the most wonderful stories, and one day his dream for adventure became my own. Then when he got sick, I saw the Harvey advertisement. I told him not to worry about me because I was going to become a Harvey Girl and see the world. It made him so happy. He passed soon after."

"I'm sorry. I'm sure he was very proud of you. Do you like your job, Miss Harris?"

"Please, call me Edie. It's getting better. I trained in Chicago then worked for a year in Kansas. When I heard about the canyon, I just had to come and see if it was the place for me."

"Is it?"

Edie shrugged. "So far it has been exciting. How about you? Do you like your job?"

"Most of the time." Wade spoke in a personal manner, something he didn't often do. "At this particular moment I do. I like being here and talking to you."

"You're very kind. You impressed me, too, from the start."

He knew that if he didn't wish to pursue Edie, now was the time to back out of this conversation. But he couldn't help himself. He wanted to know her better. "Why is that?"

"I liked the way you stopped to comfort that boy on the train. Don't take this wrong, but it surprised me to see a sympathetic lawman."

He was sorry she felt that way and hoped he could express the truth that compassion came from God, no matter what one's occupation. "Lawmen are only people. We eat and sleep and hurt like everyone else. And, Edie—"

"Yes?" She was giving him that look again.

"I'd be honored if you'd call me Wade."

"Wade," she said breathlessly. "Do you think the bandit is going to come looking for me? To keep me from"—she shrugged—"identifying him?"

He had not seen this coming, but now he recognized the look of fear. Poor thing. He needed to answer her honestly yet give her reassurance. *Lord, help me here,* he quickly prayed while she silently waited. "I doubt it," he began. "Today I rode back out to Canyon Diablo to look for clues. I couldn't find any. Since I don't know yet whom we're dealing with, anything is possible. I'll pray for you, if you'd like."

Her blue eyes widened, and her delicate mouth gaped. "You will? I mean you pray? I didn't expect that."

Wade chuckled. "There you go again, judging me."

"I'm sorry. I shouldn't have done that."

"I'm a Christian, Edie. Praying is a vital part of who I am."

"I prayed last night," she said with reverence. "For the first time since I was a child. I didn't mean to judge you before; I just didn't know grown men prayed."

"Prayer will help you get through this experience."

"My father didn't countenance weakness, even in women."

"Did he think your mother was weak because she prayed?"

"Why, I don't know. We never spoke about it."

"I'm back," Dinah called. "Sorry you had to wait."

"No problem at all." Wade gave Edie a warm, personal glance. "The time passed quite quickly."

Dinah rolled her eyes. "I see. Do you two want me to leave again?"

"Dinah!" Edie exclaimed, her face coloring. "Of course not!"

Wade chuckled and tapped the sketch. "This renegade had no idea what a favor he did for me. I can't remember an evening when I've had so much fun as I'm having with you two ladies." He continued to mix pleasure and business as they finished the drawing. Afterward, he told them it was good. He would take it to headquarters and let them know if anyone recognized the man. In the past, he would have thanked his witness and moved on. This time, he told Edie, "I'll be in touch."

❧

Edie and Dinah returned to their room, and Edie noticed Dinah's personality was subdued, compared to earlier in the evening. "Your sketch was really good."

"Oh, thanks. I enjoyed doing it."

"Is something else the matter, then?"

Dinah sighed. "I'm just feeling selfish. I love having you for a roommate, but I saw the way Ranger Sloan looked at you. I suppose you're going to get married and move on like all the others have."

Edie hardly knew how to respond. She was attracted to Wade, but she hadn't had time to think about her feelings just yet. "Now you know better than that. Didn't I tell you why I came to El Tovar?"

Dinah smiled knowingly. "We'll see. I'll just have to make the most of it while I have you."

"Seriously, why would I want to marry a ranger? When men get married, they need to show responsibility, not ride around the countryside endangering their lives."

"Now where's your sense of adventure?"

"I was just thinking of papa. He was a daring sort of man. Once he got married, things changed for him. I was born. Mama died. Papa took a job that allowed him to raise me."

"What's your point?"

"My point is that if I married Wade—"

"Wade, is it? You came to a first-name basis already?"

"As I was saying, let's imagine I married Wade. I'd want him to quit his lawman job and stay at home with me. After all, I am alone in the world. Otherwise I'd worry about him all the time. But that wouldn't be fair to him. He'd probably grow to resent it. At the very least miss it like papa did." She shook her head. "No, it wouldn't work." She was surprised to learn how she felt, but she was thankful Dinah had listened long enough for her to work it out in her mind.

"Well, at least you have a choice," Dinah said.

"What's that supposed to mean?"

"Nobody's ever interested in a plain woman like me."

"You are not a plain woman. You are kind and fun and the most talented woman I know."

"Thanks. I guess it doesn't hurt to dream."

"No. It's good to dream. Speaking of which, I think I'll read a little before turning in."

"Sure, it'll be lights-out soon enough."

Edie prepared for bed, crawled under the covers, and yawned. Pushing Wade's image aside, she opened *Armed and Dangerous*.

> *Señorita Lolita woke slowly as from a long deep slumber. She opened her eyes and saw blue sky peeking through the shade of a cactus; then she saw her torn clothing and remembered her abduction and how she had passed out when her head hit a rock. She didn't even remember traveling. Her hands were painfully tied behind her back.*
>
> *"Come see. Our captive is awake!" yelled the youngest of the band, who was in charge of keeping watch.*
>
> *The other two lumbered over and snickered. "Sleeping Beauty awakes at last!"*

Lolita's eyes snapped. "You'll never get away with this."

The cruel one laughed. "You think you can stop us?"

"When I tell my father. . ."

The cruel one shrugged and lifted his pistol. "It is our practice not to leave anyone alive to tell anyone anything."

"Drop that gun. This time you have miscalculated," said the ranger, his strong voice coming from behind a tall boulder.

Instantly the outlaws abandoned Lolita, scrambling for cover. As the bullets ricocheted overhead, Lolita let her tears fall freely. Someone had come to save her.

Edie let out a sigh of relief and placed *Armed and Dangerous* on her nightstand. But she couldn't forget the line "It is our practice not to leave anyone alive to tell anyone anything." Was that really what it was like here in the West? Could the sketch she and Dinah created help to civilize the territory?

Chapter 4

The Grand Canyon in the summertime was an exciting place to be, and Edie easily fell into the routine of her job at the El Tovar dining room. With her famous start, she now knew nearly all of the other employees and could call several her friends. Her favorite was Dinah. Ever since they had agreed to risk their lives to help the ranger with the wanted poster, they shared an undeniable bond.

Edie wondered if their efforts had been in vain. As far as she knew, the robber hadn't yet been apprehended. She hadn't heard from the ranger, either, and it had been a whole month—just as it was for Lolita in *Armed and Dangerous*. Even though the writer of the dime novel had intimated romantic feelings between the two, after Lolita's rescue, the ranger had bid his farewell and left her standing beside her father, waving and then watching until the last of his dust had settled. Only one chapter remained, but the last scene she'd read had disgusted her so much that she couldn't even bear to read it. The entire story came too near to portraying her real-life experience.

Even though she had told Dinah she could never marry the ranger, as if he ever intended to ask, she had secretly wished he would return and pursue her. Wouldn't that have been the romantic climax to her whole train robbery adventure? If the author of her dime novel knew anything about the West, Edie's ranger would not return. He would have gotten what he needed from her and would now be long gone, doing whatever lawmen did in the Arizona Territory. Supposedly the rangers left broken hearts wherever they went. It was humiliating to remember how she had believed him, truly thinking he'd be in touch. She imagined the last chapter of *Armed and Dangerous* to read something like "A ranger's first and foremost duty is always to his job."

How silly to have been taken in by his flirtatious ways, thinking he might be sweet on her. The first two weeks she had looked for him every time she entered the dining room. Now she saw what a fool she'd been. Ha! If Wade Sloan ever did return, she certainly wouldn't make more out of his congeniality than it was meant to be. She would not be duped again.

If one could choke on one's thoughts, Edie would have. For she wheeled just then to attend to her next table, and of all the unwelcome customers, hers was Wade Sloan, all six feet of him, including his shining badge and sheepish but extremely charming smile. His hands were clasped, and he leaned forward on his elbows, his fingers lightly tapping his well-groomed black mustache. He looked freshly shaved, and the Stetson on the table looked free of trail dust. She blushed, wondering how long he had been watching her. Like a warrior, she straightened her shoulders and approached his table.

"Mr. Sloan. How good to see you again. What may I get you to drink?"

He lowered his hands to the table, his eyes dancing with

amusement. "It is nice to see you again, Edie. I missed you."

She worked not to give in to his charming manner. "Well, now that you're here, what may I bring you to drink?"

"I fear you are falsely judging me again. Are you?"

"It is not my place to judge our customers, sir, only to serve them according to their wishes."

"How delightful. Then I'll have something cold. And if you really wish to please me, I'd like to see you tonight, if I may."

"Impossible."

"Nothing cold, then?"

"You know very well what I meant," Edie snapped.

His face held a flash of regret. "I have news that might interest you."

At this, Edie's guard began to slip. If she led him to believe she was turning down a personal appeal, it would be humiliating, because he probably hadn't even meant it that way, and if he had, she didn't want to give him any satisfaction. However, she did wish to know what had happened to the train robber.

She glanced around to see if anyone could overhear them, then whispered, "News about the train robber?"

"Yes. But that is not the only reason I wished to see you." His dark eyes softened, beckoned.

She really wanted to see him, and if she could do so without losing face—"I am curious about your information. And the head waitress did warn me not to mention it in the dining room, so I suppose it would be better to meet you later so I don't get in trouble. Just to talk about *you know*."

"Our regular meeting place?"

Edie nodded. "That's fine." Then she gave him a departing, and what she hoped was an impersonal, smile. "I'll be right back with your drink." As she left his table, she indulged a self-satisfying thought. She wouldn't be serving his meal as he expected since she was sharing his table with another Harvey Girl. Served him right. Anyway, his appearance had caught her off guard, and she needed time to mentally prepare herself for their meeting.

❧

Edie saw him first, seated at the same table they had used to sketch the wanted poster. When he saw her, he stood and removed his hat. His appreciative gaze swept over her slowly. He may not be interested in pursuing her, but it still felt good to know he found her attractive. Edie carefully seated herself. Normally she jumped right into a conversation, but she wanted to punish him for his desertion, so she deliberately waited for him to speak.

"You're looking as pretty as I remembered."

"After a month, my own memory began to wane. Frankly, Mr. Sloan, I hoped I had dreamed the whole situation."

"Should I begin by apologizing or giving the explanation for my absence?"

She tried to ignore his earnest expression. "You owe me no explanations, except to report on our train robber. What is your news?"

"No one at my headquarters, the Northern Detachment in Flagstaff, could identify our suspect, so my boss, Lieutenant Billy Old, sent me to Tucson. While I was there, I was asked to join a posse to chase some cattle rustlers—a different case entirely. That operation took three weeks, but it was successful. But regarding our train robber, the good news is that we now have a name. I couldn't wait to tell you. Frankly, Miss Harris, I couldn't wait to see you, either. I hope you can understand the delay. You will forgive me, won't you?"

"I really didn't expect you to call unless it had to do with the incident."

"Why not? I told you I would. I thought you knew I hoped to get to know you better."

"Isn't there a saying about rangers, something like 'A ranger's first and foremost duty is always to his job'? With that in mind, what purpose does it serve to pursue a love suit?" She saw his face pale.

"Love suit?" He gestured with his hand. "Whoa, there. There is an oath I took, but I'm not asking you to marry me, Edie."

"Of course you aren't." She straightened her shoulders. "I wasn't suggesting such a thing."

The color returned to his face, and he relaxed. He even gave her his charming smile. "Then what harm is there in enjoying the friendship of each other's company?"

"I suppose the harm would come if one of us should feel more than friendship toward the other."

"Are you trying to tell me you care for me?"

Edie's mouth fell open. She snapped it shut. "Of course not. Why do you keep making more out of this than there is?"

"I'm just trying to have an honest conversation here. During my absence, I prayed about us plenty."

"Us?" Edie ventured.

"I believe I'm supposed to follow my heart."

"Really?" Edie didn't know when she'd been more astonished. He certainly seemed to be forthright and honest, not deceiving as she had imagined him. He wasn't acting at all like the ranger in *Armed and Dangerous*. "And what exactly does your heart say?"

"It says it's going to break if you won't allow me to be your friend." He smiled again, and his eyes pleaded. "I know I can't have a real girl with a job like mine, but I get to the El Tovar pretty regular right now. I'd be honored to have you as a friend. The trail gets lonely, especially now that my partner is recuperating from a wound."

Edie sighed. "So I wouldn't be a real girl, but I'd be replacing your partner?"

He stretched out his long legs and frowned. "I'm good with a gun, but not eloquent. Don't twist my words, Edie."

"On the contrary, you're very persuasive. I suppose I could use another friend." She emphasized the last word.

"And don't forget that friends call each other by their first names. You've slipped out of the habit."

"Very well. Wade?"

"Hm?"

"Tell me about your suspect."

"His name is Shady Burt. The law calls him Shady. He's a bad sort. Already wanted for murder. And there's a bounty on his head, too."

"What happens now?"

"There was another robbery while I was gone. I'm going to ride the trains. I'm not the only one. We have a team of rangers. The good thing about this assignment is I can stop in at El Tovar quite often."

"Well, I suppose if we're to become friends, that is good news."

"I have even better news."

"Yes?"

"I'm free tomorrow. Since it's Sunday, I thought you might

like to attend the services with me."

She didn't want to admit she didn't relish a church service. "I have plans in the morning. Perhaps another time?" When she saw his disappointment, she suggested, "But I've got just the thing. After your service, we could take a picnic, and you can teach me to shoot."

Wade picked up his Stetson. "I don't know if that's such a good idea."

"Why not? I want to be able to take care of myself."

"Are you still worried about Shady coming after you?"

She nodded. "I miss the simple things, like being able to take a walk by myself. And I detest the fear I feel. I really want to do this. And you're the perfect person to help me. Please, Wade." She saw him softening.

"We would have to keep this a secret. Lieutenant Old doesn't approve of such things. Maybe you hadn't heard he's banned guns altogether in Williams. I could lose my job."

She could feel the thrill of adventure and placed a persuasive hand on his arm. "What's your heart telling you, Wade?"

He studied her a moment and gave her that smile she so appreciated. "It's telling me to give you a shooting lesson."

"Then it's a date. As friends," she quickly corrected.

His brow shot up momentarily. "A date," he repeated, an unreadable gleam in his eyes.

Chapter 5

The next day Wade lay on his side and feasted his eyes on Edie. After four long weeks apart, now only the picnic basket separated them. She lay on her stomach, her elbows propped on the Hopi Indian blanket, her sweet face supported by her dainty hands. Her legs crossed at the ankle with just her shoes visible from beneath her skirt.

Idly fingering the band on his hat, Wade felt content to watch her range of facial expressions and listen to her silky voice. It was dangerous to be getting so close to a woman, but he had always loved a good challenge. There was something exciting about Edie Harris. She wasn't sissified like so many women, and he felt irresistibly drawn to her friendship. She was far more interesting than the campfire he usually kept for company. Could it be he had grown tired of his manner of life? Grown lonely? The thought had never crossed his mind until he met Edie. He always thought the Good Book was company enough. But hadn't God made Eve for Adam? Her name was even similar.

"Is your name Edith?"

"Why yes, but no one ever calls me that."

Wade stored the information away.

"Did you ever waver over which side of the law you'd use your gun for?" Edie asked.

"No. Never did. My uncle raised me. He was a preacher. A good man, and I came to know the Lord at an early age. So no. That was not a temptation for me."

"It still seems strange to me that a man like you, who prays and reads his Bible and such, would be a lawman."

"I'm just fighting evil, simple as that."

Edie sat up. "How about teaching me a thing or two about fighting evil?"

Wade reached out and touched her arm. "I'd hoped you would ask me something like that." He reached into his pocket and pulled out a small testament. "I've been waiting for the perfect moment to give you this."

"What is it? A Bible?"

"Yes. Do you already own one?"

"No." She looked at him with a tender expression. "I think I know what this means to you. Thank you."

He placed it in her hand. "Will you read it?"

"If you wish. But what I said about fighting evil—I was referring to my shooting lesson. You haven't forgotten?"

"No, ma'am." Wade rose then reached down to help her to her feet. "Your first lesson is about to begin."

Edie thrilled to handle Wade's Colt .45. She'd always wanted to try one. She stared at the bottles lined up on a boulder about fifteen yards away. Thinking to take aim and try her first shot, she slowly raised her hands.

"Whoa. Let me show you first." Wade stepped behind her

and placed a hand on each of her arms, loosely embracing her. He softly instructed, "Now straighten out your arms. That's good."

She could hardly concentrate from his close proximity. What had she been thinking? She would never be able to hit the bottles with him breathing next to her ear. She swallowed hard and tried to concentrate. Her arms trembled slightly.

"Relax a moment. When we try again, I want you to put your index finger on the trigger. Then we'll discuss squeezing it."

Edie relaxed. Instead of pulling away, Wade wrapped his arms around her in a loose hug. He rested his chin on the top of her head while he continued to instruct. "I also want you to look through the guide and position the bottle of your choice in the guide. Ready?"

His voice sounded as if he were courting her rather than instructing her in gunmanship. She nodded, and he gently supported her arms. "Okay, look through the guide. See it?"

"Yes."

"All right, slowly now, index finger on the trigger."

Her arm began to tremble. "I didn't realize I'd be so nervous."

"Relax again."

She dropped her arms. "I cannot believe I am so unsteady."

As if he sensed his effect on her, he released her, drew up alongside her. "It takes practice to have a steady hand. Next time concentrate on keeping the gun steady. Pretend you're pouring a cup of coffee for one of your customers. When you believe you have it, I want you to squeeze the trigger."

"All right. I'll try again." He stood by her side, allowing her to lift her arms into position. Slowly she squeezed until the gun fired. "Did I hit it?"

He chuckled, "No, but don't lose heart. It takes practice."

"But my hand was steady, and I had the bottle in the guide."

"When you squeezed the trigger, you jerked. The bullet went over the top of the bottle. Next time concentrate on keeping your hands steady for a moment after you squeeze the trigger."

With understanding, Edie raised her hands, squeezed the trigger again, and sent the bullet racing.

Wade jumped and let out a whoop. "You got it, Edie! You're a quick learner!"

She stomped her foot and frowned. "No, I didn't. I wasn't aiming for that one."

Wade slapped his leg. "You're one honest woman. Now try again."

Edie kept practicing until she could hit the bottle she was aiming at about half of the time.

When she stopped to reload, Wade touched her chin with tenderness. "I'm proud of you."

Edie felt a little giddy from her accomplishment and couldn't resist the temptation to flirt back. "But I'm not sure I remember that part about keeping my arms straight and steady."

Wade quickly caught her drift. "Allow me to demonstrate again."

Stepping up behind her, he enveloped her in his embrace again. Only he quietly removed the pistol from her hand and slipped it into his holster. Then he placed one arm around her waist and turned her to face him. She looked into his eyes and saw that they were warming, from play or affection, she wasn't sure. He pulled her close, and she closed her eyes. He tightened his embrace, and his lips softly met hers. He released her, his voice husky. "If we want to remain friends, I believe we had better end this lesson."

"Yes," she breathed. "Thank you."

"The pleasure's been mine."

When they parted at the El Tovar, he took her hand and told her he would see her the next time the train brought him to the Grand Canyon. Dreamily she made her way to her room, where she lay on her bed and relived her afternoon with Wade until Dinah returned.

"How was your date?"

"Perfect. Thanks for letting us borrow your Indian blanket for our picnic."

Dinah shook her head. "All I can say is he'd better treat you right."

Edie raised up on one elbow. "I judged him too harshly before. He really is the sweetest man."

Making a face, Dinah repeated, "The tall, dangerous-looking ranger is sweet?"

"Yes, he is. I told you before that he was sent on that cattle-rustling job. He couldn't help it that he couldn't come calling."

"But sweet?"

"Well, he is. He is a godly man, and he's very kind and considerate. Not to mention strong and dreamy."

"What about all that stuff you said about not wanting to marry a lawman? As I recall, the job is too dangerous, and if you asked him to quit, he would always resent it."

"You don't understand. We're just friends. We're following our hearts."

"Come on. Surely you don't think I believe that." Dinah

placed her sketch pad on her desk and suddenly turned back to Edie. "Did he say he just wanted to be friends?"

"No. He said first he wanted to be friends, and then we'd see where our hearts led us."

Dinah crossed the room and sat on the edge of Edie's bed. "Look. I don't want to discourage you if you two are meant to be together. Only I don't want him to hurt you or mislead you. I remember how he affected you before, when he said he'd call and then didn't. Just be careful. Please."

Edie blinked back tears. "You're right, of course. I do need to be careful. Thank you for pointing that out." She swiped a hand across her eyes. "I don't know why I find myself so weepy. Father would have hated that."

"My mother always told me there's nothing wrong with a few tears. A woman is supposed to be soft. When you hold it in, you'll turn hard. Women are meant to feel compassion. It's God's way."

"You sound like Wade. He's always talking about God." She suddenly remembered his gift to her. She pulled out the testament and showed Dinah. "Look. Wade gave me this today."

Dinah's eyes lit. "He did? Maybe I was wrong about him."

"I told you he was sweet." Then, feeling like it was two against one, ganging up on her with this talk about God, she giggled. "Heaven help me."

The girls embraced. Afterward, Dinah offered to show her a few of her favorite verses.

Chapter 6

Three days later Edie had the pleasure of waiting on Wade in the dining room. She winked at him. "Hello, favorite customer."

He flashed his winsome smile. "Hello, favorite Harvey Girl."

"How's the chase going?"

He leaned close and kept his voice low. "I happened to be on the right train this time."

Edie gasped. "You mean you caught him?"

"Yes." His brown eyes darkened. "But then the justice of the peace allowed him to escape. Seems Shady has plenty of accomplices."

She felt his keen disappointment and placed a hand on her hip. "Please tell me you're not serious."

"I wish I could. Two of his gang busted him loose when he was being moved from the jailhouse to the courthouse."

"I'm sorry, Wade. Oh bother. Miss Gibson is watching. I'd better take your order."

"All right, but can we meet later?"

"Yes. How about the rooftop porch this time?"

Wade hesitated briefly then nodded. "I'll be there when you get off duty."

It seemed like eternity until Edie's shift ended. She hastened up the staircase and stepped out onto the porch, searching for Wade in the twilight. He quickly made his presence known, offering her his hand.

"You missed a beautiful sunset."

"I wish I could have shared it with you."

"Listen, Edie, I don't want to scare you, but there's something important you should know."

"What is it?" she asked, clutching his hand a bit tighter.

"Shady Burt vowed he'd get even with me. I'm not worried about myself. I hope he does come after me so I can take him in again. But I'm not sure if I should keep seeing you. He could see us together and remember you from the train. Even if he didn't recognize you, if he thinks you're my girl, there's always the chance he might take out his vengeance on you to get even with me. Do you understand?"

She slowly nodded. Although he made perfect sense, she wasn't ready to end their friendship. She liked the way that sounded—*his girl*. "But I feel so safe when I'm with you." She didn't mention how often she worried about Shady Burt when she was alone. "I suppose it will always be this way with your dangerous job. If it isn't Shady Burt, it'll be someone else."

He squeezed her hand. "I'm afraid you're right."

She looked up. The moon cast a romantic glow across his face. "What's your heart telling you this time, Wade?"

"It's telling me to trust the Lord. What's yours telling you?"

"I believe it's telling me to continue my shooting lessons. Maybe purchase a pistol."

Wade gave her a hug and chuckled. "I've not known a lot of women, but for sure I've never known one as feisty as you."

"Now you have my curiosity."

"You're such an adventuress. I never thought I'd find someone who would date a lawman. Some of the rangers are married, but most are single."

"Are you always going to be a ranger? Is that your lifelong dream?"

"I don't give it much thought. I just concentrate on my job and do my best to outwit my opponents. I don't think about the future."

She turned to face him. "Perhaps you should think about it now. I'm not sure I can pursue an association with someone who holds such a dangerous job. I wouldn't ask a man to quit what he loves doing, but I can't promise you I won't turn and run before I get overly attached to you."

He cupped her cheek and gave her that charming smile. "Oh, that's cruel. I thought you already were overly attached. I guess I have some more persuading to do. I definitely see more shooting lessons in our future."

"Look, Wade!" She turned her face away and pointed in the distance. "A shooting star. Did you wish on it, too?"

He shook his head and chuckled. "No, I'll let you do the wishing for both of us."

The breeze was sweet, rustling her skirt. "A real romantic, aren't you? What would you have wished on?"

His voice softened. "That you would be overly attached to me. Now before you object, I'd best get you back to your dormitory, as much as I hate to. It's getting late, and we don't want you to miss your curfew."

She nodded, and as they started toward the door, she marveled again at his kind, considerate behavior. Father would have liked his adventuresome spirit, but she liked his gentle side.

Wade extinguished his campfire and slipped into his bedroll, thinking about his second shooting lesson with Edie. As usual, he couldn't get her out of his mind. If only Shady hadn't escaped. Edie made light of her fears, but he could tell she harbored them. He certainly had enough misgivings for the both of them. He wanted to see Edie as often as he could, but he also didn't want to lead Shady her way. Torn as he was about it, even more crucial was the problem of where their friendship was headed. Was it even fair to hope a woman like Edie could love a man like him?

Edie's comments of late were forcing him to examine his lifestyle, something he'd never done before. He'd fallen into his ranger job, loving the freedom and challenges it afforded as well as the satisfaction he received when fighting for justice. Now he wondered if Edie would reject him because of his job if he pressed his suit.

His only other interest was ranching. But that was foolish dreaming. His small stash was not enough to invest toward such an endeavor. As far as connections, a few weeks earlier the Tucson rancher had been so pleased when the rustlers were caught, he'd told Wade that if he ever needed a favor or got ready to settle down, he'd gladly help. He gazed at the night sky and sighed, remembering the shooting star they'd watched from the El Tovar's rooftop porch. He should have asked Edie what she had wished. It might help him to know if he was setting himself up for a big letdown.

Edie was a self-professed adventuress. What if she deemed their attraction merely a pleasant diversion? Maybe she was leading him on a merry chase. He took things seriously. Most likely he'd be the one with the broken heart. Still, his heart compelled him to pursue her. He hoped the urging was from God.

The Bible verse he'd heard on the train came to mind: "For he shall give his angels charge over thee, to keep thee in all thy ways. They shall bear thee up in their hands, lest thou dash thy foot against a stone." It was easy to think about God on nights like this, gazing up at His creation. *Are You trying to tell me You're going to protect me from a broken heart, too?* The night was silent except for the sounds of nature. A coyote howled. *I never minded the loneliness before now.*

A week later Edie hurried up the steps to the rooftop porch. Like the tourist couples, she and Wade planned to share lunch and then hike the hotel grounds around the canyon's rim. Wade was waiting and rushed forward to greet her with a hug. "Mm, something smells good."

"Ham and cheese sandwiches, apple pie, and milk." Edie placed a Hopi blanket on the floor in a private corner, kneeled, and set out their lunch, cheerfully chattering. "I'm excited to go on our hike today. Miss Gibson has warned me not to do much exploring on my own. When I go with Dinah, she prefers sketching over hiking."

"That reminds me," Wade said, kneeling beside her and reaching into his tan vest pocket. "I brought you something."

Beaming, Edie gushed, "I love surprises. What is it?"

He pulled out a small package wrapped in brown paper and handed it to her. "Open it carefully."

Edie disregarded his instructions and tore into the wrapping with excitement. "Oh, Wade! It's beautiful!" She rolled the four-and-a-half-inch pistol from palm to palm. "So tiny. It's perfect. What's it called?"

"It's a Colt vest pocket pistol."

"She clutched the gun by its carved ivory grip, turning it this way and that. "I've no vest pocket like you. I wonder how I shall carry it?"

"Begging your pardon, but I've heard some women wear it with a garter." Edie blushed, and he quickly added, "Or you could keep it inside that beaded purse you carry."

"Well, I'm sure I'll find the perfect place for it."

He pointed toward the handle. "Look there."

She tilted the silver-plated weapon. "It's engraved." She peered more closely. *Armed and Dangerous.* "How did you know—Oh! That day on the train?"

He nodded. "I thought it was fitting. Let me show you how it works. It comes apart easily."

Heads together, they went over the pistol's intricacies.

Afterward, they dropped off the remains of their lunch at the dormitory and started their hike, Wade offering her his hand when needed. They fell into a pleasant camaraderie, occasionally talking but mostly enjoying each other's presence. When they stopped to rest, Edie moved away from Wade and leaned over the railing, taking a deep breath of the fresh air. "Isn't this the most amazing place? Even looking at the canyon like this, I can't grasp how vast it is. Nor how beautiful."

"Edie, please be careful."

She cast him a defiant look. "Maybe I'll just lean over a bit too far and see if a handsome ranger will rescue me."

"Don't! Edith! Get back for the sake of life!"

Edith? His scolding tone hurt Edie's pride. "Why are you so edgy?"

"I'm not. I just want you to be careful."

Giving him a frown, she noticed sweat beads breaking out on his forehead. *Strange*, she thought, moving toward him. "Are you feeling all right?"

He reached out and snatched her arm, drawing her close. "I just don't like your being so close to the edge."

Squirming around to give him another glance, she was astonished to see he was quite serious. "Why are you treating me like a child?"

"Can we just walk again?"

She stared at him in confusion.

"I'll explain if we can just walk, over there."

Edie shrugged. She took the arm he offered and let him lead her along the trail that veered away from the guardrail. "I'm waiting," she urged.

"I know it's foolish. I don't like cliffs."

"But there was a railing, and I was perfectly safe. How else could I get the full benefit of the view?"

"Accidents do happen."

"This doesn't sound like you, Wade."

He took off his hat, punched it, and placed it on again. "It's not something I can help or explain."

"Are you saying you'd be afraid to stand where I was?"

"Not afraid. I just can't breathe."

His confession amazed her. "Why?" she asked.

"I'm sure it has something to do with my parents' accident. I was just a kid when I saw their wagon go over a cliff. I was riding with my uncle. Anyway, I just can't breathe when I get that close to a precipice."

She touched his arm with compassion. "I'm sorry. I had no idea. Doesn't that hinder your job?"

He shrugged away. "It hasn't yet, but I suppose it could."

She placed her hands on her waist. "My father always said one has to face up to his fears. That's the only way to conquer them."

Wade's voice sounded gruff. "I suppose that's why you wanted to learn to shoot."

She nodded. "Look, Wade. It's nothing to be ashamed of."

"I'm not ashamed. Like I said, I'm not afraid."

"Of course not. But know what I think?"

He gave her a wry smile. "No, but I think you're going to tell me."

"You need to face this fear."

"It's not a fear."

"Whatever it is, conquer it before you have to deal with it sometime when you're chasing an outlaw. Sometime when it could really cost you your life."

"Now that's a comforting thought."

"I'm serious." She tugged his arm. "Let's go back over there, and I'll stand by the railing with you."

"Don't be ridiculous." His tone was laced with a hint of anger.

"Look, I won't touch you, I—"

"No. It's my problem, not yours."

Edie felt the burn of his rebuff. She shrugged. "Suit yourself."

Wade touched her arm. "I'm sorry. It's just that you're treating this like a game. It's not a game to me. It's not something you can fix."

Once again she saw the truth of his words. His complexion had paled until he didn't even look like an outdoorsman. "You're right. I'm sorry. I don't know what I was thinking."

"You've got to learn about a man a little at a time, Edie. You've bitten off a big portion today. Wouldn't you rather just walk and enjoy my company?"

She crooked her arm in his. "I believe I would." As they walked, she wished she could convey to him that his presence felt comforting and protective, regardless of the fear he'd shared with her. What other man would share something like that? But then, Wade wasn't any ordinary man. He was a compassionate, God-fearing man. With this realization, Edie thought she lost a bit of her heart to him. She was falling in love, and she didn't know what she was going to do about it. It felt good, but it was the scariest thing that had ever happened to her.

"Wade? You know what frightens me?"

"What's that?"

"Your job. I'm getting too attached. I find myself worrying over you every night, not knowing where you are, if you're safe."

"You could pray for me."

"Have you ever prayed about your—breathing problem?"

Wade blushed. "Edie, you've put me through more this day than a man's apt to be able to take. But in answer to your question, I don't think I have. I don't think I even ever mentioned it out loud before."

"Well, I challenge you, then."

"And I return the challenge. But don't forget that if God gets involved, nothing is impossible."

"So you're not afraid to challenge God?"

"Not at all. Don't be surprised if God reveals Himself to you."

"You, too, Ranger Sloan."

Chapter 7

Late Sunday afternoon, Edie took Wade's Bible to a large, flat boulder overlooking the canyon, a favorite place of Dinah's, and gazed with appreciation at the multicolored canyon. The time-etched walls made her life seem no more than a breath in eternity. With feelings of uneasiness, she opened the book and thumbed to the book of Genesis, where she read the creation account. Remembering Wade's request, she placed her hands on the open pages, as if they were magical, and prayed for his protection. But instead of making her feel better, the action unsettled her stomach, giving her an uneasy feeling.

She'd hoped her job would satisfy her longing for that unidentifiable something. Instead, since coming to the Grand Canyon, she was more confused than ever about how to find happiness.

As the setting sun cast rosy colors, she mused. Beauty couldn't be the key, for the canyon offered more of that than most people beheld in a lifetime. She placed her chin in her hands and gazed across the breathtaking expanse again, contemplating her situation. Wade was a godly man. The Bible on her lap was evidence of the beginning of what might be required from her, and she wasn't sure that she wanted to change or that she could ever believe like he did.

He was not without his weaknesses. Because of his confession on their last outing, she felt a tinge of guilt that she could even enjoy the view from her seat on the overhanging face of rock. Her concern for him was evidence that their friendship no longer consisted of a flirtation. He'd captured her heart with his charming smile and gentle, caring manner. It seemed love wasn't the key to her satisfaction, either. In fact, it stirred up dissatisfaction. Love hurt as much as it thrilled, and she didn't want to hurt again or lose someone again. With Wade's dangerous job, she was largely at risk.

She'd come to the West to work as a Harvey Girl, seeking adventure, and hadn't been disappointed. She enjoyed her job and found a wonderful friend in her roommate, Dinah. Perhaps she should just admit to Wade this prayer stuff wasn't working for her. She heard a rustling and looked over her shoulder.

"Dinah. I was just thinking of you."

"I didn't mean to disturb you," the other girl said. "Especially when you're studying your Bible."

"I was finished."

"May I join you, then?"

Edie nodded, explaining further, "I promised Wade I would read it and that I would pray for his safety."

"I like him better all the time."

"He's becoming a real problem."

Dinah settled in beside her. "Why? Have you quarreled?"

"No. I was just thinking how he's trying to change me. He wants me to pray and read the Bible like him. He wants me to be able to accept his job whether I like it or not. He comes and goes as he pleases. I wait and worry. And he wants to be friends when I'm feeling more than friendship."

"I don't see anything wrong with reading and praying, but I wouldn't like the worrying part, either."

"Of course you wouldn't!"

"You think he'll ever leave the rangers?"

"When I ask him about it, he doesn't say. He skirts the issue."

Dinah sighed. "That does sound like a man who isn't going to change."

"I was just thinking that I have everything I need with the canyon, my job, and you. Maybe I should just break it off with him before it goes any further. I think he'll understand, because when Shady Burt said he was going to get even, Wade was worried he'd come after me. He even suggested we not see each other. Maybe he also knows it's for the best all the way around."

"Perhaps." Dinah's expression was not so convincing.

Edie shrugged. "It's getting dark. I think I'll head back to our room. Maybe read a little before bed."

"That sounds like a good idea. When are you going to finish that dime novel so I can read it?"

"Tonight," Edie said with conviction. Tonight she was ready to face the ending.

An hour later, she opened her book and started with the end of the next-to-last chapter to renew her memory.

Lolita waved, then watched the Texas ranger ride away. She watched until his dust had settled.

"If he is a man good enough for my daughter, he will return. If he does not, he is not a man at all," said her father.

Edie turned the page and started the last chapter.

Lolita went to the well. As she had every day since the ranger's departure, she gazed down the road with longing.

"What are you looking for, señorita?"

With a gasp, she dropped the bucket and turned. Him! She blushed, her dignity returning. "Tell me first, why have you returned?"

"I forgot something."

"What is that?"

The Texas Ranger closed the distance between them and quickly drew her into his arms. "This."

She closed her eyes and savored the closeness. She was not disappointed when his lips met hers. When they drew apart, she smiled. "I knew you would come back."

"Why didn't you tell me that before? You could have saved me a lot of trouble."

She looped her arm through his. "I'm telling you now. And this time, I'm not letting you escape so easily, either."

The End.

Edie snapped the book closed. "Well, that doesn't help me at all. I still don't know what happened."

"What do you mean?" Dinah asked.

"The ending. I don't know if he quit his job or if—"

"Stop. Don't tell me. I want to read it, remember?"

"Sorry." Edie turned off the light and snuggled under the covers. *Well, this is it, Lord. If You're going to make Yourself known to me, You'd better do it soon. Once I break up with Wade, I may not talk to You much. No disrespect meant. Amen.*

Wade waited outside the dormitory, clutching a bundle of flowers from the gift shop. He hadn't seen Edie for over a week, and he wanted to make a good impression. He'd gotten a haircut, trimmed his mustache, and even bought a new shirt when he was in Flagstaff. When she came out, he stepped forward. "I missed you."

She blushed. "Thank you. I missed you, too." She smelled the offered bouquet.

Her eyes moistened, and Wade was grateful for his foresight regarding the flowers. "What do you want to do today? Go to the Hopi House?"

"Could we just walk a bit?" she asked.

Wade cast a skyward glance. "If we don't go too far. It looks like rain."

Edie clutched her flowers and nodded, gazing at the ground as they started off rather than looping her hand through his arm as usual. Normally she bubbled over with news or small talk; today she was quiet. He sought for something to say that might interest her. "I heard some gossip in the gift shop. They said a woman named Olivia Gregory just had a baby. Do you know her?"

She gave a wobbly smile. "I heard that news, too. I wait on her husband sometimes. He used to be a manager here. Now he's a lawyer in Williams and is working on the canyon's national park status. Olivia was a Harvey Girl. Everyone is happy for her."

Even talking about happiness, Edie looked sober. Her behavior troubled Wade. Normally she would have spilled out such news before they'd gone ten paces.

"Is something bothering you today?"

"Yes. I—" A crack of thunder rent the air. Edie pointed toward the east. "Oh. Look how dark it's gotten."

"I'm glad I'm staying at the hotel tonight. Shall we take cover in the lobby?" he suggested.

She nodded. "We need to talk."

"We can talk about whatever you want. Anything that makes you happy. I just want to see that smile of yours lighting up your face."

Inside, they sat near a window where they could watch the rain and lightning show.

"Just in time," Wade said a bit too cheerfully.

She sighed. "The weather seems quite appropriate."

Wade took her hand. "Tell me what's bothering you. Did something happen at work?"

"Just look at the pine trees, their tops bending to the wind." She pointed. "I'm going to miss this place so much."

Wade's heart plummeted. "What do you mean?"

"I'm putting in for a transfer."

He scooted to the edge of his chair. "But I thought you loved it here. You just said you did. Why?" Suddenly he understood. "It's me, isn't it? You want to get away from me?"

"There's no easy way to say this, but yes. I have enjoyed our times together, but it's getting too complicated."

"Is it what I said about Shady Burt?"

"He's a small part of it. Mostly it's because I'm falling in love with you, and I can't do that."

"Why not? I know we haven't known each other long, but I've known for weeks that I love you, too. This is a good thing, Edie. Don't fight it," he pleaded.

"Please don't make this hard." She laid the bouquet in her lap and swiped tears from her cheeks with the back of her hand. "I don't know when I'll get a transfer, but I'd rather we didn't see each other again in the meantime."

Her unexpected rejection caught him off guard, but he knew he needed to delay her leaving the territory and disappearing forever. He had to convince her to stay long enough for him to figure out a way to win her over.

She picked up the bouquet and started to rise.

"Wait. You don't need to transfer. I promise I won't bother you. I'll respect your wishes."

She hesitated. "But you often come into the dining room to eat. You stay at the hotel."

"I won't sit at one of your tables. And I won't seek you out if that's not what you want."

There was a lull in the storm, and Edie glanced toward the door. "I don't know. I thought it would be easier if I didn't see you again."

"Let's try. If it's too hard, then you can transfer. Better yet, I can. You love it here, and you love Dinah."

She looked at him. "Really?"

Wade nodded.

"I'm sorry, but I just can't love a ranger. Please try to understand. I'm sorry—" She turned and hurried away.

Wade slumped back into the armchair and stared at the

closed door, then watched her pass outside the window. So that was her reason. If he was honest with himself, he could understand why she felt like she did, but what he couldn't understand was why she didn't even give him a chance to make a choice. The rain started up again. With a storm of rising emotions, he turned away from the window and left for the privacy of his room.

❧

Edie hurried across the street, past the dormitory toward the edge of the forest. She lifted her skirt and waded through the wet grass and brushed by the dripping evergreen branches until she reached privacy. She flung her flowers on the pine-carpeted ground and leaned against the nearest tree, sinking to the earth. Placing her face in her hands, she allowed the sobs to come.

He hadn't even argued, hadn't offered to quit his job, hadn't begged her to change her mind, and she was miserable and didn't know what she was going to do. A crash of thunder and a torrent of rain added to her suffering. *Oh bother,* she thought, placing her arm across her forehead to protect her face. Rising, she lifted her skirt with the other hand and had no choice but to run toward the dormitory. A few steps and she returned and groped the ground for her scattered flowers, then ran again for the dormitory. Her only comfort was that the rain would wash her tearstained face.

Chapter 8

Wade finished his coffee and put out the campfire. The first several days after Edie's rejection, he could think of nothing other than his utter distress and loneliness, but as the days grew into a week, his mind focused on something different—Edie's challenge.

It simmered until it prompted him toward action, so he'd packed his saddlebags for an indefinite stay and mounted his horse.

Now from a distance, he saw his destination, Canyon Diablo Bridge. *Diablo* was Spanish for "devil." The Lord was urging him to make peace with the demon that had robbed him of so much peace. And this was the perfect place to do it. He didn't know what to do to restore his friendship with Edie, but he knew what to do about his—fear. Yes, fear.

The bridge was so high it seemed surreal, its steel bracings strong enough to hold a moving train. He was going to camp here tonight and haunt that bridge every day for as long as it took for him to overcome his fear. And every day when he reached the summit, he was going to pray for God to change Edie's heart and remove her fears just as he trusted Him to bear away his own fear and pain.

He surveyed the area first, looking for the perfect place to make camp. On each side of the bridge, the bluffs sloped dramatically with giant boulders and scraggly plants. He tied his horse and looked for a path to the bottom but saw nothing. He finally chose a place on the top by some scrub bushes for shade. While his horse was sampling the vegetation, he walked toward the bridge. Just thinking about his task tightened his chest. The closer he got, the more panicked he felt.

Once on the bridge, he managed one step at a time, peering down often to acclimate himself to the height. He was only about a sixth of the way when he heard a train's whistle. A burst of energy fed his muscles. Common sense vanished. Frantic to outrun the train rather than climb down the trellis or let the locomotive rattle past him, he raced until he reached the end of the bridge; then he gave a mighty leap and stumbled. Momentum rolled him another thirty feet downhill. A rocky ledge stopped his fall. He lay there, gasping for air. Above him, the train rumbled across the bridge.

Wheezing, he crawled up the embankment, pebbles and stickers becoming embedded in his hands. He pushed to a standing position and sprinted off in the opposite direction until he reached camp, where he sank flat to the ground, stomach down, and lay there until his breathing returned to almost normal, all the while berating himself for not taking the train schedule into consideration.

When he could speak, he recited the verse he had heard on the train about God's sending His angels to protect him. In God's mercy, the humor of it struck him—*"They will keep him from striking his foot against a stone."* He had been mighty glad for that stone ledge. His chuckle turned into gales of laughter, and there all alone in Canyon Diablo, he laughed at himself until the tears came.

Edie stood at the coffee urn filling a tray of cups and genuinely tried to put her heart and soul into her work, but it didn't relieve her misery. She reminded herself of why she had come to the Arizona Territory as a Harvey Girl—to make her father proud. She argued with her heart that she had not endured training and come clear across the country just to mope over a man. Her hand trembled, and coffee sloshed over the rim and onto her starched white apron.

Oh bother. Now she'd have to run across the street to the dormitory to change. She started toward the head waitress, but Dinah caught her eye.

"You all right?"

"I spilled again. Honestly, Miss Gibson is going to think I'm doing this on purpose to get out of work."

"Nonsense. I'm sure she's spilled a cup or two in her day. She knows by now that you are good at your job. It's Wade, isn't it?"

Edie nodded. "It's been a week since we parted ways. I keep thinking I'll turn around and see him sitting in the dining room. Know what I mean?"

Dinah nodded. "You miss him. He'll be back. Don't worry. It's almost quitting time. We'll talk later. Here, let's trade aprons, and I'll go fetch a clean one."

"You don't have to do that."

"Hurry, before someone sees," Dinah urged.

Edie smiled. "Thanks. You're the best." She watched Dinah leave. She really was the kindest woman.

❧

The following day, Wade climbed the bridge again, this time making it to the halfway and highest point. There he prayed about his attachment to Edie and felt his spirit urging him not to give up on her, so he prayed for God to soften her heart to the gospel. Maybe her reluctance to accept Christ was the chief factor keeping them apart. He would bring it before the Lord each day and trust God for His best.

Afterward, he did some exploring and discovered a trail that wound its way to the bottom of the canyon, so he moved his camp down into the valley by the stream.

As the week continued, Wade lost track of the days. But one morning visitors entered what he now considered his canyon. He watched the three men lead their horses to a rocky pocket close to the top of the bluff. The men congregated on a nearby ledge. Wade retrieved his binoculars from his saddlebag and focused them on—Shady Burt! The nerve of the outlaw to return to the very place they had attempted a robbery! They had about two hours before the train came through. He needed to make a plan, and he knew it wasn't going to be to his liking.

❧

Edie went to her room exhausted and hosting another headache, the third in a week. It had plagued her all day. Dinah suggested she lie on the bed and allow her to place a cool cloth on her head.

"How's that feel?"

"Much better." After days of fighting an escalating feeling of physical weakness and emotional despondency, Dinah's kindness caused Edie's fragile countenance to shatter. Her tears fell, and her shoulders shook uncontrollably.

"Poor girl. Go ahead and cry it out," Dinah soothed.

Edie sobbed all the more while Dinah patted her shoulder. Finally, Edie gulped, "I'm sorry. I don't know what's wrong with me."

Dinah used the cloth to dab at her face. "Everyone needs a good cry once in a while. You've been through so much."

"I have?"

"Why yes. You recently lost your father. You learned a new job. You love a man you can't marry. It's time you realized you can't carry all your burdens yourself."

"But I've always detested weakness."

"Why?"

"Papa wouldn't have liked it."

"Pretending everything's all right when it isn't has only made you sick."

Edie protested. "But what am I supposed to do?"

"I've learned the best way to cope is to take my concerns to God. He changes my heart, and I find peace in the situation."

"I could use some peace. I'm miserable."

"Would you like me to pray with you?" Dinah asked.

"Please."

With Dinah's help, Edie simply asked God to forgive her for living a life without Him and to bring her Dinah's kind of peace. Amazingly, He did. She'd found her unidentifiable something at last.

❧

Wade kept a keen eye on the three robbers. If they climbed the bridge's steel trellis, they could jump onto the train as it passed over the bridge. The last time they had disappeared quickly. Now he knew how they'd made their escape. Behind the horses was a well-hidden hollow area, almost like a cave. He'd bet they even stored supplies in there.

His only plan of action was to surprise them by lowering himself over the edge of a narrow ledge directly above them. He studied the area. It wasn't a frightening drop unless he missed his footing when he landed. If he did, he could fall off the lower sheer cliff and tumble to his death.

He counted the reasons he should attempt the capture. First, it was his duty. Second, the robber had escaped once and made threats. He didn't want to see the man go free, especially since there was the chance he might recognize Edie. Third, there was always the possibility that someone on the train could be injured or killed. Last, he'd come to this bridge to make peace with his fears. If he walked away, he wouldn't be able to live with himself.

He knew he probably wouldn't be able to capture all three men. Usually, at first sight of a lawman, the renegades scattered and fled. He'd go after Shady first, because headquarters thought he was the gang's leader.

He checked his pocket watch. Not much time for weighing the pros and cons. The train would arrive soon, which meant he needed to implement his plan before the robbers left their hideaway and started up the trellis. Once they were out in the open like that, Wade wouldn't be able to sneak up on them.

He took off his Stetson. *Lord, I'm not ready to die. But Your will be done, not mine. Keep me safe if You will. Amen.*

The next several minutes, Wade moved in and out of cover, climbing and getting into position. If all went well, it would be easy to surprise them. They thought they were the only ones in the canyon. He hoped they'd surrender without a gunfight but knew he probably wouldn't be so fortunate. He took his pistol from his holster, checked it for ammunition, and moved to the edge. His ear to the edge, he could hear voices but couldn't distinguish their conversation.

He hunkered down and lay on his stomach, ready to slide feet first. He would land facing them and hope for the best. If his feet didn't hit solid ground, there were some scrub bushes that might save him.

Ready. Set. Jump!

Chapter 9

Releasing his grip and dropping was the hardest feat Wade ever remembered doing. Somehow he managed it. As he fell, the landscape blurred, his stomach lurched to his throat, and he concentrated on planting his feet and keeping hold of his gun. A strong urge to toss the gun and grab hold of shrubbery tempted him, but thankfully he didn't give in to it.

He landed in a crouching position with a loud grunt. Quickly he drew himself up and leveled his gun at the scattering, wide-eyed trio. "Freeze. Hands in the air or I'll shoot!"

In response, a bullet whizzed past his left ear. He dropped and rolled, then scrambled for cover beneath a creosote bush on the very edge of the ledge. The trio backed up into their protective hideaway behind a cover of bushes. Wade could see red cloth and took a shot. It thudded into its fleshy target.

A flurry of gunfire caused puffs of dust to rise from the nearby ground. He froze. A bullet nicked his thigh and tore his trousers but otherwise did little harm. He lay low until the firing ceased then peeked around the creosote. A thatch of brown hair gave away another robber's position. Wade shot, and a yell pierced the air. The remaining man made a run for it. Wade scrambled out into the open, not paying attention to his wound, all his efforts zeroed in on the chase. Before Shady Burt could reach his horse, Wade's bullet penetrated the renegade's leg, and he fell to the ground.

"Throw me your guns!" Wade ordered.

Shady did as directed, rolling on the ground, cursing, and clutching his leg.

On Sunday Edie joined Dinah for her first church service at the canyon. It was held at the hotel, and a Harvey employee named Robert Thatcher preached. Edie felt immeasurable joy and peace, better than anything she'd ever known. She only hoped to be able to share her experience with Wade sometime. That would make it all the sweeter. She even looked for him in the service, but he wasn't attending.

Afterward, the two women were invited to join a group of Harvey employees planning to hike partway down the canyon on Cameron's Trail. The two girls agreed to the plan and after lunch paid their dollar for the hike and joined the others in line. Edie inhaled a deep breath of the canyon's fresh pine air then started down the white, sandy path.

"The first overlook is less than an hour away," Dinah explained as they made their descent. "From there we'll see Roaring Springs Canyon. I'd like to stop there to sketch the sandstone layers and the red rocks visible from the area. But if you'd like to go on with the group, I don't mind."

Edie cast a look behind her, realizing how much harder the return climb would be. "I should probably take it easy my first time."

"You could make it all the way to the Supai Tunnel. But you would be exhausted."

"I don't need that on my day off," Edie laughed. After that they spoke little, concentrating on their breathing and taking in the untarnished wilderness in its encompassing beauty with its strange and exotic plant life and small canyon creatures scurrying out of harm's way.

At the overlook, the group stopped to rest and sightsee. Since she was not hiking farther and would have plenty of time to look around once the group moved on, Edie took off her glasses and carefully placed them on a flat rock. She used a white lace handkerchief to wipe the sweat off her brow. Her hair had come partly loose, so she worked to secure it. Then she heard the awful sound. *Crunch!* She wheeled about. *Oh bother!*

A fellow Harvey Girl named Sarah Jane had climbed on the rock. She lifted her booted foot and pulled out Edie's crushed spectacles with a cry of remorse. "Oh no! Look what I've done."

Edie reached for the glasses. "May I see them?"

"I'm so sorry. Here." She relinquished the mangled spectacles.

One lens was shattered. The other featured a large crack. The frames were bent and distorted. Edie silently wondered how she would get by.

Sarah Jane looked just as stricken as Edie felt. "I'll pay to have them replaced. I'm so sorry."

The girl's twin sister, Mabel, came looking for her. "The group's getting ready to leave—Uh-oh. What happened?"

Sarah Jane hesitated. "I broke Edie's glasses."

Mabel sympathized. "You won't be able to go on now, will you, Edie?"

Edie replied, "I wasn't planning to. Dinah's going to stay and sketch. I'll just keep her company."

"But I've ruined everything for you," Sarah Jane moaned.

"Nonsense. Please go on," Edie said. "And don't worry about a thing. See," she said, putting them on again. "I can still wear them. I have one lens."

"You will let me pay for them?" Sarah Jane pressed.

"We'll see. You two had better go, or you'll be left behind."

"Are you sure you'll be all right?" they asked.

"I'm fine."

"Very well. I'll check on you later at the hotel." Sarah Jane gave a final hesitant look then hurried off with Mabel to catch up with the others.

Edie waved them on, but when the girls were out of earshot, she gave a great sigh of disappointment and repeated what she'd kept under her breath before, "Oh bother!"

Dinah touched her shoulder. "We can return now. I wouldn't want you to get another headache."

Edie shook her head. "I'll be fine. Let's stay." Even though she had one lens, the crack distorted her view. She didn't want to complain, but she wondered how she would survive without them.

Dinah situated herself with her sketch pad. "We'll leave well before dark, then, and I'll help you. I'm sure you'll have no trouble getting off work to get a new pair."

"I suppose not." They sat in silence for a while. Dinah sketched, and Edie picked the shards of glass out of the shattered lens.

"Did you ever do something you regretted but didn't know how to fix it?"

Dinah cast her a sideways glance. "Yes. What is it you regret? Wade?"

"You know me so well."

"What about him do you regret?"

"Running him off."

"You think you would marry him now?"

"Since I've been praying about it—yes, I think I could."

Dinah gave her a warm smile. "Then I shall start to pray that you will have the opportunity to tell him."

Edie felt a rush of hope. "You think God would do that for me?"

"He might. If it's in your best interest from His point of view. It doesn't hurt to ask."

Hoping for the best, Wade strode into the El Tovar's dining room. So much had happened in the past few days, and he needed to give Edie the good news—Shady Burt was now behind bars. He'd been disappointed the other two had gotten away. Evidently he'd only grazed them with his bullets. However, Shady was the one he'd most wanted to capture.

Wade knew he had promised not to see Edie, but given the fears she harbored over Shady, he felt the man's capture was a good reason to break his promise and initiate a conversation with her. He also wanted to tell her how he had accepted her challenge and how God had helped him overcome his fear.

Seating himself at a table she usually served, he searched the dining room for her. When Dinah appeared to wait on him instead of Edie, he thought his heart dropped all the way to the bottom of the canyon.

"Ranger Sloan. Nice to see you. Here's a menu."

Wade didn't miss Dinah's attentive expression, sure it had something to do with the situation between him and Edie. "I was hoping to see Edie. Is she working today?"

Dinah's expression fell, and he sensed an ally. "I'm sorry. She's gone."

"You mean she's not at the El Tovar?"

She shook her head. "I'm sorry. She left this morning. Took the train to Williams."

That was all he needed to hear. Familiar with the train schedules, he knew if he left right away, he might be able to intercept her before she made her next connection. He had to. He didn't even know where her home was in Chicago. "Excuse me, please," he said, bounding up and running from the dining room.

"Wait!"

He heard Dinah's appeal, but there was no time to wait. He felt the other customers' eyes on him, but it didn't matter. He had to catch that train. Had to tell Edie that Shady had been captured. Who was he kidding? What he had to tell her was that he loved her and he would do whatever it took to make her his own.

By the time he had saddled up, he'd figured out that he always knew he would be willing to give up his job to marry her. Why hadn't he told her that before? And now, with the reward money, he could set up a ranch and—"Giddy up! Need to catch that train."

❧

Edie folded her hands in her lap and watched the scenery whir by. As Dinah claimed, it was easy to get the day off. Because the Harvey Company stressed a neat appearance, one look at

Edie's pitiful spectacles caused an expression of horror on Miss Gibson's face. She had strode straight to Manager Niles, Edie in tow, and the next thing Edie knew, she had a train pass in her hand and was being escorted to the exit. Miss Gibson's parting admonition was to enjoy her time off and not return until she had a new pair of glasses. She bit back a smile at the memory. Edie looked forward to today's adventure in Williams even though Dinah wasn't with her to share the fun. To be truthful, the only thing that made her a little nervous was the train ride itself. However, she had prayed and was carrying her tiny Colt in her purse.

Edie remembered reading her dime novel on her last train ride. Regrettably, she had taken it to heart, even letting it prejudice her against Wade, at least until she had read the last chapter. But the ending hadn't satisfied her curiosity. She never knew if the ranger had quit his job. Too late she came to realize she couldn't judge Wade by a fictional character just as she couldn't judge him by her father's preferences. She bit her lip, remembering how Wade had cautioned her against judging him from the beginning. Too bad she hadn't listened. What was important was finding God's will in the situation. She hoped it included Wade. Even if it didn't, she wanted to tell him her good news someday.

"Where you going?" inquired the gray-haired woman seated across the aisle.

Edie turned. "Williams. To get new glasses."

"Ah. You one of those Harvey Girls?"

"I am. Did you enjoy your stay at the canyon?"

The loud screeching of steel interrupted their conversation, and Edie inwardly panicked.

"Why we stopping?" the older passenger asked.

This couldn't be happening again! Edie couldn't help but look out the window. This time there was no frightening face. However, neither were they anywhere near a train station. As the train came to a complete stop, hissing and wheezing, Edie placed her beaded purse on her lap, placed her hand inside, and clutched her Colt's pearl grip.

Chapter 10

What's going on?" the gray-haired woman asked again.

Although Edie had a good idea, she refrained from giving her opinion. Waiting until the woman looked away, she slipped her Colt from her purse and hid it in the fold of her skirt. Her mind raced. What if Shady Burt recognized her? He had promised Wade revenge. Could she really pull the trigger? Was Wade somewhere on the train?

The door to her car flung open. A tall man with a handkerchief over the greater portion of his face strode into the car, causing a collective gasp from the passengers. He gave them a menacing glare. "Get out your valuables and nobody gets hurt. I'm going to pass my hat. Put 'em in." He pushed his hat at the closest man and aimed his gun at the man's head. "Go on."

The man didn't hesitate, pulling off his watch and withdrawing his billfold and plopping them into the hat.

"Pass it on!" the outlaw sharply reprimanded.

The man shoved it to the fellow beside him. The outlaw followed the course of action with the point of his gun, while his steely eyes kept constant vigil over the other passengers.

Edie's heartbeat raced. At least it wasn't Shady. The man's gun was much larger than hers. It was no match. She needed a plan.

The hat was about one-third of the way up the car. The outlaw grew increasingly impatient, increasingly greedy. "Hurry up!" He swung his gun around at the passengers. "Have your valuables ready! The next one ain't ready, I'm shooting." Everyone scrambled to get items from their bags.

When the mild commotion started and the robber was distracted, Edie knew it was time to act. She'd aim to wound, not kill. Surely then one of the men in the car would jump in to help. With a big gulp, she stood and stretched out her arms to aim, but her cracked and missing lenses blurred her vision through the gun's sight. In all the excitement, she hadn't remembered her impairment. But it was too late to retreat. The robber had already seen her gun.

He sneered in delight. Then ever so slowly, he brought his own gun around. Edie tried to keep her pistol steady. *Just pouring a cup of coffee—steady, steady.* The evil man was going to shoot her, and she didn't know if she could even pull the trigger. Then the dizziness came.

Wade rode hard and took a shortcut, hoping to be able to intercept the train when it arrived at Williams, but he caught up with it well before the station. Once he spotted it in the distance, he kept it in his line of vision. When it slowed at the same juncture where Shady Burt's gang had robbed it earlier, Wade grew suspicious. Remembering that some of his gang members were still on the loose, he spurred his horse and galloped toward the halted train.

Seeing two horses tied to a nearby tree, Wade dismounted and bounded onto a nearby platform.

Knowing one robber usually went after the engineer, Wade easily found his first intruder. Thankfully, his back was to the door, making Wade's job easier as he stole up behind him, raised his Colt, and whacked him on the back of the head. The man slunk silently to the floor. The engineer grinned. "I hoped one of you boys would show up. There's at least one more with the passengers. I'll tie this one up."

Wade felt a rush of energy as he started into the first car. He silenced the passengers' surprised shrieks with a finger to his lips and a flash of the badge on his vest. He moved forward, passing through each car. All he could think of was that Edie was on this train! He paused when he heard a commotion sounding from outside the door of the next car. Slowly he stole inside, hoping the passengers would remain calm and allow him to do his job, and hoping against all odds that Edie wasn't inside this particular car, but nothing prepared him for the scene he came upon.

The sight sent a jolt of fear through Wade worse than any he remembered, including Canyon Diablo. *His girl* stood with her arms outstretched, aiming her pistol at the robber. And the outlaw had his gun pointed back at her. It was a standoff Edie couldn't win. What was she thinking?

The outlaw made a move Wade recognized all too well. He flew into action. "I wouldn't do that!" he warned, preparing himself to take out the other man quickly.

The robber jerked and turned.

At the same time Edie's gun fired. Her bullet hit a chandelier directly over the outlaw, and instantly the light crashed down on his head. Edie and the outlaw fell at the same time. Wade hurried to scoop up the outlaw's gun and place it in his belt, then quickly stepped over him and rushed toward Edie. He sank to his knees and cradled her head with his hand. Had she taken a bullet?

"Edie?" She didn't respond. Frantically he ran his eyes over her clothing, searching for signs of blood, but there didn't seem to be any.

"She fainted," a gray-haired woman said. "That's all. But she got that robber good, didn't she?"

Wade lightly tapped her cheek. "Edie. Wake up, girl."

She stirred, opened her eyes. "Oh, Wade. I knew you'd come!"

"Are you hurt?" he asked.

"No." She shook her head. "Just frightened."

He drew her close. "It's all right now. You got him."

"He's not dead?"

"I doubt it. You hit the chandelier, and it fell on his head. But look at you. You must have broken your glasses when you fell."

"No." She shook her head. "They were already broken. That's why I missed my shot."

"You mean you weren't aiming for the chandelier?"

"Not at all."

He chuckled. "Oh, Edie. You're the most honest person I know. I've got to make sure he gets tied up before he gains consciousness. Let me help you to your seat. I'll be back shortly."

❧

The passengers around Edie pressed close, congratulating her on her quick thinking. The gray-haired woman fanned her.

"Please, I'm fine now. I just need some air," Edie insisted.

"Of course, dear," the lady said. "But you were magnificent. Even with those broken glasses." As the woman backed away, Edie heard her say, "She's one of them Harvey Girls, you know."

Edie slunk back in her seat, wishing everyone would just turn away and leave her be. She had a more important matter to think about. If God had given her a chance to tell Wade she'd changed her mind, then she needed to do it, no matter how humiliating or frightening it seemed. He said he'd return shortly. She thought she saw love in his eyes when he bent over her earlier, but that didn't mean he would forget and forgive her earlier rejection.

She leaned into the aisle to see if Wade was still there.

He was already returning to her. When he reached her seat, he asked, "May I sit? I don't have long."

Her pulse quickened. "Yes, please."

"Once the train starts, it's only a short time until we reach Williams. Then I'll have to turn in these outlaws and return for my horse and theirs, too. But I have to know. Are you running away from me? Because I'm here to do everything in my power to persuade you to stay."

"I've been praying that God would give me a second chance with you."

"Praying?"

"Yes. God's been changing my heart. I'm ready to marry a ranger, if there's one who will have me."

Wade removed his Stetson. "I don't think there is, Edie."

Her face fell. She nodded. "I understand."

"But would you consider marrying a ranger that turned rancher?"

Her heart swelled with hope. "You're giving up your job for me?"

"I always wanted to try my hand at ranching anyway. I went to the hotel to tell you we captured Shady Burt. With the reward money and some connections with a rancher I helped in Tucson, I've got enough to buy a small spread. Do you think you could marry a rancher?"

"I could marry you. I love you. The rest will work out."

"I love you, too, Edith. But why were you running away?"

"I wasn't!" Edie shook her head adamantly. "I was only going to Williams to get a new pair of glasses."

"What a relief. When Dinah told me you were on the train, I thought you were headed back to Chicago. I rode like a tornado to intercept you."

Edie smiled. "You did? I thought you probably hated me."

"I love you. And right now I'd really like to kiss you."

"Then kiss her, Ranger," said the gray-haired woman.

When Wade drew her close, Edie felt the love well up in her. They kissed to the passengers' cheers then drew apart in embarrassment. Wade leaned close and whispered, "You are one armed and dangerous lady!"

Epilogue

Two months later

The newly married couple stood arm in arm atop the crest of the Diablo Canyon Bridge. They waved. Dinah waved back from far below. She was sketching them on the bridge. It was her wedding gift to them. Not only was it the very place they had first met, but also Dinah hoped the picture would serve as a reminder of how they had overcome their fears.

"I'm so glad Dinah agreed to spend her vacation on our ranch," Edie said.

"Me, too. She's right, you know. God used you and that verse to help me overcome my fears."

Edie pulled her coat tight to ward off the early autumn chill. "What verse is that, dear?"

"You know, Psalm 91: 'For he shall give his angels charge over thee, to keep thee in all thy ways. They shall bear thee up in their hands, lest thou dash thy foot against a stone.' Don't you remember? Right after I entered your passenger car that first day we met? A passenger quoted it out loud."

"No, I didn't hear it."

"But it was loud and distinct."

"Maybe it was just for you to hear."

"I have never memorized a verse so easily before. It just stuck in my head."

"Exactly." They quietly contemplated the miracle verse and what God had accomplished with it. "This canyon may be named *Diablo*, but God used it for His glory, didn't He?" she asked.

"Indeed, He did."

A mischievous look came over Wade's face. "Want to give Dinah something really good to sketch?"

Edie cautiously backed away. "I'm beginning to recognize that look."

But Wade was too quick for her. He soon had her cradled in his embrace.

"What's she going to think?" Edie whispered, snuggled against his warm coat.

"That we're in love?"

DIANNE CHRISTNER

Dianne Christner is a full-time historical Christian romance writer. She loves the traveling and research part of her job. After living in the same home for twenty-six years, she and her husband, Jim, are building a new house on two and a half acres of desert. They love the outdoor-living style of Phoenix. Dianne's son, Michael, and his wife, Heather, live in Phoenix and just started their family with a little girl named Makaila. Dianne's daughter, Rachel, and her husband, Leo, live in Houston, Texas. You may visit Dianne's Web site at www.diannechristner.com.

The Richest Knight

Nancy J. Farrier

Dedication

For my Grandpa and Grandma Rhine,
who raised eleven children on a small farm during the depression.
I loved hearing that Grandpa claimed to be a millionaire
because God blessed him with so many children.
Thanks, too, to my Aunt Ruth, whose love of the
Grand Canyon led her to work there in her retirement years.
Her enthusiasm made this story a joy to write.

Prologue

San Francisco, 1909

"Franklin, you can't possibly be serious about this."

The anguish in his mother's voice churned the food in Franklin Knight's stomach into a lead weight that held him immobile in his seat. From around the table his brothers and sisters were staring openmouthed. At the head of the massive dining table, his father's countenance was so dark Franklin expected lighting bolts to be shooting his way any minute.

"This is preposterous." Miranda Knight shot an imploring look at her husband. "Tell him, Eugene. He can't leave home right now. We need him to run the ranch while you're campaigning for office. Charles and Daniel are too young to handle such weighty matters."

At the mention of their names, Franklin's younger brothers bristled. He knew they both chafed at the way their parents loaded all the responsibility for management of the ranch on Franklin, giving him authority over his siblings as the eldest.

That was one of many reasons Franklin intended to ride out in the morning to start a new life somewhere else. He'd been planning and praying about this for a long time.

"Your mother's right." Anger tinged Eugene's words with more harshness than normal. "We're counting on you to be here. You've worked with Jason and the other hands for several years now. They know what to expect from you. These boys have spent the last few years away at school. They won't know the first thing about running a place the size of ours."

"Jason is the best foreman in California. If Charles and Daniel listen, he can teach them all they need to know." Franklin leaned back, smiling up at Emma as she took his plate so the dessert could be served. He'd left half his food, but his appetite had fled with the start of this conversation.

"What about Charlotte?" Tears glistened in his mother's eyes. "She's expecting an engagement ring on her birthday next month."

"Mother." Franklin said a short prayer for the right words. "Charlotte and I have nothing in common other than family status. She's only interested in me because of our name and money, the same as all the girls before her."

"Franklin, that's a terrible thing to say." Miranda pressed her handkerchief to her temple, her face pale. "I believe Charlotte loves you. You're a very handsome man."

"If I were one of the ranch hands, my looks wouldn't matter at all." Franklin could feel his frustration building. "Charlotte wouldn't give me the time of day if I couldn't court her in the style she's accustomed to."

"That's enough." Eugene's fist slammed the tabletop, making the dishes clatter. "We've been patient with you. You've rejected every girl your mother has deemed worthy. Charlotte comes from a very respectable family. An alliance will increase our holdings and be to our benefit. I don't want to hear any more of this nonsense."

Silence bore down as Franklin's siblings stared down at their plates of dessert. Their father's anger was so rare that Franklin knew some of the younger ones had never heard him roar like this.

"I'm sorry, Father. I don't want to go against you, but I can't marry Charlotte. Money isn't everything, yet that's what it has become to this family, not to mention to all your friends."

Eugene leaned forward. His lip curled in derision. "So what is important to you, son? That religious tripe of yours?"

Franklin's heart pounded. He tried to pray but couldn't think of what to say. "I believe God is calling me to get away from here for now, to follow Him wherever He wants me to go."

"So just like that you'll give up all your inheritance? Everything we've raised you for?" Eugene's words were met with shocked glances from around the table. "Because that's what will happen. If you walk out now, you won't inherit the manure from one of the barns. You'll be penniless. Then see what girl will have you."

"That's one of my points." Calm flowed through Franklin. He folded his napkin and pushed his chair back from the table. "If a woman doesn't believe in Jesus and only wants me for my name or my money, then she isn't the right one for me."

"Franklin, you can't go." Miranda sobbed aloud.

"Leave him." Eugene's dark gaze made Miranda sink back into her chair. "He's made his choice." His heavy brows drew together as he looked back at Franklin. "You can leave now. I won't have you taking any of the horses. They belong here. You can take some of your clothes and that mule you insisted on keeping. That's it."

"Thank you, sir. Since I bought Moses with my own money, I appreciate your letting me keep him." Franklin was at the door when his mother's teary voice stopped him.

"Franklin, where will you go?" she asked.

"East." He strode from the room, knowing exactly where he was heading. He didn't want to let his family know. His father couldn't be trusted not to try to influence Franklin's life with his money and power.

Chapter 1

El Tovar Hotel at the Grand Canyon, 1910

Peering into the large silver coffeemaker, Lillian Robinson pinched her cheeks to give them some color and tried her best to quell her jittery nerves. In the distance she could hear the train whistle, the signal she and the other Harvey Girls had come to recognize as their personal call to work. In a few minutes the dining room at the Grand Canyon's El Tovar would be teeming with people expecting a superb meal. The Harvey Girls were there to make the diners' luncheon a relaxing and memorable time.

Although she'd been working here for three weeks and had the routine down, Lillian couldn't help feeling unsettled. She'd overheard her manager, Mr. Niles, talk about some of the men who would be meeting with him today. Lillian had prayed hard about getting the right table. This was the day she would meet her future husband. She had to be at her best.

"Lillian!" Constance Gibson, the head waitress, called to her as she headed for her station. "Come here." Lillian could hear the woman's disapproval. She didn't use that tone with the other girls. For some reason Constance didn't like Lillian. She knew her clumsiness had tested Constance to the limit of her endurance.

"Yes, Miss Gibson?" Lillian met the woman's gaze, knowing this time she had nothing to hide.

"Your cheeks are red. Have you been using rouge again?" Constance frowned at Lillian. "Let's check." She led the way to a sink in the back.

"I haven't used anything, ma'am."

"Well, after the last time, I can't very well take your word for it, can I? I've never known a woman so determined to snag a husband." Constance's eyes narrowed. "Don't think I didn't hear who is coming in for the noon meal today. If I know you, you've wangled some way to get them at one of your tables." Wringing a wet rag, Miss Gibson began to scrub at Lillian's cheeks. Biting her lip, Lillian ignored the disapproval and kept her smile at bay. The head waitress was playing right into her hands. Now her face would be certain to have some color.

"Okay, get to your station. Hurry." The chatter of voices could be heard from outside telling them the visitors were coming. "Lillian." The head waitress halted her one more time. "Pay attention to what you're doing. You're here to serve the customers. Don't be clumsy."

"Yes, ma'am. I'll be careful." Lillian whipped back around to get to her place. Her toe caught on the rug. She stumbled but didn't fall. Casting a quick glance over her shoulder, she saw Miss Gibson roll her eyes as if she were asking God why He gave her this particular girl.

As she trotted across the dining room, Lillian smiled at her roommate, Dinah Weston, one of the few Harvey Girls who had befriended Lillian. Most of them seemed to want to keep their distance. She understood. She hadn't encouraged friendships because she wanted to focus on finding the right husband. That was crucial in her plan for life. She couldn't spend the rest of her life being someone's servant. She had to find a wealthy husband, not end up like her parents with too many children to feed.

The next several minutes were too busy for Lillian to notice who was seated where. Her tables filled up fast. She brought water, coffee, and tea and smiled until her cheeks felt molded in place. Most of the people here had come up on the train and were anxious to see the canyon for the first time.

"How long does it take to walk along the canyon?"

"When do the Hopis dance?"

"Have you seen the Indians dancing?"

"Are they dangerous?" The heavyset woman who asked this question stared at Lillian with eyes widened in trepidation as if she expected them all to be murdered at the end of the show.

When Lillian first fielded these same questions at the beginning of the season, she'd had to bite her lip to keep from laughing at the absurdity. Now she took it all in stride, smiled, and assured the guests that all the entertainment was safe and provided for their enjoyment.

When Mr. Niles and his guests entered the dining room, Lillian's hands shook so much that she sloshed water over the rim of the glass she was filling. She apologized and grabbed a rag to mop up the wet spot. Forcing herself to take a deep breath to calm down, she hurried for another pitcher of water and more glasses. The men were heading in her direction, but they could get either her table or one of Dinah's. *Please,* she prayed.

From behind the coffee urn, Lillian watched as the men started toward Dinah's last table. Seated next to them would be a family with two excited young boys. The manager glanced in that direction, then ushered his group to one of Lillian's tables in a quieter area. Lillian breathed a silent thanks.

For the first time, she took a moment to look over the three men accompanying the manager. She recognized Mr. Kemper, the banker from Phoenix, who visited the canyon on a regular basis. Rumor said he enjoyed time away from a very formidable wife. The rotund man mopped perspiration from his florid face. When Mr. Kemper came in on the train, the manager tended to be later than usual because the banker wasn't used to the altitude or physical exertion.

Across the table, facing her, sat a middle-aged man whose sharp, handsome features seemed familiar. Lillian wondered if she had seen him here before with someone else. He came from money. She could tell by the expensive cut of his clothes and the way he carried himself.

The fourth man had his back to Lillian. She didn't recognize him from the waves of brown hair or the broad shoulders. Something about him made her wonder if he was as comfortable in this setting as the other men. Her hands shook as she prepared the coffee and water she would take to their table.

The men were discussing the menu as she approached their table. They all drew back their menus to allow her to fill their coffee cups. Mr. Niles smiled at her as she served him last. He had specified that the guests were always to be taken care of first.

"Good afternoon, Lillian." The manager rested the tip of his finger on his menu. "I believe we're all ready to order. Is that right, gentlemen?" The other three nodded.

Lillian took out her order pad and looked up to meet the eyes of the fourth man. His deep blue gaze caught and held her, stealing the breath from her lungs. One wave of his brown hair swooped down on his forehead. The lights shone on the thick mass, bringing out hints of gold. His square jaw framed an arresting face, one she could look at forever. Lillian caught her breath and forced her thoughts back to her work.

Mr. Kemper was just finishing his order, and she hadn't heard a word he said. Flustered, she didn't want to admit her lack of attention, especially not in front of the manager. She opened her mouth, trying to figure out how to get him to repeat his preference when the sharp-faced man said, "That sounds very good. I'll have the same as Mr. Kemper."

She could feel heat creeping into her cheeks. At least she would have some color and not look as pale as death. From across the table, the man who had caught her eye spoke. "I believe I'll have almost the same as Mr. Kemper and Mr. McClean, the ham steak and mashed potatoes. Instead of the Brussels sprouts, I would prefer the string beans."

Complete relief flooded through Lillian. She glanced again at the blue-eyed stranger and couldn't help noticing the way his mouth quirked up. He was aware of her dilemma. He'd ordered that way to help her out so she wouldn't be embarrassed. She knew just from the expression in his eyes and on his face. Gratitude washed through her. Handsome, rich, kind, and thoughtful. Here was the perfect man.

Mr. Niles chimed in with his order, encouraging the other

men to include dessert. They all added either éclairs or pie to their selection. Lillian jotted down everything and hurried off to give the order to the chef. She knew her feet weren't touching the ground. Today she'd met *him*, the man who would rescue her from all her problems. She had to bite her lip from doing something stupid like breaking into song. All along, she'd told herself this would happen, but now that her dream was coming true, she wanted to pinch herself to know she was awake.

The next half hour Lillian almost ran from one table to the next, refilling coffee cups, delivering food, making sure everyone was satisfied with their meal. She wanted to give extra attention to the manager's table—to a certain man whose blue gaze followed her around the room—but she didn't have time to do more than she did for the rest of the customers. Besides, most of the time the men were in serious conversation when she stopped by their table.

She was thanking two young couples who had come to the canyon together for some sightseeing when she noticed the manager was signaling her to come. Many of the customers were heading out the door, eager to walk along the rim of the canyon or to purchase some of the Indian souvenirs and other gifts available.

"Lillian, I believe we're ready for our dessert now." Mr. Niles smiled at her as she gathered the empty plates. "I believe I would like my pie with a scoop of ice cream on top, please."

"Yes, sir." Lillian forced herself not to look at her future husband. She would not begin to count his money or plan the wedding. She had to finish with the lunch crowd. When she got off work later, she could inquire about his name, position, and holdings. Then she would have time to dream.

Mr. Kemper's eyes lit up as she set éclairs in front of him and Mr. McClean. Rounding the table, she bent to put a slice of raisin pie in front of Mr. Perfect when Mr. McClean spoke.

"Mr. Knight, I know you're the head mule skinner here at the canyon, but I still prefer the idea of hiking down to the point. Perhaps we can arrange for some of my people to be taken down on mules and those who want to walk can do so."

Time stopped. Sound faded. Lillian stared at the man who had been Mr. Perfect until a few seconds ago. A mule skinner? He worked with mules? How could this be? She hadn't seen him around. There must be a mistake.

"Lillian." Mr. Niles snapped her back to reality. Lillian jumped. The plate of raisin pie clattered to the table in front of Mr. Imperfect. The slice of pie with mint ice cream leaped from the saucer in her hand. The pie rolled through the air, flinging bits of apple across his lap and the floor. She stared in horror as the ice cream hit Mr. Knight in the mouth, plopped onto his chest, and slid down to rest next to the ruined pie.

Chapter 2

Franklin stared at the mess in his lap. Back home, he had been in a couple of food fights with his brothers—outdoors, of course. He'd even made his sister Nellie so mad she'd flipped a spoon of peas across the table at him, which almost sent their cultured mother into a faint. Of course, he'd known Nellie would use any excuse to get rid of her peas. Never had he been hit with ice cream. He couldn't resist licking the sweetness from his lips as the mound puddled on the hem of his jacket.

Looking up at Lillian's horrified gaze, he thought if she turned a darker shade of red, she would be as purple as a plum. He winked. "I didn't order ice cream, but it is good."

The other men at the table chuckled, except for Niles, who appeared to be struggling to contain his anger in front of guests. Lillian glanced at her boss. Under the scarlet of embarrassment, her face whitened. She jerked a rag from her pocket.

"Here, let me clean this up." She still clutched the empty pie plate. Leaning over, she started to scrape the dessert onto the saucer. Uncertainty seemed to halt her as she realized the delicacy of where the sweets were resting. Lillian plunked the plate back on the table. She lifted the cloth and began to smear the streak of ice cream that had left a trail down his jacket. "If you'll get your clothes to me, I'll see that they are cleaned and returned to you."

Franklin could see the sheen of tears on her long lashes. A strand of fine blond hair came loose, curving down past her cheek, outlining the delicacy of her oval face. He almost had to sit on his hands to keep from smoothing that lock of hair back and assuring her that all would be right. One glance at Niles told him that might not be true anyway. Although firm, Niles had always been kind to the people who worked under him. Franklin couldn't imagine why he was coming down so hard on this beauty.

"I can have these taken care of at the laundry. Don't worry. Accidents happen." Franklin used the same tone he would use to comfort a frightened horse or mule. His lips twitched as he thought of what Lillian would think of the comparison.

"Lillian seems to have more than her share of accidents." The manager's sharp tone had the upset girl straightening so fast her cloth whipped against Franklin's jaw.

"I'm sorry, sir. I didn't intend for that to happen." Lillian clutched the rag until her knuckles turned white.

"Lillian, I know what's going on. I know you wanted us in your section." Niles glowered at her. "We'll talk later in my office. I'll speak with Miss Gibson, too."

The girl looked as if she wished the floor would open up and swallow her. Franklin picked up the saucer she'd set on the table and tugged the cloth from her hand. With a few deft movements he scraped the pieces of pie and melting lump of ice cream onto the plate. He swiped at the remainder of the crumbs.

"Good as new." He flashed a smile as he handed her the dessert. She blinked rapidly as she took them from him.

"Excuse me. I'll bring you another piece, sir." Lillian rushed away before anything more could be said.

Franklin wanted to turn in his seat to watch after her. He wanted to go find her and comfort her. He sighed. She had felt the same attraction he had. When their eyes met, he knew she acknowledged the connection. Still, he didn't understand what had happened to upset her so much.

"I don't think the girl meant for that to happen." Andrew McClean frowned at the manager. "Don't you think you were a little hard on her?"

Niles waited to reply until Lillian returned to set a new dessert in front of him. She didn't lift her puffy, red-rimmed eyes to look at any of them. He watched her retreat back toward the kitchen. "Lillian has kept no secret about what she's looking for while she's working here. The girl is looking for a husband."

Mr. Kemper laughed. "Isn't that what most young girls are looking for when they come out west?"

"Most of them aren't as vocal about wanting a man with money. I don't think Miss Robinson cares about age or looks, only about money."

"I've known plenty of young women like that." Mr. Kemper took a last bite of his éclair, wiping a smear of cream filling from his lower lip. "In fact, I believe a girl should concern herself with her future husband's ability to provide for her and her children."

The manager pursed his lips. "I suppose you're right, but I don't think she should be telling everyone in sight that all she cares about is a wealthy man." He slid a bite into his mouth.

All the attraction Franklin had been feeling for Lillian faded into hurt. How had he even considered wanting to know her? He didn't agree with the banker at all. There were more important things for a woman to look at when she wanted to marry. Money mattered very little compared to having a good Christian husband who would provide spiritual support. He believed that with Jesus as the cornerstone of a marriage, everything else would fall into place. He'd seen enough of the dissatisfaction money could bring. The wealthy never had enough. Look at his family.

"Gentlemen, if you'll excuse me." Franklin set his fork on his empty saucer. He almost never ate in the dining room, but he did love their raisin pie. "Mr. McClean, let me know when you want to schedule the trip down the canyon. The hikers won't be able to travel at the same pace as the mule riders, but we should be able to work something out."

"Will you be the one leading the mule trip?" Mr. McClean folded his napkin and placed it on the tablecloth.

"I usually have two of my men take groups down, but if you request me, then I'll accompany your group."

"That would be good. I want to assure the people I'm bringing that the best will be in charge." Mr. McClean's dark eyes bored into Franklin almost as if he were trying to say something else.

"Thank you for your confidence." Franklin pushed in his chair. "My men are every bit as good as I am, or I wouldn't let them lead a trip down. Customer safety is our first concern."

On his way out the head waitress intercepted Franklin and insisted on taking his jacket for cleaning. She apologized several times for Lillian's clumsiness, telling him the girl would be reprimanded. No matter how Franklin insisted it was only an accident, everyone else seemed equally determined to accuse Lillian of being deliberate.

The hot sun beat down. Franklin couldn't wait to get back, wash off the sticky mess, and start working. He wanted to finish up in time to take Moses, his mule, out for a ride in the quiet of the forest late this afternoon.

"Lillian, I don't know when I've been so mortified as I was at lunch today." The manager's lips were so taut with anger they were only thin lines in his hardened face. His eyes almost spit fire across the desk to where Lillian sat at attention in a straight-back chair. Next to her, Miss Gibson sat with her hands clenched together in her lap.

Opening her mouth to apologize, Lillian changed her mind. If the first ten apologies hadn't helped, why should she keep repeating a phrase that wasn't even heard? There was no way to go back and right the wrong. Her father would say this man was beating a dead horse. Not only that, but the animal was beginning to stink. She'd been in here for a half hour already. All she'd heard was how mortified he'd been when she spilled the dessert.

"We have standards to uphold here, Lillian." The manager's eyes narrowed as if he were thinking she had no standards. "Harvey Girls have a certain name. There are expectations that come with being one of the girls."

"Yes, sir, I know." Lillian struggled to keep her tone even. She couldn't lose this job. Yes, she'd made a mess of things today, but her comfort was that she'd made an impression on Mr. McClean. He might not be her first choice of men at that table, but after she found out Mr. Knight was a mule skinner, Mr. McClean had become the only choice.

Mr. Niles sat back in his chair and steepled his fingers beneath his chin. Lillian waited, hoping the tirade was over but suspecting this was only the lull in the storm.

"What do you think we should do with you, Lillian?" Mr. Niles leaned forward again, his clasped hands resting on the desk, fingers pointed at Lillian. "I'm sure you understand there has to be some disciplinary action."

"Yes, sir." Lillian swallowed hard against the lump at the back of her throat. She couldn't think of anything that would help her or change her. She'd always been flighty according to her parents. Clumsy or Easy to Startle should be her middle name. What kind of punishment would change her nature?

"I don't know what to suggest for punishment, sir." The words caught in her throat.

"Miss Gibson, do you have a suggestion? After all, Lillian's behavior is your responsibility."

Lillian hadn't thought it possible for Miss Gibson's spine to get any straighter, yet it did. "This Friday some of the young ladies are going to Williams on the train for an evening out. I would ask that Lillian not be allowed to go."

"But. . ." Lillian gritted her teeth together as the head waitress shot her a glance. The woman knew how much all the girls looked forward to these times away from the isolation of the canyon. As much as she loved it here, Lillian wanted the chance to get out, to get a few personal items that weren't available here.

Constance seemed to know Lillian's thoughts. "If you have something you need from town, I'm sure one of the other girls would be willing to pick it up for you. I believe Dinah is going to pick up some paints she ordered. She would be happy to shop for you." Her eyes showed no sympathy as she watched Lillian's reaction. "I know this is a hardship, but the alternative is to let you go. We can't have you ruining the reputation of the Harvey Girls."

Lillian caught herself as her mouth started to drop open. She clenched her teeth together so hard her jaws ached. Ruin their reputation? Because she'd had an accident? Despite the ridiculousness of the accusation, Lillian kept her head high.

"Do you have any more to add, Lillian?" Mr. Niles drummed his fingertips on the desktop. She wanted to slap her hand down on top of his to stop the noise.

"No, sir." The words came out stilted, but Lillian didn't care anymore.

"Bear in mind this isn't your first infraction. Every time has appeared to be accidental. I'm beginning to wonder." He paused as if to give her time to defend herself. Lillian kept her mouth closed. "If this happens again, we may have to do more than take disciplinary action. Is that clear?"

"Yes, sir." Lillian stared at a point over his shoulder, breathing deeply to keep her calm.

"In that case, you may go."

"Lillian." Miss Gibson spoke as Lillian got to her feet. "You won't be needed at this evening's meal. We have a smaller party, and some of the more responsible girls will be serving."

Lillian grasped her skirt with fingers that itched to throw something.

"I'd like for you to spend this time contemplating ways to keep these accidents from happening." Miss Gibson's tone could have frozen fire.

"Yes, ma'am. I will." Lillian didn't begin to relax until she was out of the El Tovar. She didn't pay attention to where her feet were taking her. Since it was near the dinner hour, most of the guests were gathering in the main room of the El Tovar, waiting to get in the dining room, so the grounds were almost empty.

Tears burned in Lillian's eyes, spilling down her cheeks. She hated to cry, yet she couldn't stop. She stumbled into the pine forest. Shadows lengthened beneath the tall ponderosas. Plucking her handkerchief from her pocket, Lillian blew her nose, ignoring the moisture blurring her vision.

Following the path around a tall tree, Lillian didn't see the protruding root. Her toe caught on the edge. She fell forward, flailing her arms. Instead of meeting the dirt, her face smacked against a broad chest. She closed her eyes, wanting to sink into the ground as strong arms wrapped around her.

Chapter 3

"Here, now, nothing can be that bad." A hand brushed moisture from Lillian's cheek. "Are you okay?"

She nodded, keeping her eyes closed. Lillian couldn't bear to see who was witnessing her utter humiliation. For the moment she was breathing in the faint scent of sweat and mules. He brought back memories of her father and the way he smelled after a day plowing fields, when he would throw her up in the air and catch her to him. The unexpected rush of longing for her family brought a fresh round of tears.

"I didn't mean to make you cry more by keeping you from falling." Amusement tinted the man's voice.

"You didn't." Lillian pushed away from him. She kept her eyes downcast as she wiped her face on her apron. "Thank you."

"Want to talk about it?" he asked.

"No, thank you. I need to be going." Lillian tried to step around him, wanting to be on her way before she further humiliated herself. Faster than a striking snake, his big hand grasped her arm.

"Have you walked in the woods much?"

"No. I usually walk along the rim of the canyon on my time

off." She tugged, but his grip was firm. Still staring at the man's worn boots, Lillian wished he would let her go. She wanted to be alone in her misery.

"This time of day there are certain critters to watch out for. I'll walk along with you." At his announcement, Lillian's gaze flew to his face. She gasped.

"Mr. Knight. I didn't realize it was you." Her face felt as if her color could rival that of the fiery sunset. "I don't need anyone with me. I'll be fine."

"I don't suppose you've had the chance to meet Uncle Jim." The beginning of a smile tugged the corners of his mouth.

"I don't know any of your relatives." Lillian's mind raced in confusion. Had she been introduced to any other Knights? "Do they work here at the canyon, too?"

He chuckled. The humor made his gray-blue eyes sparkle and lit up his whole face. "I'm talking about Jim Owens. He's not related to me. Everyone calls him Uncle Jim."

"No, I don't believe I've met him." Lillian fell into step with Franklin when he tugged on her arm. "Why would this Uncle Jim influence my decision to walk alone?"

"Well, he's working hard on holding the record for killing the most mountain lions here at the canyon." Franklin's eyes still held such humor that Lillian wondered if he was teasing. Yet she remembered that Miss Gibson and Mr. Niles had mentioned the problem with the big cats and cautioned the girls to be careful. In her haste to be alone, she'd forgotten the admonition.

"I've never even seen a lion when I've gone for walks." Lillian wished he would release her arm. He didn't have a tight hold, yet she could feel the impression of each fingertip as if he were branding her through her sleeve.

"You won't see them along the rim where there are so many people and so much open country. At least, not very often. The big cats prefer the forest where they can approach undetected."

Lillian shuddered. Her gaze traveled over the dense thickets of trees and undergrowth that could hide several large animals.

"This time of day is the best time to spot them. The deer like to come out to feed, so the mountain lions like to catch some supper, too. They aren't real picky about what they catch."

"Have any been spotted around here?" Lillian asked. She moved a fraction closer to Franklin's side.

"One of my men saw one the day before yesterday. I went out to Uncle Jim's to get him to hunt it before one of the guests or workers could be injured." He chuckled again. "Jim has a sign on his cabin that says, 'LIONS CAUGHT TO ORDER, REASONABLE RATES.' "

"And just how many lions has Uncle Jim killed?"

Franklin rubbed his jaw with his free hand. "He has marks up for each cat. I'd say it's somewhere around two hundred by now."

Lillian stopped. Her mouth fell open. "Two hundred? Lions? From here?" Her gaze flew to the surrounding woods. "That's like an army of cougars, isn't it?"

Laughing, Franklin started walking again. "They don't travel in packs like wolves. Besides, Jim hunts them all over the area, not just around the El Tovar and the canyon." His gesture took in the area around them. "We don't have hundreds of pumas circling the buildings at night."

She couldn't help laughing at the ludicrous picture. She wasn't sure how true the lion story was, but Franklin had helped her forget her troubles for a moment and lightened her day.

"If I come out here by myself again, I'll be sure to carry a juicy steak to throw at any cats that stalk me."

"Feeling better?" His question caught her off guard.

"Yes, thank you." She looked away from the intensity of his gaze. What was it about this man that pulled at her so? "It seems I'm ruining the reputation of the Harvey Girls by my clumsiness." She shrugged. "I needed to get away, and I promised to think about being more coordinated."

He raised an eyebrow. "Thinking about coordination will help?"

She laughed. "Not in my case. I've been perfecting my clumsiness since I was a child. When you're good at something, you find it hard to give it up."

Another grin split his handsome face. "Isn't it nice to be good at something?"

"Yes." She swept her skirt around a bush that intruded on the path. "I think perhaps I should have chosen something else to excel at, though."

For the past few minutes, Franklin had been trying to tell his fingers to release Lillian's arm. His hand seemed to have a mind of its own. He had never been so aware of a woman before, and he'd escorted many society girls of his mother's choosing. Even though he knew Lillian to be just another gold digger, he couldn't make himself walk away from her.

What is this, Lord? Yes, I'd like to marry, but I want a woman who puts You first, before anything, including me. Franklin sent up the silent prayer, hoping God would take away the intense attraction he felt toward Lillian. This is why he'd left the influence of his parents and their money. He didn't want to live his life under the dictates of finances and the power that came with riches.

"Look at that." Lillian's words jerked Franklin from his reverie. He glanced over to where she pointed. "Someone left a mule tied up?"

"He's mine." Franklin turned them onto the side path leading to the mule.

"Yours?" Lillian asked. "You mean he belongs to the Harvey Company. He's one of the mules they use to take guests on trips down the Bright Angel Trail, isn't he?"

"No, Moses is all mine." Franklin released his hold on Lillian and strode ahead to untie the mule. Moses stood with his head drooped a bit, his long-lashed eyes half closed, his ears flopped toward the ground. Most people would think he hadn't even noticed their approach, but Franklin knew better. This beast probably knew everything that was going on within a quarter-mile radius.

"Moses?" Lillian's mouth quirked up, her full lips trembling with the beginnings of a smile. "You named him after Moses in the Bible?"

"You got it." Franklin couldn't help grinning as he patted the mule's shoulder. "He has more objections to what I ask him to do than you could count. But if I'm patient and explain why I want him to do the job, he carries through even on the toughest chores. I'd say that the Moses in the Bible had one tough chore leading all those Israelites. He had plenty of arguments, too, but after God explained things, Moses did what he was supposed to do. Most of the time, anyway."

Lillian nodded. She stepped toward the mule. Franklin

opened his mouth to warn her to watch out, since Moses didn't usually take to someone right off. His mouth stayed open as he watched in amazement as his cantankerous partner lowered his head to allow Lillian to scratch that special spot. Without any coaching, Lillian seemed to know just the right place to touch the animal.

"I can't believe he let you do that." Franklin shook his head. "Moses isn't the friendliest mule around. He's always cautious around people he doesn't know."

"Oh, he recognizes someone who understands him." Lillian's smile brightened the deepening shadows. "I didn't realize how much I missed home. My father has mules. One of them is marked just like Moses."

"Where is home?" Franklin moved closer, draping his arm across Moses's neck.

"Nebraska. My parents have a small farm there."

"What made you leave?" Franklin asked.

She leaned closer to Moses, breathing in his scent. Franklin knew what she was doing, because he'd done the same thing many times.

"I'm the oldest of ten," Lillian said. "I felt like I'd been raising kids all my life. We didn't have any money, so I thought I'd try to get away. One less mouth to feed should help. Anyway, the others are old enough to do my chores and care for the baby."

He could read between the lines. Lillian loved her family. If Franklin were a betting man, he'd say that Lillian sent money home to her family any chance she got. He better understood her desire to find a man who had more than enough money to support her. His heart began to soften. Besides, Moses liked her right at the first, and Moses had great judgment. More than once God had used an unusual means to get a message across to Franklin. He knew God had orchestrated this meeting in the woods to help him lay aside some of his doubts. Somehow he was certain Lillian wasn't the money grabber he'd thought she was.

Giving Moses a quick hug, Lillian stepped back. "Thank you for talking with me." She turned her gaze on Franklin. Once again he felt the strong pull toward her. "I'd better get back to the El Tovar. Mr. McClean asked me to meet him after the evening meal to walk along the rim. I wasn't going to after talking with Miss Gibson and Mr. Niles, but I feel so much better now, thanks to you."

Franklin's grip on Moses tightened. The mule swung his head around to gaze up at his master with expressive brown eyes, as if asking what was wrong. Franklin loosened his hold and patted the animal's neck. "I'm glad I could be of help." The words almost choked him as he realized his help had led her to seek out a man only because she was interested in his money.

Lillian backed away a few steps. She gestured to the side. "I can see the lights coming on through there. I should be safe from mountain lions. Good-bye." She gave a small wave as she backed away then turned to hurry off into the twilight.

Chapter 4

Even though Lillian knew Franklin was watching from behind her, the short walk in the shadowy woods had her peering around trying to detect any sort of movement. She'd never realized how many branches pine trees had—places to conceal a crafty mountain lion while he waited to pounce on some delectable, unsuspecting prey. She tried to appear unconcerned, but her stomach clenched at every rustle in the grass.

The lights of the El Tovar were the best sight she'd seen in some time. As she entered the lobby, the happy chatter of satisfied guests surrounded her with a haze of normalcy. Lillian gave a last glance over her shoulder, wondering if Franklin had headed on to the stables to put up Moses. She refused to dwell on the way her heart responded to his every glance and touch.

"There you are, Miss Robinson." Andrew McClean approached from the dining room, his honed, attractive features made more so by his welcoming smile. "I expected to see you working." He reached out and clasped her hand. Lillian allowed him a quick squeeze before she tugged free.

"There weren't as many customers tonight, so I didn't have to work." She straightened her skirt, well aware of the disapproving gaze of Mr. Niles from across the room. "I went outside to enjoy the fresh air."

Andrew took her elbow, guiding her toward the queue at the door. "You might not want to walk, then. Would you rather watch the Hopi dancers?"

"No, I always enjoy a walk along the rim in the twilight." Lillian flashed him a quick smile, hoping he didn't think her childish. "Sometimes I even go in the rain. The canyon is so beautiful with the clouds down below you like that."

"Well then, I'm delighted to have someone experienced to show me around." He smiled as they exited into the balmy evening.

"Is this your first trip to the Grand Canyon, Mr. McClean?" Lillian asked.

"Yes, it is. Mr. Kemper is my banker. He's been telling me of the canyon's beauty. I have some business investments in Phoenix. I came up here to see about bringing some of my best customers to the Grand Canyon for an outing."

"Investments?" Lillian's heart pounded. *Mr. McClean must have a lot of money.* "What kind of things do you invest in?"

"My family is in the hotel business." Andrew smiled down at her. Although Lillian felt none of the connection or excitement she'd experienced looking into Franklin Knight's eyes, she allowed Andrew to pull her a little closer to him as they walked. "We have hotels in most of the large cities back east—Boston, New York, Philadelphia, even Chicago. My family thought it was time to move out west. My brother was sent to San Francisco. I came to Phoenix."

"So you're kind of like the Harvey family?"

"Yes, I guess that would be a fair assumption. My father knew Fred Harvey for years." Andrew grinned. "In fact, for a time they were in competition with one another to see who could have the best hotels. Mr. Harvey had a brilliant idea with following the railroad and establishing the Harvey Houses. We've stayed with individual businesses instead of a chain of places all named alike."

"What is the name of your hotel in Phoenix?" Lillian asked. Her head was spinning with the thought of how much money this man came from. He had to be the reason God brought her here. Andrew must be the right husband for her, even though he was quite a bit older. She pushed away the image of gray-blue eyes that made her blood rush. God wouldn't expect her to marry a mule skinner.

"Right now we don't own any. I've invested in a couple of large hotels that we might take over. I'm acting as an adviser to improve the holdings and the clientele." Andrew closed the gap between them, releasing Lillian's elbow and tucking her arm through his. Her skirt brushed across his boots, they were walking so close.

Lillian held her breath, waiting for the tingling to start, the same type of electricity that sparked when she stood this close to Franklin. Nothing happened. To hide her disappointment, she gave Andrew a bright smile. Her mother used to say that sometimes love developed over time. Perhaps her love for Andrew would grow in the next few days that he would be here.

"Mr. Kemper and I are leaving tomorrow afternoon." Andrew's fingers wrapped around hers where they rested in the crook of his arm.

"I thought you would be staying on to see what the canyon has to offer." Lillian tried to conceal her frustration. She didn't want to appear pushy.

"We had lunch with the head mule skinner. I've arranged to bring some people up in two weeks. Some of them will take the mules down canyon; the others will hike. I'll be taking the hiking group down, and I'd like for you to join me."

"Oh, but I have to work." Lillian forced a smile. "Unless you happen to come on my day off, I can't go."

"I'll speak with Mr. Niles." Andrew reached over to wrap a wayward strand of her golden hair around his finger. "As a friend of the Harvey family and a man of means, I'm sure I can convince him to let you have the time off."

Excitement surged through Lillian, despite the niggling doubt about breaking her contract and the problems that would bring. She wanted to believe the slight euphoria had to do with her nearness to Andrew and not the opportunity to go down into the canyon. She'd wanted to do that since she'd first come here. Now she not only would have the chance to do something she longed to do but also would be accompanying her future husband. In the next two weeks she would have plenty of time to dream about the possibilities for her future. She could almost picture the gorgeous ring Andrew would place on her finger when he proposed.

❧

Watching from the shadows in the fast fading light, Franklin couldn't take his eyes off Lillian. Even from here he could tell she didn't light up with McClean like she'd done with him. Some of her sparkle had faded, yet she continued to walk closer than she should and allow him little privileges that should belong only to her betrothed. When McClean touched her hair, Franklin had to fight to contain himself. He wanted to challenge the man, to ask his intentions. Although he didn't know McClean well, Franklin had heard the family name. He knew men of McClean's type, and they weren't the kind with whom Lillian should become involved.

Moses nudged Franklin on the shoulder, reminding him that supper should have been served an hour ago. Although he'd eaten some while tied in the woods, the mule still wanted to get to his hay at the stables.

Stepping back, Franklin slung an arm over his companion's withers. "Just a few more minutes, boy. I can't help feeling like she needs someone to watch over her. I know McClean acts like a gentleman when others are around, but I'm wondering if he'll carry through when he has her alone."

The soft *clop* of the animal's hooves didn't echo in the evening air. As the cacophonous chattering of the groups of people fell behind, the symphony of night noises took over. Cicadas whirred. In the distance, Franklin heard the cry of a mountain lion. He hoped Jim Owens caught this one soon. The big cat was too close to civilization for comfort.

"Evenin', boss." A couple of Franklin's wranglers materialized out of the dark.

"Evening, boys." Franklin nodded at the pair. They were probably headed to meet some of the girls up by the dorms. Most Harvey Houses frowned on any mingling between male and female employees, but here at the canyon the rules were somewhat relaxed. The closest town of any size was Williams, a hundred miles away by train. That meant life could get pretty lonely for unattached men and women even with the entertainment room provided for them. There were still strict rules to enforce propriety, but that was to be expected.

"You boys remember we have a large party going down canyon in the morning. I'll need you rested up and ready to help out by first light." Franklin made the admonition despite the fact his employees were the best workers he'd been around. No matter how late they stayed out, they would all roll out of bed on time, ready to go.

By the time the wranglers moved on, Franklin had lost sight of Lillian and McClean. Moses had one hoof cocked. His head drooped, and his long-lashed eyes were closed. Franklin gave the reins a light tug. "Come on, boy. Let's see if we can see her one more time to make sure she's all right. I don't want that scoundrel taking advantage of her. She doesn't have the sophistication of the ladies he's used to."

Franklin wondered whom he was trying to convince, himself or his mule. Lillian may not be a society girl, but Franklin could tell from the little he'd been around her that she'd been raised with good morals. He'd be willing to guess her parents were God-fearing people who had raised their children to believe likewise.

If that was the case, then where had Lillian gotten this idea of looking for a rich husband? Didn't she read the Bible? There were many types of wealth. He believed that truth with his whole heart. Her parents might not have been gifted financially, but what about spiritual gain? Wasn't that worth more than fine jewels? So how was he to get this point across to Lillian?

Lord, I could use some of Your wisdom. I don't want to see

Lillian get hurt. I feel like there's a war going on inside me. I left home to get away from girls like her, yet I'm drawn to Lillian. Show me Your will, Lord. Please let Lillian know how precious she is in Your sight, and show her that You can provide for her.

As Franklin finished his prayer, he spotted two indistinct figures up ahead. They weren't walking now but rather were standing very close. He frowned, thinking a shaft of moonlight might have trouble getting between the two of them. This had to be Lillian and McClean. He hadn't seen any other couples walking in this direction.

He fought the urge to mosey over and interrupt before McClean did something to offend Lillian. Before he could move, he saw the smaller figure stumble back. He heard a cry as she fell to the ground. Giving Moses's reins a hard tug, Franklin hurried to offer help.

"Lillian." McClean squatted down beside her. Franklin knew the other man had heard the sound of hooves approaching. He stiffened before straightening up and turning to face Franklin. "Mr. Knight. Is that you?"

To someone like Lillian, McClean's question might have sounded innocent. Franklin had been schooled in innuendos and nuances people used to convey different messages. His advantage was that McClean didn't know it. The man wouldn't expect Franklin to pick up on his subtle message to back off.

"Mr. McClean. Is someone hurt?" Franklin tried to keep his tone even, an employee asking about a guest. Franklin knelt next to Lillian. "Miss Robinson. Are you okay?"

"I'm fine." Her smile looked strained. "Still clumsy, though. I tripped over something and fell." She didn't meet his gaze.

Franklin couldn't help glancing around at the smooth path. He knew Lillian might wonder why he was so concerned, but he didn't care. He wanted to know what had happened.

Chapter 5

For over a week, Franklin didn't see Lillian except from a distance. Since he ate with his men, he had no reason to be in the dining room when she was working. Every evening he'd gone walking in the forest near the El Tovar, hoping to see her again. To his disappointment, she didn't trip and fall into his arms one time. When he recalled the feel of catching her, his arms ached to hold her again.

This morning, Sunday, Franklin hurried toward the El Tovar for the church service held outside in the fresh air most of the time. Cloudy skies meant they would meet indoors today. Robert Thatcher, a former employee, had become a minister and came to the canyon once or twice a month to lead the services. Many of the guests and workers enjoyed the opportunity to worship together.

This was the first time in weeks Franklin had been free to come to the services. He always tried to arrange the time off, but the last few times he'd had to lead unexpected mule trips. Today he was hoping to see Lillian at the services.

Subdued murmuring could be heard in the hallway outside the room that served as a sanctuary on Sundays. Franklin nodded or spoke politely to the several employees he knew. He scanned the room, trying to find Lillian. When he realized she wasn't there, disappointment made him sink into a seat at the back of the room rather than at the front, where he usually sat. Most of the chairs were filled.

As the singing started, the few empty spots in the back were taken until the only available seat in the room was in the corner next to Franklin. Closing his eyes, Franklin concentrated on the familiar words of the hymn. Guilt chased through him as he realized he'd come to the service not to seek God and worship Him but to see Lillian. *Lord, forgive me. I have my priorities mixed up. Help me focus on You and only You.*

For the rest of the song, Franklin kept his eyes closed, allowing the words to bring him to a place where he could meet with God. The heaviness of his heart lifted. He sighed with relief as he opened his eyes.

He hadn't heard or felt anyone sit in the seat next to him, but sometime during the music Lillian had come in and taken the only chair left. He took in her porcelain profile, the rigidness of her back, and the way her hands clenched together in her lap. Something was wrong. Franklin couldn't recall anything that would have caused her to be upset with him, anything he'd said or done wrong. Instead, his thoughts kept returning to the night she was with McClean and fell. Had something else happened?

For the rest of the service, Lillian didn't look at Franklin. He tried his best to pay attention to the message, but no matter how many times he dragged his thoughts back, they kept wandering away. By the end of the service, Franklin had to admit he couldn't tell anyone what the visiting preacher had said.

"Lillian." Franklin put his hand on her arm to stop her from leaving. She halted but didn't turn. "Could we take a walk?"

"I have to be ready to serve lunch." Lillian still faced the door.

"You won't need to be there for another hour." Franklin kept his grip on her elbow, ignoring her gentle tugging. "It's a beautiful day. I won't keep you long."

She was silent as the congestion in the room eased. When the way was clear, she glanced over her shoulder. He caught a glimpse of something in her eyes. Fear? Uncertainty? "A short walk would be nice."

The temperature was almost perfect. The cool air held a scent of moisture. The clouds amassing overhead suggested the possibility of rain before too much time passed. Franklin led Lillian to the privacy of the forest path where they'd met before.

"Are you all right?" He thought she looked too pale.

"I'm fine." Lillian pasted on a smile so forced Franklin knew no one would be fooled into thinking it was sincere.

"Has something been bothering you?"

She hesitated, glancing back at the hotel. "Why do you ask?"

He guided her around a fallen tree. "You aren't your usual cheery self. I thought maybe you'd had more trouble in the dining room."

Relief softened her features. "No. I've been very careful not to throw pie at anyone." This time her smile was genuine.

Franklin chuckled. "Let me know if they get any of that mint ice cream in again. That stuff was so good, I'd let you throw it at me any day."

Lillian gave a little laugh. "I heard we're supposed to get a new shipment the day after tomorrow. I'll let you know if any mint comes in."

Now that her mood had lightened, Franklin drew in a deep breath and broached the subject he'd wanted to bring up. "You know, Lillian, I can't tell you what to do, but I'm concerned about you and Andrew McClean."

She stiffened but didn't say anything.

"He's very well-to-do, but I don't believe he has the best intentions toward you."

She halted and faced him, her eyes sparking with anger. "You're right. You can't tell me what to do. I have a reason for agreeing to accompany him next week. He is a gentleman." At the last statement, she looked away again.

"Is he?" Franklin asked quietly. "Why did you fall down that night, Lillian? Did he do something that startled you?"

She jerked her arm free. "What happened is none of your business. I have to go."

He started to reach out and stop her then dropped his hand to his side. As she hurried down the path to the El Tovar, Franklin watched her shoulders droop. She looked as if she were swiping away tears. He had to force himself not to run after her.

Entering the dormitory the back way, Lillian breathed a sigh of relief that the hall was empty. Even her room was deserted, for which she was grateful. Right now she couldn't face anyone, not even Dinah.

She hadn't meant to yell at Franklin. He'd only been concerned for her. She knew that, but she also knew what God wanted for her. Hadn't she prayed about this often enough?

Flinging herself on her narrow bed, she allowed the tears to come. That night along the canyon rim, she'd been afraid.

Who was she, a girl from a small farm in Nebraska, to know how to be with a suave, smooth gentleman of Andrew's caliber? He was used to society women, not some country maid. He'd expected her to be willing to kiss him. He hadn't meant anything by it, had he?

Lillian remembered shoving back from him and losing her balance. She needed time to adjust to his touch. That was all. In time, Andrew would evoke the same emotions she felt when she was around Franklin. Andrew was the right man for her. She had to have a man of means. She just had to.

Yes, her parents had put on a show of being content and happy, but she knew they couldn't have been. How could anyone be content with the same food day after day or clothes that were threadbare?

She closed her eyes. Thoughts of this morning's message swirled in her head. The scripture passage from First Timothy had seemed to be directed right at her. She could still hear the preacher's low, sonorous tones. *"Having food and raiment let us be therewith content. . .rich fall into temptation. . .love of money is the root of all evil. . .that they be rich in good works. . ."* What was it he'd said about God providing for His people? As exhaustion claimed her, Lillian remembered that even though they'd been poor on the farm, they always had food to eat and clothes to wear. Had that been God's provision? Not an abundance, but enough. Were her parents truly happy?

"Lillian, what are you doing?" Dinah was shaking her shoulder, concern evident in her plain features.

Lillian sat up. Rubbing her eyes, she stared at her roommate in confusion. "What is it?"

"You've got about fifteen minutes until the lunch crowd

starts. Your station isn't ready. Hurry up; I'll help you." Dinah raced from the room.

Lillian leaped off the bed, rinsed her face in the washbasin to clear away the cobwebs from her brain, and headed out the door. As she hurried down the hall, she checked the pins in her hair.

By the time she reached her station, Dinah was already setting things out. Lillian began to help. "Thanks, Dinah. I don't know why I fell asleep like that in the middle of the day."

"I do." Dinah gave her an odd look. "You haven't been sleeping at night. You toss and turn as if one of those cougars you asked about is after you."

Lillian's face warmed. "I'm sorry to keep you awake."

Dinah's touch on her arm was comforting. "Don't worry about it. I only said something because I'm worried about you. You aren't your usual self, Lillian. If you want to talk, I'm here." With that she hastened to her station as they heard the noon bell sounding.

For the whole lunch hour, Lillian worked in a daze. She kept hearing Dinah's words echoed in Franklin's voice. Hadn't he said almost the same thing to her? She refused to dwell on their concern. She'd been under great stress not to make any more mistakes on the job. That was what kept her awake. It had nothing to do with Andrew. He was an answer to prayer. She would have to relax and not allow her job concerns to keep her, or her roommate, awake at night.

That afternoon, Lillian sat on the porch and watched the rain. Thunder boomed in the distance. She breathed in the fresh scent. Everything would be fine. All her worries would wash away like the earth was washed by the rain. After lunch today Miss Gibson had complimented her on doing well with her serving. Lillian knew things were looking brighter.

In a few days, Andrew and his party would be arriving. Hiking down into the canyon would be great fun. Mr. Niles had already told her he'd approved her day off to accompany the party.

She ignored the twinge of uncertainty that spiked through her at the thought of spending the day with Andrew. She wouldn't learn to have wifely feelings for him unless they spent time together. He was right for her; he would be her future husband. She closed her eyes, breathed deeply, and tried to picture Andrew's face. But instead of Andrew's sharp features, all she could see was wavy hair, a strong jaw, and humor-filled gray-blue eyes staring back at her.

Chapter 6

You goin' along today, boss?" One of the mule skinners slapped Franklin on the back as he passed by. Franklin tugged the cinch of Moses's saddle as he glanced over his shoulder to see Perry Davis grinning at him.

"Yep, I'm going." Franklin gave Moses a pat before turning around. "I'm not riding lead, though. You are. I'll be on the tail end."

"Eatin' dust." Perry grinned.

None of the mule skinners liked that position. They ended up with enough grit between their teeth to dam up the Colorado. Franklin had chosen to bring up the rear in the hope that he would see more of Lillian as she hiked. As a rule, the mules outdistanced the walkers, but if he didn't have the responsibility of the lead mule skinner today, he might be able to lag back and watch her longer. He'd made sure to tell McClean that the hikers should start off first so they could all meet up at the designated spot for lunch.

"Let's move out, boys." Perry took the reins of three mules, leading them from the stable area.

The others fell in behind him. Franklin brought up the

rear on Moses, leading the two pack mules carrying supplies for lunch. A total of nine riders were coming today. Since they were also meeting the hikers below, there were three mule skinners besides Franklin. The extras would help corral the people and make sure no one fell off the point in their eagerness to see down into the canyon. Franklin was always amazed at the nerviness of tourists. They didn't understand danger until it bit them on the nose as they fell.

After tying the mules to the hitching posts, the men did a last check of the cinches and equipment. The guests would be coming anytime. Franklin walked to the head of the trail and looked down. Far enough down that they resembled miniature people, he caught a glimpse of the hikers. Lillian's blond head was easy to pick out. There were five other hikers besides her. Of the five, only one was a woman. Even from this distance, Franklin could tell she came from money by the way she carried herself.

The guests arrived then—seven men, two with their wives. Franklin listened as Perry gave the instructions on riding mules into the canyon. Even though most people were used to riding horses, taking a mule into the canyon could be unnerving. The animals were surefooted, but they tended to walk close to the edge. When a guest saw the depth of the drop-off, the natural inclination was to rein the beast toward the inside of the trail. Mules didn't take well to orders contrary to what they wanted to do.

Since they had extra hands, Franklin held back to let the dust settle a little before he followed. They wouldn't need him to keep an eye on the guests anyway. The scenery passed by all but unnoticed. Every chance he got, he watched down the trail to see if he could get a glimpse of Lillian and the other hikers. Although she walked every day along the rim, Franklin wasn't at all sure she was ready for the strenuous hike planned for the day. As images of rescuing her and carrying her back up to the top on his mule flitted through his mind, Franklin assured himself he was only thinking of her well-being.

He had to admit Lillian's party had made good time. They were closer to the meeting place than he would have thought by the time he caught up to them. Franklin wasn't far behind the other mules, but he guessed the hikers weren't expecting him at the exclamations of surprise he heard. They all moved to the edge of the path to allow him and the pack animals room to pass. On this road, mules had the right-of-way.

Most of the men called a greeting or at least nodded as Franklin passed with his mules. The society woman held a kerchief to her nose. Franklin bit back a smile. From the sour expression on her face, he could tell this jaunt wasn't what she'd thought it would be.

McClean stood next to Lillian, his hand on her elbow. Something in his gaze told Franklin the man was aware of all the reasons why Franklin had come down the canyon with the mules. As Franklin tipped his hat to Lillian, McClean jerked her arm. Lillian stumbled on the loose rock, almost falling against McClean's chest. Looking smug, the man put his arm around Lillian as if steadying a clumsy girl.

Tugging the reins, Franklin pulled Moses to a stop. "You all right, Miss Robinson?" She didn't meet his gaze. Her cheeks had reddened. She nodded.

"I'm fine, Mr. Knight. Thank you for asking." She hesitated. "Just a bit clumsy on this trail."

"I'll see you up ahead, then." Franklin slapped the reins on Moses's neck to set him in motion. His jaw ached from being clenched so tight. Why had she done that? Why did she always stick up for that man? Had he been wrong, thinking she wanted to help her family? Was money that important to her? Was pride?

❧

Shaking out a wrinkle in the split-skirted walking dress Dinah had loaned her, Lillian tried to calm the burning in her stomach. Andrew and his party had arrived two days ago. He'd made it very clear that he wanted to spend time with Lillian. She'd made excuses about working and having cleanup to do. *He's rushing things. Once I spend more time with him, I'll be fine*—so she told herself over and over, yet still she kept putting off walking with him or even sitting with him on the porch in the evening.

Mrs. Carver, the only other woman hiking, had turned up her nose at Lillian from the first. Lillian had overheard her say something to Andrew about waitresses and their reputation. She'd even implied that Andrew had other motives for seeing Lillian than to seek her hand in marriage. Lillian had been horrified at the intimation.

So far, today hadn't been the exciting outing she'd thought it would be. The canyon had proved to be fascinating, but she found she had to be on guard all the time. Andrew always wanted to have her close to him, much closer than she wanted to be.

When she'd looked back to see Franklin riding up on Moses, her heart had leaped in her chest. She didn't know why she wanted to climb up on the mule with him and ride away from this group. *Because Moses reminds you of home, of growing up on the farm,* she told herself. That was all. It had nothing to do with Franklin.

"I do think they could have a separate trail for those stinking beasts than the one we're on." Mrs. Carver's petulant tone sent chills down Lillian's spine. She hadn't known one woman could complain so much. Within a half hour she was whining about everything from the heat, the smell, and the possible danger of snakes to every part of her that might ache now or the next day. Her husband had even offered to take her back to the top, but she refused to be left behind, which told Lillian the woman wasn't really too bad off.

Two hours later they arrived at the point where they would have lunch. Franklin and one of the other mule skinners were setting out sandwiches, fruit, salads, and cake. The other mule skinners were with the riders walking near the edge of the point. The mules gave the impression of sleeping in the corral, heads drooping, long ears hanging down except for an occasional flick at an exasperating fly.

"I believe I'm ready to sit down." Andrew pulled Lillian with him to one of the blankets spread out on the ground. "Sit with me." He sank to the ground and tugged so hard she almost landed in his lap.

To tell the truth, getting off her feet sounded good to Lillian, but she didn't want to sit with Andrew. "I think I'll wander over to the edge and see the view." She tried not to grimace as she surged back to her feet. Her legs muscles were on fire. She didn't want to get cramps, but she had to get away from Andrew. He'd been too attentive.

"I'll go with you." Andrew's smile seemed a little strained.

He grabbed her hand, which already ached from being held so much today.

They sauntered off at a slow pace. Lillian tried not to notice the way Franklin watched them from where he was working. She wanted so much to sit with him and talk. If she heard any more about investments, hotels, and society life in the East compared to the West, she thought she would scream.

"Thank you for being so gracious today." Andrew smiled at her as they looked down into the canyon. "I know Amanda Carver can be trying. Thomas does dote on her."

Guilt flooded through Lillian. Why was she thinking such awful thoughts about Andrew? He was nice, and she knew he cared about her. "Thank you."

"I'd like to dote on you, too, you know." His proprietary gaze made her want to squirm. "I know we don't know each other well, Lillian, but I would like you to consider coming to Phoenix with me. We could have such fun in the city. There are parties to attend, concerts, various outings. I know you would have a wonderful time. I'd spoil you."

Warmth flooded through Lillian. Excitement stole her breath. Andrew was asking her to marry him. Yes, this was fast, but he wasn't young anymore. He needed a wife to help him, to be there for him. He would want a family. Turning to face Andrew, she caught a glimpse of Franklin's tense features as he talked with a guest a few feet away. Had he heard Andrew's question? Did he still disapprove?

Her face warmed. "This is so sudden, Andrew. Will you give me time to think about it?"

"Of course." He stepped closer. Lillian's heart pounded. Did the man intend to kiss her in front of all these people? She took a step back. Franklin's eyes widened. He lifted his hand toward her. Andrew glanced over his shoulder. His smile still in place, he moved nearer to Lillian. She didn't understand Franklin's alarm. He ran toward them as Lillian took another step back.

Andrew whirled to face Franklin. The rock under Lillian's feet shifted. Too late, she remembered how close to the edge they'd been standing, the stomach-swirling drop. She reached out to grab Andrew. He took a backward step toward her, bumping into her. The ground dropped away.

Chapter 7

Already surging forward, Franklin thrust McClean to the side and threw himself to the ground as Lillian fell. Her terrified gaze met his. Her mouth opened, but no sound came out. Franklin's fingers closed around her wrist. He couldn't stop her motion. Lillian swung around, and her head smacked into the rocks. In an instant she became deadweight.

Shouts from behind him told Franklin his men were coming fast. They knew the dangers with tourists and would have been watching. Perry slung himself down next to Franklin, inching forward until he could reach down and grab hold of Lillian's arm.

"I've got her, too, boss." Perry's dark eyes met Franklin's. "Ready to bring her up?"

"Ready." Franklin's muscles began to ache. Together he and Perry inched Lillian up the cliff face. Franklin didn't want to consider the fact that she hadn't moved or even moaned since her head hit the wall of rock. He wanted to pray, but pulling Lillian up safely took all his concentration. *God, please,* was all he managed.

"Almost there." Perry's voice showed the strain of pulling

Lillian up when she couldn't help them. The awkward angle didn't help.

When he felt hands on his ankles, Franklin reached his other hand over the edge and grasped the shoulder of Lillian's dress. The fabric wouldn't stand much strain, but he hoped it held long enough for him to get a better grip on her arm.

He and Perry tugged together. Lillian slid up a little more. Franklin grabbed the upper part of her arm. "I've got her. Ready?" He glanced at Perry, whose sweaty face was close to his. Perry nodded. He'd gotten a second grip on her dress at the side.

They jerked as they surged upward. Lillian popped over the edge. They scooted back, getting her out of danger. The white of her face made a sharp contrast with the stream of blood coursing down her temple. Franklin bent to examine the cut.

"Is she all right?" McClean stepped close.

Franklin shoved his fists into his pockets to keep from attacking the man. Hadn't he known better than to allow her to stand so close to the edge of the cliff? "I don't know yet."

Perry gave him a quick glance. He jumped to his feet and took McClean by the arm. "Come on, mister. Let's step back and give Mr. Knight some room. He's had plenty of experience with injuries, but he needs to concentrate. In fact, why don't you folks go on over and have your lunch? The boys here will see that you get served."

The other wranglers took their cue from Perry. They led the party to the blanket-draped rocks that served as a table. Perry turned back to kneel beside Lillian. "How is she?" His tone was grim. Perry knew how bad head injuries could be.

"She's breathing okay. This cut isn't as bad as it looks. Head wounds always bleed like there's no tomorrow." Franklin dabbed at Lillian's head with his moistened handkerchief. Some of her color had returned. She moaned. Franklin didn't think he'd ever heard such a sweet sound. He blew out a breath and glanced up at Perry.

Perry grinned. "I'd say you've got it bad, boss."

"What?" Franklin wasn't sure what the man meant.

"This little filly means a whole lot more to you than a guest on a trail ride." Perry chuckled. "Looks like she'll be fine. I'll go have some lunch and leave you two alone."

"Perry." Franklin watched the mule skinner saunter off without a backward glance. He looked back down at Lillian as her eyes fluttered open. He watched the emotions chase across her face; fear, relief, wonder, and something else he couldn't quite grasp.

"I fell." She started to sit up, gasped, and dropped back. Her face paled again. She raised her hand. Franklin grabbed her fingers before she could touch her wound.

"You hit your head. You have a small cut, but you'll be fine." He smiled down at her. "Other than the headache."

She winced. "Yes, I can feel that." Wonder lit her blue eyes again. Franklin felt himself getting lost in her gaze. "You caught me. I would have died, but you caught me."

He tried not to squirm under her adoring look. "It's my job to see that everyone is safe." His words came out gruffer than he intended. A shadow crossed her face. He knew she was thinking she was just another guest to him. No one special. Is that what he wanted her to think? Franklin knew without a doubt that would be a lie. Lillian was someone special to him. For the first time he admitted to himself that he might be falling in love with this blond-haired beauty.

❧

Resting with her back against a rock, Lillian wanted to close her eyes and sleep for a week or two. Maybe a month. Her head pounded like a herd of mules were parading through. Her scalp throbbed from the cut, which had quit bleeding. Franklin had wet a cloth with cool water and tied it around her head. She knew she must look like a refugee from a war.

"You sure you can't eat something, Miss Robinson?" The young mule skinner Perry knelt next to her with a plate of food. The thought of trying to take a bite made her stomach pitch and roll like the wash hung out in the Nebraska wind.

"No, thank you." She managed a small smile. "A nice hammock under some shade trees might be nice." Her attempt at humor made his eyes light up. "Come to think of it, though, that would only work if there was no breeze."

"Is this man bothering you, Lillian?" Andrew stood over them, frowning.

This was the first time he'd come to check on her. He'd been busy talking with all the people he'd brought on the trip. She'd been hurt, but she realized this trip was business for him. Perry rose, brushed off his pants, and walked away. Andrew knelt beside her.

"I've been talking with some of the men who rode mules down. One of them has agreed to hike back out with my party so you can take his mount. I didn't think you'd be up to the walk."

Guilt flooded through her. She'd been feeling sorry for herself, yet all along Andrew had only been thinking of her welfare. "Thank you, Andrew. You're too kind." She attempted another smile. "I'm not sure I could make it out of the canyon on my own. This was a beautiful hike, though. Thank you for asking me to go."

"I meant what I said earlier." Andrew took her hand in his. "I know you're not up to making any decisions now. I'll be back in two weeks, just passing through. I'd like you to leave with me."

"I have a contract to fulfill." Lillian didn't know why she was hesitating. Wasn't this what she'd wanted? Shouldn't she be elated at the thought of marrying Andrew?

Andrew's indulgent look told her he thought she was a silly girl. "I'm sure we can find a way to get you out of your contract. I've been told there are a lot of Harvey Girls waiting to come to the canyon to work. I don't think Mr. Niles will have any problem finding one to replace you."

He patted her hand. "I'll let you rest now. It's time to start the walk out of here. Think about my offer. I'll talk to you in the morning before I leave." He leaned forward to press a kiss to her brow.

Three hours later, Lillian fought to sit upright on the mule. Franklin had sent all the others on ahead, giving her a little longer to recover before they started the strenuous ride to the top.

"Okay?" He stared up at her, his eyes darkened with concern.

"Fine." She managed a whisper, having no idea how she would stay on this beast for the next few hours without fainting.

"We'll take it slow. Your mule will lead out. Give him his head, and he knows the way home." Franklin patted the mule's neck. The sound ricocheted around the inside of Lillian's skull. She grimaced, an expression Franklin must have taken for a smile, because he smiled back.

The trip up was interminable. Franklin stopped several times as if he sensed Lillian's need for a break from the constant motion.

He'd been so considerate. At each stop she found she wanted to be closer to him. His strength, his character, the kindness in his stormy eyes called to her in a way no other man had.

Her mule stopped. Lillian swayed. Her grip on the pommel loosened. She couldn't hold on any longer. She slipped to the side and had no strength to stop her fall. Strong arms caught her before she even left the saddle.

"Perry, can you take her mule? Leave Moses here for me. I'll carry her up to her dorm." Franklin's voice wrapped around her like a blanket of comfort.

Rocks crunched underfoot. Lillian snuggled closer to Franklin's broad chest. He felt so good, so strong. She wanted to stay here forever, yet she had to make a decision about Andrew. How could she choose Franklin when she knew Andrew was the answer to her prayers?

She faded in and out of consciousness. She heard the murmur of voices. Mr. Niles? Miss Gibson? She tried to wake up, but her brain wouldn't respond. The strong arms carrying her lowered her to a bed and released her. Lillian wanted to cry out in protest. Instead, darkness closed in, and she drifted away.

Chapter 8

Standing against the hitching post, leaning back against Moses, Franklin watched the door of the El Tovar. Everything in him thrummed with anticipation. Four days had passed since he'd carried Lillian into her room. Every day he'd inquired about her welfare. Today she was back at work. Her roommate, Dinah, had come to Franklin saying Lillian wanted to talk to him after the noon meal was over.

The door swung open. Lillian stepped out, still dressed in her Harvey Girl uniform. The starched apron had something dribbled down the front. Franklin bit back a smile. No matter how she tried to be careful, Lillian always managed to spill something. He would have to be quick so she had time to rest and change before the next meal.

He started toward the steps, wanting to save her walking too much. He knew she must be tired after serving two meals today. She would need to rest before suppertime. Her blond hair glinted like gold in the midday sun. Lillian took his breath away even with the circles under her eyes and the strain of exhaustion lining her face. He wondered if this tiredness was from more than the injury.

"No, don't come down." Franklin held his hand palm out to stop her. "There are a couple of free chairs over there. We can sit outside and enjoy the fresh air."

Lillian halted at the top of the steps and smiled at him, causing an ache of longing to sweep through him. He wanted to hold her, to protect her, to have her beside him as his wife for the rest of his life.

"Thank you for coming." Lillian tilted her head to the side as he took her elbow. Her clear blue gaze seemed to be looking into his heart. He wondered if she could read how much he'd come to love her in the last few weeks.

"I was hoping to see you. Are you feeling all right? How's your head?"

She reached up to touch the spot above her temple where she'd been cut. "It's just a little tender."

"Still having headaches?" Franklin asked.

"Not too much. Only when I try to overdo." The way she winced as she turned her head told him she might have overdone today by working both meals.

Quiet settled between them. Franklin relaxed back in his chair. From the corner of his eye, he could see the lines of strain on Lillian's face ease, and she, too, rested. He could get used to this. Franklin could picture them in a home of their own, sitting on the porch in the evening watching their children at play. He'd never pictured this scene with any woman before. He'd often wondered if he ever would.

Thank you, Lord. You knew the right woman for me. Please help me to convince her we'll be right together.

Before Franklin could speak, Lillian started to talk. "I wanted to have the chance to thank you. You saved my life." Her voice caught. She swallowed hard. "If you hadn't been right there, I would have fallen down into the canyon." A shudder rippled through her. "I don't know how to say more than thank you for my life."

Franklin shifted in his seat. "It's nothing. I was glad to be there."

"Just doing your job. Right?" Lillian's eyes held hurt.

"Yes, it's my job to protect the people I take down canyon, but I'm not usually close enough to grab someone who's falling." He took her hand and squeezed. "I believe you're alive now because God had me that close for a purpose. He's the one you should thank for saving your life."

She closed her eyes. "I have. Many times." Her gaze caught him again. "I know God brought me here for a purpose. I've prayed so long for the right husband, and now I believe I've found him."

Franklin's heart soared. Ever since the other night when he carried Lillian up to her dorm, he'd known she'd had a change of heart. The way she snuggled close to him made him realize they were perfect for each other. Somehow she must have sensed it, too.

A smile washed most of the strain from her face. Pulse pounding, Franklin knew this was the time. Before she could say anything else, he tightened his hold on her hand and slipped to one knee. "Lillian, I know we haven't known each other long, but I feel like I've waited for you forever. I agree God brought you here for a purpose—for me. Will you consent to marry me?"

Her mouth dropped open. The color fled from her cheeks. Shadows of emotion chased through her eyes. "Franklin, I had no idea."

Dread swept through him. Had he misinterpreted the way she'd clung to him the other night? Hadn't he prayed about them? Hadn't he heard clear instructions from God about this proposal?

"What do you mean?" he asked.

"Andrew is coming back this week. He's waiting for my answer to the question he asked." She tugged her hand free from his. "He's the husband God has for me. I'm sorry." Her eyes filled with tears.

Anger coursed through Franklin. "Why? Why do you want a man old enough to be your father? Is it just the money?"

She drew back as if she'd been struck. "It sounds so shallow when you say it like that." She looked down and plucked at the stain on her apron. "Since I was a child, I loved to hear stories about a princess being carried off to a castle by her handsome prince. I know this sounds stupid, but I wanted to be that princess. I want to live in a castle with my prince." When she looked at him, her gaze was so full of misery Franklin had to glance away.

"A castle can be a wonderful place, or it can be drafty and cold." He took her hand again as he sat back in the chair beside hers. "A castle doesn't have to be big. Remember in the Bible Paul says he learned to be content wherever God had him? That's what we need to learn, too."

"I can't do that." Tears began to trickle down her cheeks. "I know God wants me to marry Andrew. I prayed about it."

God, please give me Your words. He longed to wipe the tears from Lillian's cheeks. "Lillian, consider this carefully. Andrew McClean has quite a reputation, and not always a good one. If you marry him only for money, you'll be miserable." He squeezed her hand again, releasing her when she pulled away. She stood up, and he knew he was losing her. "Please consider if you truly listened for God's answer in this matter. Will you do that?"

She stood a minute staring down at him. He could almost see the war going on inside her. Her shoulders slumped. She put her hand to her head. "I have to go inside now."

He watched as she fled, feeling as helpless as a baby to stop her from making a major mistake. *God, please watch over her. Help her make the right choice. Not me, Lord, but You. Always Your way.*

❧

Exhaustion claimed Lillian again. The evening meal had been a disaster. At least this time she'd only spilled the water pitcher. Water wouldn't stain the way tea did. Miss Gibson had looked as if she wanted to head the lynch mob that would be coming to Lillian's room tonight. She sighed. To tell the truth, the woman had been more than patient in putting up with Lillian's clumsiness. None of the other girls had this problem.

Doing a quick wash and slipping into her nightgown, Lillian got into bed before Dinah could come back to the room. She didn't want to hear anything her roommate had to say. Ever since she'd told Dinah about Franklin's and Andrew's proposals, Dinah had been trying to get Lillian to reconsider. She even had the temerity to suggest Andrew might not have meant marriage. Dinah, too, said she'd heard rumors about Andrew McClean and his possible disreputable ways. Well, Lillian wasn't listening to rumors or to any more lectures.

She closed her eyes as the door opened. Dinah wasn't quiet as she came in and prepared for bed. Lillian feigned sleep. She tried to keep her breathing even as she listened to Dinah move around the room. When her bed dipped, she knew Dinah hadn't fallen for her ruse.

"Lillian, I need to talk to you again."

Lillian rolled over to look up at Dinah's solemn gaze as she sat on the edge of the bed. Although Lillian knew her friend had her best interests at heart, she still wished Dinah would leave her alone. She tried to focus on some of Dinah's artwork on the wall across from her but couldn't bear to hurt her friend by ignoring her.

"I heard you gave your notice tonight. You're not even going to stay and fulfill your contract. Why?" Dinah asked.

"I don't have to tell you." Lillian hated the defiant tone of her voice, but she couldn't seem to help herself. "Andrew wants me to marry him now."

"Has he actually used the word *marriage*?" Dinah asked.

"I'm sure he did." Lillian's stomach churned. She couldn't remember anymore how Andrew had worded his proposal.

"Well, after what I heard tonight, I don't think he did." Dinah looked angry enough to spit nails.

"I don't want to hear any more rumors. I thought you were a good Christian girl, Dinah. What would God say about you spreading gossip? Besides, you have your own secrets. I saw you hiding that drawing of a man in the box under your bed. What is he to you?"

Guilt flashed across Dinah's face, making Lillian want to groan at her harsh words. Sorrow made Dinah's plain features look more drawn as she bit down on her lip. "He's nothing. I only want to keep you from doing something you'll regret, Lillian. I care about you."

"Then let me take care of my own life, and I'll let you take care of yours." Lillian tried to smile. "I've prayed about this, Dinah. I know what God wants for me."

"Do you?" Dinah's soft question hit a sore place in Lillian's heart.

Lillian opened her mouth to reply, but the words wouldn't come. She nodded instead.

"Okay." Dinah's eyes held a note of sadness as she eased up off the bed. "I'll not say anything more." She crossed the room to extinguish the light before crawling into bed. "But I'll keep praying for you to do the right thing, Lillian. Your heart knows. Good night."

In the darkness, Lillian fought the tears burning the back of her eyes. The lump in her throat felt like it was the size of a boulder. Andrew would arrive tomorrow on the train. He would be taking her away with him to get married. Why didn't she feel the elation she'd expected? Why was her heart so heavy? Why were her dreams full of Franklin and those incredible eyes of his?

Chapter 9

Sitting on her bed in her traveling clothes, Lillian reread the letter from her mother. Her family was doing well. Rain had been plentiful. Looked like a good harvest coming up. They would have a little extra for some necessities.

Lillian, I can't thank you enough for the monies you have been sending to us. I've put some away to help us through the harder winter months. We did as you asked and your father bought the children a bag of sweets at the store last week when we were in town. They all say hello and thank you. I have also put enough aside to buy shoes for everyone when the cold weather starts. What a blessing to have shoes for the children to wear to school.

Tears blurred Lillian's vision until she couldn't read any more. Just when her resolve had wavered, she'd received this letter as a reminder of why she had to marry Andrew. Although he'd never asked about her family, she knew he wouldn't mind helping her parents out after the wedding. When he had so much, he would want to share a little with the needy, especially if they were his wife's family.

She closed her eyes. Franklin's face swam into focus. Just the thought of his smile set her heart pounding. She could still feel his strength as he carried her to her room. She ached to be close to him, to hear his deep voice, to see the kindness in his eyes. She loved him. That thought hit her hard enough to double her over. She gasped. How had this happened? Why couldn't Franklin have been the man with money?

God, I know what You want for me. Give me the strength to carry through.

Wiping her eyes on her sodden handkerchief, Lillian rose from the bed and picked up her packed bag. She had to get to the train station to meet Andrew. He'd sent a message that he wouldn't be staying overnight after all. He wanted her to be ready to board the train with him now.

Her feet wanted to drag. She'd already said good-bye to the other girls. They were all getting ready for the lunch crowd anyway. Slipping out the back door, she walked to the station without looking back. This door of her life had to close forever. She was following what God wanted. Wasn't she?

The whistle of the train had her picking up her pace. She needed to be there in time to board. Her heart ached as she thought of how much she wanted to drop her bag and race to the stables to find Franklin. She wanted to see him one last time and tell him. . . What? What would she say? *I love you, but I have to marry Andrew for his money?* How would anyone ever understand this need she had to provide for her family? This was the work God had given her to do, and she had to do it. Squaring her shoulders, Lillian stepped onto the platform as the train huffed and hissed to a stop.

"There you are, my dear." Andrew pulled her into an embrace. Lillian stiffened then tried to relax. The feelings would come. Given time, she would enjoy his embrace as much as she longed for Franklin's.

"Come, let's get your bags on board." Andrew picked up her worn traveling case and looked around the platform.

"That's all I have." Lillian could feel the flush working up her cheeks.

"Well, that's fine, then. We'll have to get some things made when we get to Phoenix anyway." Andrew took her arm and helped her up the steps of the train. "We'll be riding in here." He escorted her to the luxury car, one she'd never seen before. The chairs were plush enough to get lost in or to allow for sleeping.

Andrew ran his hand down her arm. Lillian repressed a shiver.

"I hope you don't mind. I reserved a room in Flagstaff for a few days. I thought we might enjoy some time to ourselves before it's back to work in Phoenix." The gleam in Andrew's eyes made Lillian uncomfortable.

She had to clear her throat twice before she could speak. "So we'll be getting married in Flagstaff?"

His forehead creased for a moment before Andrew managed another smile. "I have some special surprises in store for you, my dear. You'll see."

Dread stole her breath. Dinah's warnings whispered through her mind. "We are getting married, right?" Lillian remained standing, despite Andrew's attempts to help her into a seat.

"You worry too much." Andrew's smile became strained.

"I have to know." She forced her shaking legs to hold her up.

"We will have a wonderful time, Lillian. I can show you

wonders and buy you things you would never have otherwise." Andrew reached out to touch her hair. Lillian drew away.

"I send money to my family each month. Will I still be able to do that?" She clenched her hands in the folds of her skirt so he wouldn't see how badly she was shaking.

"My dear, I don't take on charity cases. My money is for me and my family, not yours." Andrew frowned. "You can't expect me to throw my money down a hole like some churchgoing do-gooder."

Anger gave Lillian the strength she needed. How had she ever allowed herself to be deceived into thinking Andrew was God's answer to her prayer? The floor beneath her feet shifted. The train whistle blew a shrill blast.

God, why is this happening? I prayed about my need. This is Your answer, isn't it? She closed her eyes. The pastor's words from a few Sundays ago came to mind. *"Having food and raiment let us be therewith content. . .rich fall into temptation. . .love of money is the root of all evil. . .that they be rich in good works."*

Lillian could picture how rich her parents were. They were content with their life. How many times had her father said he was a millionaire because he was blessed with so many children? Didn't her parents abound in good works? She could hear God saying, *You prayed, but you didn't ask. You told Me what you wanted.*

"God, what do You want?" Her quiet question received an immediate answer.

❧

Leaning his head against Moses's shoulder, Franklin breathed in the tangy scent of stale sweat and mule. Why had he opted to stay this morning instead of leading the mule trip down canyon?

He knew the answer before thinking the question. Lillian was leaving today. He had some wild dream about persuading her to stay, telling her one more time he loved her, watching her kick McClean off the El Tovar porch as she leaped into Franklin's embrace. He groaned aloud. That was about as realistic as being able to fly across the canyon with wings like a bird.

"Moses, you should be glad you don't have to worry about women." The mule flopped one ear backward as if listening, though his eyes remained half shut.

"God, I don't know what to do. She rejected me, but I still can't get her out of my mind. She's made her choice." He clenched his jaw, fighting the anger at the thought of how wrong Lillian's decision might be. "Tell me what to do, please."

"Hey, boss." Perry strode toward him from the corrals, where he'd finished seeing to the mules that hadn't been used in today's ride. "One of the boys saw your lady friend heading for the train station with her bag. Don't tell me she finally hit the wrong guy in the mouth with the ice cream." He grinned at Franklin, who knew the mule skinners had heard the story and loved that their boss had been the victim.

Forcing a weak smile, Franklin tried to think of a reply, but all he could do was picture Lillian walking to meet McClean at the station. She was leaving with the man today. She would be married. Not his wife. McClean's.

"You know, boss." Perry rested his arm across Moses's rump. "If I had a girl I thought that much of, I wouldn't be moping around while she was preparing to leave. I'd be fighting for her." He grinned. "Maybe not physically, but at least I'd show up and give her one last chance." He chuckled. "Then again, maybe I'd even do a little physical fighting."

Franklin's sour mood lightened. Perry had a way of making things look brighter. He stilled. Was this God's answer to his prayer? Should he give Lillian one last chance? A moment of quiet told him what to do. God didn't want him to give up without one last attempt to convince Lillian to do the right thing.

"Thanks, Perry. I think I'll ride on down to the station." Franklin clapped the mule skinner on the shoulder, untied Moses, and mounted.

"Can I come watch?" Perry's eyes twinkled.

"No fighting." Franklin tried to look stern. These mule skinners were a rough bunch, but they were good guys. The only thing they liked more than watching a fight was participating in one. "Besides, if there was a fight, I'd have to charge you a quarter to watch, and I know you don't have the money to waste."

"Aw, you're right." Perry dug his toe in the dirt like a chastised young boy then grinned up at Franklin. "Go git her, boss."

Today Moses would try the patience of Job. If he'd been the one leading the children of Israel, they would have taken a hundred years to cross the desert instead of forty. No amount of coaxing or threatening would convince the mule to pick up his pace.

"If you don't quit lollygagging, I'll leave you in the forest to have dinner with the mountain lions." At Franklin's threat, Moses flipped one ear up and down and snorted as if to say he knew an empty threat when he heard one.

The train whistle echoed through the trees. Franklin could hear the engine straining as the train started up to leave the station. He and Moses left the cover of the trees in time to see the last of the cars heading down the track.

Franklin's hope plummeted. She was gone. Following her dream. She would be rich. He prayed she would be where God wanted her to be. As for him, he would treasure the time he'd known her. He patted Moses. "Maybe someday I'll be able to forget."

He didn't have to close his eyes to remember her blue eyes or the way the sun glinted off her golden hair. He could still feel her slender form as she rested in his arms. Bowing his head, Franklin couldn't quell his longing to know what it would feel like to kiss Lillian. The image of them growing old together hadn't ever faded. Now she would grow old with another. His heart ached. He couldn't seem to summon the will to move.

"I don't suppose you've seen a handsome prince looking for a princess, have you?"

Franklin jerked his head up, startling Moses. The mule took a couple of sideways steps and stopped. Lillian stared up at him with luminous blue eyes. She held a small traveling case, both hands wrapped around the handle. Her smile wobbled as if she were fighting tears.

Taking a deep breath, Franklin tried to still the pounding of his heart. "I don't know a single prince." He watched as disappointment crossed her face. "However, I do know a Knight on a mule who would love to have a princess if she's willing to have him."

Her smile rivaled the beauty of the day. Tears coursed down her cheeks. Franklin swung off of Moses. Lillian dropped her bag as he pulled her into an embrace. She laid her cheek against his chest. He knew this was part of God's plan for them.

"I'm so sorry, Franklin. I've been giving God orders instead of listening to His instructions." Her breath hitched out on a sob. "I thought I had to be the provider for my family. God showed me that He is capable of doing the job. They don't have to have plenty. He's given them enough."

She drew back to look up at him. Tears sparkled like diamonds on her lashes. "Is your offer still open, Mr. Knight?"

"It is, but I don't want some forward woman." He released her and dropped to one knee beside the deserted station. "Lillian, will you marry me? Just as I am, no matter what?"

She nodded, biting her lower lip.

"I don't think I heard that." He pressed his lips to the back of her hand.

"Yes, Franklin, I'll marry you." She reached over to stroke Moses on his nose. "I don't know why I got hung up on the prince instead of considering a knight on a strong charger."

Franklin laughed. He stood and gathered her close again. "The only thing Moses might charge is the feed bin." He sobered and cupped her cheek. "I love you, Lillian. I'll love you forever." He could see her love shining back at him in her gaze.

Chapter 10

The sunlight coming through the window glinted off the simple ring on her left hand. Lillian moved her hand from side to side, smiling at the way the plain piece of jewelry pleased her. Like most girls, she'd dreamed of a fancy ring with a beautiful stone. Now, however, she realized the ring only symbolized the commitment and oneness in the marriage relationship.

She glanced over at Franklin to find him watching her, his gray-blue eyes filled with so much love her breath caught in her chest. Franklin Knight. Her husband. The man she loved with all her heart. The man God had given to her.

He smiled, and she delighted in the way his eyes crinkled at the corners. She smiled back. "I see you're finally awake. You've been missing all this scenery, you know."

"The only scenery I want to look at is you. You're the most beautiful thing around." He stroked his finger down her heated cheeks. "I love you, you know."

"I think I've heard that somewhere before." Lillian couldn't stop the broad grin. She'd never thought she could be so happy. The past few weeks had been wonderful. She'd gone back to work at the El Tovar to fulfill her contract. Franklin had come every day to see her, insisting they should have a proper courting time.

Two days ago, at the end of the season but before everyone left, they'd exchanged their vows. Yesterday afternoon they left the canyon to head to California. For the last few weeks, Franklin had talked with her about his need to go back and mend the rift between him and his family. God had impressed on him the need to share his faith with them, and he had to do it. Lillian agreed.

The conductor called the name of the station where they would be disembarking. Franklin stood to gather their bags. Lillian straightened her skirt, trying to shake out some of the wrinkles.

She wished she could do something about smoothing out the hitches in her nerves. She could feel a thousand butterflies fluttering in her stomach. Franklin may love her, but what would his family think? He hadn't said much about what they were like, only that they lived on a ranch north of San Francisco. She imagined his father must be one of the hands, and maybe his mother was the cook. He'd seemed reluctant to say much, so she hadn't pushed him.

"If you want to wait at the station with the bags, I'll head over to the livery and get a wagon for us." Franklin set their cases next to a bench. "I won't be gone long. We'll have a four-hour drive to get to the ranch."

"I'll be waiting." She placed her hand on his arm, stopping him. He looked down, his gaze troubled. "I love you, you know. I'll love your family, too."

"I hope so." He gave her a brief kiss on the cheek.

"I know I will. God loves them, doesn't He?" She could see from the way he relaxed that she'd said the right thing.

"Be right back." He squeezed her hand before striding out the door.

"Franklin Knight. It's good to see you after all this time. Where you been?" Weldon Grimes, the owner of the livery stable, held out his hand to Franklin.

"Been off earning a living." Franklin shook the man's hand.

"Heard you had a split with your family." Weldon shook his head. "Imagine having to earn a living with your roots. I'm glad you're back. Those brothers of yours could use a little of your good example."

Franklin stiffened. "I haven't heard anything where I've been. Are they all right?"

Weldon scratched his head. "Well, with your father running for the senate this fall, they'd better straighten up. They've been in some trouble. I'll let you hear about it from your folks, though, not from me."

"I need to rent a wagon." Franklin glanced over at the rigs for rent.

"I don't have any wagons." Weldon pointed at the buggies available. "You can have one of those. They don't hold much, but I can have Charlie bring your bags out in the morning." He looked puzzled. "I always thought you traveled light."

"I used to." Franklin's heart lightened at the thought of Lillian waiting for him at the station. "Until I got married two days ago." He couldn't help grinning at the way Weldon's mouth dropped open. Franklin didn't tell Weldon that most of their baggage consisted of gifts and new clothes he'd bought for Lillian.

"Well, congratulations, boy. Your family know?"

"Not yet," Franklin said. "That's why I'll take you up on your offer of the buggy. We'll get there a little faster."

Within minutes, Franklin was back at the station loading their overnight bag in the buggy. "Charlie will bring the rest of our things out tomorrow." He handed Lillian up to the seat. "We should be at the ranch in about two hours this way."

The fall air was cool. Gathering clouds promised the possibility of rain. Each mile that passed heightened Franklin's excitement. He knew this was what God wanted him to do. This was the right way to be going.

"Lillian, you asked me what we would be doing." Franklin gazed down into her clear blue eyes and lost his train of thought. He pulled the buggy to a stop on the deserted road, took her in his arms, and kissed her breathless. Her cheeks had reddened by the time he stopped. Her eyes glowed.

He blew out a breath. "Sorry, got sidetracked."

"I'm not complaining." She gave him an impish grin.

He laughed and hugged her. "I've been doing a lot of praying about what God wants me to do. I know you have, too."

She nodded.

He continued. "I think I need to stay at the ranch for a while and help out. My brothers are having some problems. I'm hoping I can lead them to Jesus. They really need Him."

He paused a moment, wondering just how deep in trouble those boys were. "My father will need some help, too. He's. . ."

Lillian placed her hand on his arm. "You don't have to say more." Her smile warmed him. "We'll do whatever you think is right."

"There are things I need to tell you about my family."

Franklin stared out at the hills around them. "They're different from me."

"I would expect that to some extent." She laughed. "After all, if they don't know Christ, they won't be like you. Now don't say any more. I know I'll love them when I meet them. Are we getting close?"

"Just around this bend." Franklin fell silent as they topped the hill overlooking the ranch. He stopped the buggy and watched Lillian's eyes widen. "This is my family's home." He gestured at the sprawling two-story mansion below. "They raise cattle and horses. I'm the eldest son. I gave up any right to an inheritance when I left to go to the canyon."

"You mean your family owns this ranch?" Her tone held a note of awe, but that was all. He could see no greed or longing in her gaze.

"Among other things, yes." He waited.

She turned to smile up at him. "Then I can see why you wanted to come back. They do need to hear about Jesus. I'm willing to work here right alongside you. We'll do our best to be a godly example to them and to their friends. I know now that having money without knowing Christ makes a person as poor as the poorest beggar."

Franklin couldn't speak. He pulled her close to his side. Lowering his mouth to her temple, he kissed her. "Your love makes me the richest I ever want to be."

NANCY J. FARRIER

Nancy recently moved to Southern California with her husband, John, and her three youngest daughters. Nancy's son and grandson live in Tucson, Arizona, and her oldest daughter lives in Portland, Oregon.

Although she grew up with a love of reading and making up stories, Nancy didn't write seriously until 1995 when God made it clear He wanted her to use her talent for Him. Now she loves sharing her faith and the message of the gospel through her writing.

Since then, Nancy has written seven novels and three novellas for Barbour Publishing, and she has also coauthored a nonfiction book for them, *Prayers and Promises for Mothers*. Before having any books published, Nancy wrote numerous articles and short stories for many Christian magazines.

Nancy enjoys hearing from her readers. You may contact her at njfarrier@yahoo.com.

Shelter from the Storm

Darlene Mindrup

Dedication

To Devon, Remko, Tim, and all those men and women who are serving (and have died serving) our country during this time of War on Terror.
May God be with you all.
"We're proud of you!"

Prologue

El Tovar Hotel at the Grand Canyon, 1926

Dinah Weston thoughtfully studied the girl sitting across from her. It was almost like looking into a mirror twenty years in the past, despite the difference in hair and eye color. Although not much to look at with her mousy brown hair and freckles sprinkled across her nose, Katie Halloran definitely had class. Her clothes and the regal way she held herself indicated a wealthy background. Still, looks could always be deceiving; that was one thing she had learned over the years. Miss Halloran had arrived at El Tovar sporting a multitude of bruises that had finally faded until they were almost indistinguishable. Dinah wondered about the girl's background.

"What can I do for you, Miss Halloran?"

Dinah noted the way Katie Halloran's fingers were twisting her handkerchief nervously in her lap. If she didn't cease the movement soon, the beautiful lace-edged hanky would be nothing more than a tattered shred.

"Um. . .I heard about the accident."

Although Dinah managed to keep her surprise from showing, she wondered how the news had spread so rapidly among the customers. One of her Harvey Girls had taken a serious fall only this morning while taking the trek by mule to the bottom of the Grand Canyon. How serious was still uncertain, but it would be some time before little Betty would be back to work. The accident left Dinah shorthanded at a critical time, since several of her girls had been sent to New Mexico to the El Navajo for the Indian ceremonials and two others were home on vacation for several weeks.

"Yes," she finally answered. "It was unfortunate. But you needn't concern yourself, Miss Halloran. I assure you that service will not suffer." How she intended to keep that promise was something she would have to work out later. Right now she needed to be the voice of encouragement.

The dark blue eyes that met Dinah's were filled with a peculiar luminosity. Something strange in that look touched Dinah's heart, and she unconsciously frowned.

"I know this is going to sound heartless," Katie told her, biting nervously at her lower lip, "but I wondered if I might take Betty's place." She rushed on. "I know what the job entails. I've been carefully watching for the last three weeks. I know I could do it!"

A multitude of thoughts ran through Dinah's mind at this announcement, but the one uppermost was that this woman could very well be an answer to her prayers. It wasn't unusual for women to approach her asking for a job, but this one was unique. She seemed almost desperate, yet she had been staying here at the El Tovar for nearly four weeks now, which only the wealthy could afford to do.

She took a moment to study Katie more thoroughly. The Harveys had always been particular about the type of women they wanted as Harvey Girls, and one of the stipulations was that they had to be attractive. If not for the fact that Dinah's family had been friends with the Harveys, Dinah doubted even she would have been accepted. Although Katie Halloran wasn't attractive in the traditional sense of the word, there was something different about her.

"Are you a Christian, Miss Halloran?"

Surprised, Katie looked up from the twisted hanky in her lap. Dinah didn't miss the tight swallow before the girl answered.

"Yes, Miss Weston, I am."

What was that look that flashed through her eyes so suddenly? Fear? Embarrassment?

"Can you tell me why you want this job?" Dinah asked gently.

The blue eyes met hers once again, and Dinah couldn't help but notice the honesty that shone through. "I'm almost out of money," she replied just as quietly.

More curious than ever, Dinah sat back to contemplate this strange turn of events. She might have dismissed the idea out of hand entirely if not for that niggling little voice at the back of her mind. That voice had never let her down before, and she didn't expect it to now. Taking a deep breath, she smiled at Katie. "I think something can be arranged."

Chapter 1

The resounding peal of the gong from the train station platform sent Katie Halloran scurrying to her station in the dining room, along with every other Harvey employee in the El Tovar Restaurant.

She smiled at Cleo, her coworker, and brushed a hand down the immaculate white apron that attested to the fact that she was one of the proud and respected Harvey Girls. It had been four weeks since she had approached Dinah Weston, a long and grueling four weeks, but now she was through with her training and would finally receive her own income. The thought sent her spirits soaring, though her body was once again battling a strange nausea and dizziness.

"Are you all right, Katie?" Cleo's concerned face seemed to move in and out of Katie's suddenly blurred vision. Placing a hand to her churning stomach, Katie forced a smile.

"I'm fine."

"You don't look fine," Cleo began, only to be interrupted by the first round of customers from the train. From that moment until the last of the passengers headed out the door to board the train thirty minutes later, no one at the hotel had a second to themselves.

Katie sighed with relief as the last customer laid a tip on the table and departed. She leaned against the wall for support, her limbs feeling like the jelly she had served only moments earlier.

"Katie."

Katie turned, smiling halfheartedly at Dinah. "Ma'am?"

"You don't look well, Katie. I think you should go and lie down for a while."

The suggestion was a welcome one, but Katie felt the need to protest. "I haven't cleaned my station yet."

"I'll do it for you," Cleo offered.

Katie hadn't even heard the girl approach, so swamped was she in her own misery.

"Enough said," Dinah told her inflexibly. "Go and lie down. I certainly hope you're not coming down with something."

"I think it's just the heat," Katie murmured, but she knew from Dinah's tone of voice that she was not to be disobeyed. Katie squeezed Cleo's arm lightly as she passed her.

"Thank you."

Cleo grinned cheerfully. "You can do the same for me sometime."

Katie stopped to get a glass of cool water from the kitchen as she passed. Albert, the cook, took one look at her and started tutting.

"You no look so well." Reaching over, he plopped some ice in her glass from the tub he was returning to the refrigerator. His Italian accent was not as marked as when Katie had first been introduced to him a month ago. Like most of the Harvey House cooks, Albert was a chef imported from Europe, and he felt his importance. Everyone knew it was the food that brought people back time and time again. That and the cleanliness. Even out here in the wilds of Arizona.

Sighing with exasperation, Katie shook her head. "I wish everyone would stop saying that. I must look like a hag."

Albert tilted his head to one side then slowly shook it. "No," he told her, "you could no look like a hag ever. Maybe like the cat the dog drug in, hey?"

Katie couldn't help but laugh at his saucy grin. She thanked him for the ice and retreated to the dormitory where her room was located. Although she shared the room with Cleo, she was glad now for the time alone as she tried to sort out what was happening to her.

She lay down, closing her eyes against the spinning room and trying to still the churning in her stomach. It was no good. Jumping from the bed, she ran for the bathroom.

Ten minutes later she crawled, shivering, beneath the covers on her bed. Even in the extremely warm temperatures of July, she felt chilled.

Dinah entered the room a few minutes later, balancing a cup and saucer in one hand. She closed the door behind her with her foot and set the cup down on the table next to the bed.

"I thought you might like a cup of tea."

Katie smiled wanly. In the short time she had been here, the people had become like family to her. Dinah reminded her so much of her own mother, so gentle and caring. The thought brought a tightness to her throat. The grief from her parents' death only six months earlier was still too near the surface.

Slowly she sat up in bed, relieved to find the nausea subsiding. She eased the cup and saucer toward her. "Thank you," she told Dinah.

Dinah settled herself on the mattress next to Katie and placed a cool hand against Katie's forehead. Her narrow-eyed gaze settled on the younger woman's white face.

"You don't have a fever."

Katie shook her head. "I told you, I think it's only the heat. I think I overdid it yesterday when I went exploring."

Dinah looked relieved. "That's probably true. You *were* gone a long time."

As Katie sipped her tea, she felt her insides returning to a more normal state. She sighed with relief.

"Your color is returning," Dinah told her, rising from the bed. "Do you think you'll be all right to work the evening train?"

Katie nodded. "I'm fine, really," she told the other woman.

The manager stared dubiously at her for several seconds before she finally smiled. "All right. We'll see you downstairs."

Katie stared at the closed door a long time, her thoughts in turmoil. Miss Weston was so good to her, as were all the other Harvey employees, but what would they say if they knew the truth? Would they still think as highly of her if they knew she was a runaway wife?

Hard on the heels of that thought was the possibility that was disturbing her most. Could she be pregnant? *Dear God, please don't let it be so!*

Her husband had touched her in that way only once during

the entire three years they had been married, and the horror of that night was still with her. Theirs had not been a love match but rather one of political and financial ramifications. She had agreed to the match because her father had asked it of her, and knowing that he wanted only what was best for her, she had acquiesced. But would her father have arranged the match if he had known the kind of man Darius O'Neil was? She just couldn't believe such a thing of her father, the one man she loved above all others. Besides, even she hadn't known the kind of man her husband was. He had never sought to touch her, always treating her with polite courtesy and always mindful of her welfare, but treating her more like a sister than a wife.

It was only after her father's death that Darius had shown his true colors, although there had been hints of erratic behavior before then that she had ignored, believing them to be something associated with most men. She supposed it was fear of her father that had held Darius in check, but after that barrier had been removed. . .

She closed her eyes against the memories, trying to push her thoughts back into the recesses of her mind. Still, one thought kept nudging its way forward. Could she be pregnant from that one awful night?

Going to the bathroom, she washed her face, patting it dry as she stared at herself in the mirror. She frowned. There was no discernible change that she could see, but could one tell after only two months? Unconsciously her hand went to her abdomen. What on earth was she to do if it turned out that she *was* pregnant? Blinking against the tears that threatened, she hastened from the room.

When she returned to the restaurant, she had herself somewhat in control, but disturbing thoughts continued to dodge around in her mind. She would just have to cross bridges as she came to them. Didn't the Bible say each day had enough trouble of its own? She certainly had to agree with that.

She found her station spotless, and she smiled with gratitude at Cleo. "Thank you, Cleo. I really appreciate your taking the time to clean everything for me."

The other girl shrugged, searching Katie's face in a way that brought heat to Katie's cheeks.

"No problem."

Together they began restocking supplies for the evening meal. Although it would be several hours yet until the train arrived, more people would be arriving by car throughout the day. The El Tovar had seen the area grow from several thousand visitors at its inception to almost two hundred thousand in the last year. People came and went all through the day, so everything needed to be prepared before she and Cleo could have time to themselves.

When at last she was free from her duties, Katie decided to take a walk to her favorite spot, a small pine tree close to the canyon's edge that struggled against the perpetual wind. Katie seated herself beneath it, leaning back against its spindly surface.

The grandeur of the canyon never failed to amaze her. Spread out before her in a panorama of age-old beauty, the steep canyon walls edged downward to the mighty Colorado River below.

Lifting her gaze upward, she watched a majestic eagle

circling high overhead. Its cry of freedom brought forth an answering cry from deep in her spirit. For the first time in six long months, she felt really free and finally able to let down her guard. It had been two months now since she had fled the security of familiar things and headed out into the unknown. She knew that without the knowledge that God was in control of her life, she never would have had the courage.

Still, that niggling worm of doubt crept into her mind. Was she in God's will, having fled from her marriage? She would never consider divorce, content to live her life alone, but then again, she could not countenance staying with an abusive, philandering husband.

She closed her eyes, rubbing her forehead with one hand against the headache inching its way once again through her temple. She didn't know what she was really supposed to do, so she did the only thing she could. She prayed. The Lord was her comfort and solace, and all her life her mother had taught her He would never leave or forsake her. Only during those dark months had her faith wavered. Here among the magnificence of one of God's mightiest creations, her faith had grown once again. It was impossible to see the wonder of the canyon and not be moved by its beauty.

She finally stood up, shielding her eyes against the sun's bright rays. The cool wind made the temperatures feel much chillier than they actually were. At least up here they had the wind. A visitor from Phoenix had mentioned that in the valley, the temperatures were a soaring one hundred ten degrees.

Continuing her walk, she ambled along the canyon rim, watching other people marveling at the beauty of the canyon, or else dodging in and out of the El Tovar or the equally popular Hopi House. Designed by Mary Jane Coulter, the building resembled a Hopi pueblo complete with sandstone walls and tiny windows. It was one of Katie's favorite places to spend her time; she was intrigued by the beautiful Harvey museum collection of Navajo blankets and other Indian novelties.

Fascinated by the unique jewelry the Indians made, Katie had been unable to resist purchasing a few trinkets for herself. Since Harvey Girls weren't allowed to wear jewelry, she didn't know when she might put them to use—if ever. Frankly, after long days, she fell tiredly into bed at night only to rise and start all over again. But she wouldn't trade the work for anything. She had grown to love the people of El Tovar, and they were very good to her. She had missed that sense of family so much since her parents had died.

The sun began its descent to the horizon, and she knew it was time to return. The evening train always brought customers who wanted to spend the night, and that was always more work for everyone.

Noticing the dirt stains on her uniform apron, she hurriedly raced to the dormitory and changed it. It was forbidden for even a spot to show on their uniforms. It was a good thing the Harvey Company did all the laundry, because Katie wouldn't have had a clue how to go about doing it. Pampered all her life by an adoring father and mother, she had learned very little about keeping house, or anything else for that matter. Her college education had consisted of subjects such as mathematics and science, but very little else. Training in domestic matters had been considered unnecessary since she would one day be the sole heir of her family's fortune.

Her first month here had been hard for that very reason, but she was intelligent and quick to pick up on new ideas. It was that adaptability that had helped her to excel to the point where she now proudly wore a number seven badge on her uniform instead of the number fourteen she had originally been given. One day, she promised herself, she would wear the number one badge. And who knew, she might even attain the position of manager one day. With a wry twist of her lips, she stopped her daydreaming and rushed downstairs and back to the hotel to make certain once again that her station was in pristine order.

When the train pulled into the station, the mad rush began. Although the train would leave later in the evening, many would choose to stay just to see the sunset over the canyon. Also popular in the evening was the Hopi dance at the Hopi House across from the hotel. Katie never tired of seeing the Indians in their full regalia performing dances that had been a part of their heritage for hundreds of years. In many ways, she envied them their free lifestyle.

The travelers who had disembarked and now filled the restaurant made a cacophony of sound, their voices mingling Dutch, Spanish, and myriad other languages. Only last week a famous silent movie star had visited the canyon. Katie had watched as the woman was hounded by hotel guests and reporters alike and thanked God for her anonymity. Well she knew how frustrating such attention could be. But whereas being a movie star was a *choice*, Katie had been born into the limelight. Only here in the obscurity of the West did she feel comfortable, though she had experienced a close call last week when a reporter from back east had stared at her as though he knew her.

"Katie."

Startled out of her reverie, Katie turned to find Cleo just behind her.

"Your food's up," Cleo told her, giving her a peculiar look. "You look kinda pale again. Are you sure you're all right?"

Katie smiled. "I'm fine. Just thinking."

"Well, you'd better get a move on before Dinah sees you."

"Right." Katie hurried to retrieve the plates for two of the last guests. When she finished, Cleo caught her by the arm.

"Do you want to go to Flagstaff on your day off? I thought it would be fun to see a movie. We have a choice between a Western or Buster Keaton."

Katie hesitated. As accustomed to hiding as she had become, she found it hard to let go of the feelings that coursed through her each time she thought of leaving Grand Canyon Village. She knew she was being paranoid, but the feeling still persisted that something dreadful was about to happen. That choking feeling of panic was riding her hard lately, and she wasn't sure why. Remembering the eagle from that morning and the heady feeling of freedom that swelled through her, she realized she had to get on with her life and stop living in fear.

"Sure, I'd love to go with you," she finally agreed. "My vote is for Buster Keaton. I've heard that *Battling Butler* is really funny."

Cleo grinned. "Great! We'll catch the morning train and make a day of it."

Katie turned to smile at her friend, admiring not for the first time Cleo's effervescent personality. "That will be fun."

Cleo's look moved past Katie's shoulder, her eyes widening with appreciation. Katie knew that look. There had to be some good-looking male standing just behind her. Fixing a smile on her face, Katie turned to the customer. Her own eyes widened, but not with appreciation.

"Hello, Katie."

The shock of seeing her brother-in-law standing before her sent cold tingles shooting all through her body, and the room suddenly began to spin crazily. The hard green eyes staring into hers slowly started to pale and blur. She only had time to register Clay's quick look of concern before she crumpled to the floor.

Chapter 2

Katie awakened in a room shrouded in darkness, the light of a single lamp telling her night had already fallen. For a moment, she was disoriented, unable to recall how she had gotten here; then a shadow moved in the far corner and materialized at her side. She caught her breath sharply.

"Clay."

He studied her in cold silence. Taking her wrist, he glanced at his watch as he counted the beats of her pulse. Being a doctor, he probably thought she was about to have a heart attack as he felt the staccato cadence. Her thoughts were running along much the same lines. She hadn't seen Clay since her parents' funeral, and she was amazed at the change in him. Although he had always had a lean physique, his body now held the rugged lines of someone familiar with physical exercise. His sandy brown hair had bleached highlights, evidence of time spent in the sun. The evidence was also there in the darkness of his skin. If he had been handsome before, he was devastatingly so now. She felt again that funny little twist of her insides at his mere presence, but she firmly pushed the feeling away. Surely she had gotten over her adolescent crush years ago. She wondered where his wanderlust had taken him to this time, and what ironic streak of fate had brought him to El Tovar.

"What are you doing here?"

His condescending snort made her flinch. Dropping her wrist, he fastened an angry green glare on her.

"I might ask you the same thing."

He seated himself next to her on the bed, effectively pinning the covers against her legs with his weight. She couldn't bring herself to meet his eyes.

For the longest time, silence reigned in the room. When Katie finally glanced up, she caught his look and was surprised to find it full of sympathy. Her face colored hotly, and she quickly turned away. *He knows I ran away!* Had Darius told him? Probably so, and as usual, Darius had probably involved Clay in things that didn't concern him. She didn't think she could be more ashamed than she was at that moment, though why she should be the one to feel shame, she hadn't a clue.

But exactly how much did he know? She started to ask him, but just then something more pressing suddenly occurred to her. She leaned forward and grabbed his wrist, her panic evident in her voice. "What did you tell Miss Weston?"

The lack of emotion in his face was unsettling. "I told her I was a friend of yours from back east and that I was also a doctor. She found that reason enough to allow me to examine you. She just went to the kitchen to get you something to drink." He looked at the door then back at her face. "She should be back any minute, so you'd better explain fast."

There was no way Katie was going to tell her husband's brother what had happened that night that sent her tearing off in a wild, tearful rush. Clay and Darius had always been close, so he probably wouldn't believe her anyway.

She released her death grip on his arm and moved her body as far away from him as the small bed allowed. Biting her lip, she stared at the beautiful painting of the canyon that hung on the wall next to the bed. She had purchased the painting from Dinah some time ago, awed by the woman's artistic ability.

"Katie."

The softly spoken word compelled an answer. She closed her eyes tightly, glad he was no longer holding her wrist, because her heartbeat had increased its rhythm tenfold. Finally, she looked at him. His eyes were gentle with some unnamed emotion. He reached out and lightly brushed a tear from the corner of her eye.

"You already know, don't you?" she asked him softly.

His lips drew together in a tight line, and he pulled away from her. At first she thought he wasn't going to answer, but sighing, he pushed a weary hand back through his tumbling brown locks.

"Yes, I know about Delia."

Katie stared at him wide-eyed for several seconds and then burst into hysterical laughter. His wary look scanned her from head to toe, obviously concerned over her irrational behavior. She shook her head reassuringly, still chuckling. Despite her laughter, a sob was lodged in her throat.

"I'm sorry," she told him, the tears she had been holding back so long finally surfacing. "But which one is Delia?"

She hadn't meant it to come out like that, but she was hanging on to her emotions by a mere thread. He stared at her in dumbfounded silence as the meaning of her words finally registered. He began to shake his head slowly from side to side, his eyes narrowing in unbelief.

"Are you saying my brother was having an affair with more than one woman?" The look that transformed his face was alarming, and Katie tried to move even farther away from him. He reached forward, grabbing her by the wrist, his face now so close to hers that she could see the evening shadow of his whiskers. His crushing grip brought a small cry from her as his fingers bruised her skin. "How long has this been going on?"

She tried to pry loose from his hold, terrified by his anger. Memories of that last night with Darius caused fear to pulsate through her body. This was Clay, and he was Darius's brother. She had always believed them to be so different, but perhaps that wasn't entirely so. Perhaps they were more alike than she realized.

"Please, Clay, you're hurting me," she whispered.

Although those same words had had no effect on Darius, Clay released her wrist as though he had been burned. He quickly rose and moved away from the bed. His apologetic look did little to still the fear that had caught her in its paralyzing grip.

"I'm sorry, Katie. I'm so sorry."

The huskiness of his voice spoke of feelings held tightly in check. He was still angry, she could see that, but the anger seemed not to be directed at herself. Was he apologizing for hurting her, or for his brother's treachery? Whichever, his emotion had been frightening.

There was a knock on the door, and Dinah came into the room with a tray. She glanced from one to the other. Sensing the tension in the room, she fixed a narrow-eyed gaze on Clay.

"I thank you for your services, Dr. O'Neil. But Miss Halloran needs to rest now."

Clay's eyebrows disappeared beneath the hair that had tumbled across his forehead. The look he fixed on Katie spoke more clearly than words. *Miss Halloran?* it said.

She begged him with her own eyes not to betray her. They still had much they needed to discuss, and she could only hope he would keep her secret until they did. Katie gave a soundless sigh at his slight nod of acquiescence.

"I'll see you tomorrow," he said, the words sounding more like a threat than a promise. He opened his mouth as though to say more, then closing it again, he gave Dinah a slight nod and left the room.

❧

The next morning Katie found herself relieved of her duties for the day. Although she argued hotly, Dinah was adamant. No doubt Clay had used his medical influence to see that she had time for them to finish their interrupted conversation. The thought made her stomach churn to such an extent that she thought for certain she would have to rush for the bathroom again.

She slowly tugged on her favorite sapphire-blue silk charmeuse dress, tying the ribbon belt at her waist and checking to make sure that the portion of her stocking showing from her calf to her ankle had no runs. She knew she would have to face

Clay sometime, but the dread she felt made her movements slow and clumsy. Growing frustrated with herself, she gave herself a lecture that soon stiffened her backbone. After all, what could Clay do to her?

She set her chin firmly, buckling on her black patent leather shoes while continuing to berate herself.

Brushing her hair, she twisted it into a French roll. Although the Harveys had recently allowed some girls to wear their hair bobbed in the style of the day, Katie still liked hers long. She didn't think she would ever get used to the shorter hair that so many girls sported nowadays.

Perching a blue velvet hat on her head, she looked in the mirror and heaved a dispirited sigh. Regardless of the exquisite clothing, nothing, absolutely nothing, would ever make her into a beauty. She disregarded the heavily fringed blue eyes that most considered her best feature.

Deciding she was finally ready, she straightened her shoulders and marched down the stairs and across to the El Tovar. The beauty of the morning reached out to embrace her, and she paused on the porch. The sun had risen brightly, but she noticed wisps of clouds on the horizon, a possible precursor of a storm to come. The summer monsoon had reached Arizona, and Katie had been amazed at the ferocity of the storms that came with it. At this height, the power of the lightning was awesome indeed.

Although she had awakened early, Clay was dressed and waiting for her in the restaurant. He rose and pulled out the chair across from him, motioning her into it. Katie glanced around apprehensively and realized there were few people in the restaurant this early in the morning. After witnessing Clay's anger the previous evening, she suddenly felt very unsure of herself.

Clay seated himself, giving her a quick perusal. The fine-cut navy blue worsted suit he wore spoke of wealth and culture, but Katie was more concerned with what might be hidden by that veneer of charm and civilization. Darius had looked and dressed the same, but beneath all that sophisticated appeal hid a demon.

"Feeling better this morning?" Clay inquired, and Katie blinked her eyes at the intrusion into her thoughts. His silent scrutiny was unnerving.

"I feel fine," she assured him hastily, reaching for the menu one of the Harvey Girls handed her. Katie smiled at her. "Thank you, Anne."

After they placed their order, Clay leaned back in his seat and studied her through half-closed lids.

"So where were we?"

Katie sighed in exasperation. "May we please hold the interrogation until after breakfast? I don't think my stomach can handle it right now."

"Cleo told me about your problem."

Katie dropped the glass she had just lifted, and water splashed onto the table. Jumping up, she threw him an angry glare. "Now look what you made me do!"

He rose with her and began mopping up the spill with his napkin, his lips twitching in amusement. "*I* made you do?"

Katie's glare intensified. "You enjoy shaking me up, don't you?"

He stopped wiping the spill and leaned forward until their hands on the table almost touched. "Oh, Katie," he said. "I only wish I could." His soft voice and intense look caused a surge of feelings to rise and then settle in the pit of her stomach. What on earth had he meant by that?

Anne hurried over, allowing Katie to break loose from a look that made her suddenly short of breath.

"Here, let me seat you at another table."

After they were seated again, silence hung like a blanket around them. Katie wasn't certain if she could swallow one bite of the meal Anne was placing in front of them. What exactly was Clay trying to say to her? Did he really enjoy shaking her up in such a way? Darius liked to do the same, but his teasing was always unkind and hurtful. She didn't trust Darius, and at this point she found herself unable to trust his brother, too.

They finished their meal with a minimum of polite conversation. Clay wiped his mouth and threw down his napkin. The way he was watching her made Katie feel like a specimen under a magnifying glass.

"I've hired us a car. I thought we might go on a excursion."

Without realizing she was doing so, Katie used her napkin and began wiping the fingerprints from the saltshaker on the table. Clay placed a restraining hand over hers, and she jumped as though she had been scalded. Clay grinned, and some of her tension eased.

"You're off duty, remember?"

She met the smiling eyes across from hers. Laughing lightly, she folded the napkin on the table. "I guess the training goes deep."

His look suddenly turned serious. "Let's go. There are things we need to get cleared up."

Katie took a deep breath. She might as well get it over with, because once Clay got hold of something, he was like a bulldog. Rising, she followed him out to the car. He opened the door to the Cadillac Fleetwood, and she settled into the luxury of the car, a luxury she had gladly given up in exchange for a life of freedom.

"I hope you know where you're going," she told him nervously.

He grinned his devil-may-care grin, and Katie felt herself relax again. This was more like the Clay she remembered.

They traveled for some time before Clay pulled off the dirt track and parked close to the canyon. He glanced at her, his mouth parting as though he were about to say something. Turning, he quickly got out of the car. Going around to her side, he helped her out and pulled an Indian blanket from the backseat of the car. She followed him to where he spread the blanket in the shade of a large ponderosa pine tree. He bowed from the waist.

"Your throne, madam."

Katie couldn't stop the smile that tipped one side of her mouth. If not for the niggling thoughts pecking at her peace of mind, she could have relaxed and enjoyed herself. She knew Clay was trying his best to put her at ease.

After she was seated, Clay seated himself next to her. He leaned down on his side, propping himself up with one arm. While he watched her, Katie studiously avoided looking at him. Instead, she concentrated on the magnificence of the canyon before her.

"Why did you run away, Katie? If you knew Darius was unfaithful, why didn't you just go to my father, or even to me?"

Katie answered him with something between a sigh and a laugh. She looked down at him, her mouth slanted in a wry smile. "That would have been a little hard to do, Clay. You're never around." Something indefinable passed so swiftly through his eyes, she couldn't be certain of what she had seen. "Besides, what could you have done?"

He moved so quickly his face was close to hers before she realized it. His breath feathered softly across her cheek.

"I could have been there for you."

She frowned, moving away from his disturbing nearness. Clay's attitude of late made her decidedly uneasy. She glanced back out over the canyon. "Why are you here, Clay?"

"You know why. I'm here to take you home."

She clenched her teeth so hard she thought they might shatter. Fixing him with a glare, she told him in no uncertain terms, "I'm not going back with you. El Tovar is my home now."

"You expect me to believe you are happy being a waitress?"

"I'm not a *waitress*! I'm a Harvey Girl!"

His face darkened with growing anger, and she jumped up to move away from him, her heart thundering in her chest. She hadn't noticed before just how much he looked like Darius when he was angry.

He must have read the fear in her eyes, because he shook himself slightly and took a deep breath. He got up and held his hand out to her. His brows knit with confusion.

"I would never hurt you, Katie. Don't look at me like that."

She had already had a taste of his anger, and it had left a

lasting impression. Would he hurt her? Even if she believed him, she knew the same could not be said for his brother. Again, vivid pictures of that violent night passed through her mind. She felt the color drain from her face.

"I won't go back, Clay, and you can't make me."

His chest rose and fell rapidly in his agitation. His hands clenched at his side. "We'll see about that."

Chapter 3

The trip back to El Tovar was fraught with a tense silence. Katie turned over in her mind ways to convince Clay she was serious about not returning with him, but she was very aware of Clay's ability to get his own way.

She glanced at him now and recognized the rigid set of his jaw. This was not going to be easy, and she could see no way out of it without telling him the whole truth, something she was loath to do. Still, she would do so if it meant being allowed to remain at El Tovar.

She opened her mouth to speak, but he forestalled her.

"You realize that if I tell Miss Weston the truth, you will lose your job."

Her stomach clenched tightly, and bile rose to her throat. That was exactly what she had been afraid of. "Would you really do that, Clay?"

He threw her a look that spoke volumes. "You've given me no reason not to."

Katie's anger rose against him. "So I should just go back with you and live with a man while he parades his women in and out of my life?" She clenched her teeth so hard, he surely must have heard. "I think not!"

Clay suddenly pulled the car to the side of the dirt track and came to a stop in the shade of a tree. He turned on her, his eyes glittering dangerously. "I'll talk to him."

"I don't *want* you to talk to him. I just want him out of my life!"

"Have you thought about what all is at stake here?"

Katie sighed. Closing her eyes, she began rubbing her neck to try to ease the strain of taut muscles. "I suppose you're talking about money," she said flatly.

He leaned back against the door of the car and gave her a hard stare. "Among other things."

She met his look. "What other things?"

"How about your reputation, for one?"

She snorted softly. "My reputation! I don't care one whit about my reputation!"

Before he could stop her, she climbed from the car. She had to get away from his nearness. Somehow, just being close to him clouded her thoughts. She walked closer to the canyon's edge. Folding her arms across her stomach, she stared out over the canyon to the El Tovar in the distance.

Clay came up behind her. From her peripheral vision, she could see his hands reach out to touch her, and she tensed; but then he slowly dropped them to his side.

"I care, Katie."

She turned on him angrily. "Well, *don't*! Just go away and pretend you never saw me. Darius is welcome to anything that was mine, including my money. I don't want it. I don't *need* it."

She touched his arm and felt the muscles tighten beneath her fingers. She couldn't help the tears in her eyes. "I've made a life for myself here, Clay. I'm happy here."

He sighed heavily, his look dubious. "You expect me to believe that? You've never had to work a day in your life, and you expect me to believe that you *enjoy* it? I've seen how hard the Harvey Girls work. Regardless of what you call it, it's still being a waitress, waiting on everyone's beck and call."

She pressed her lips tightly together trying to choke back the words that were bursting for release. "I'm staying, Clay. If you cost me my job, I will just go somewhere else."

His eyes darkened with anger until his pupils shone black. Once again, she felt a pang of fear. She stepped back, her chin lifting defiantly.

"Wherever you go, Katie, I will just follow."

Katie's mouth parted in astonishment. She knew Clay could be ruthlessly determined, but this tenacity was beyond her comprehension. There must be more at stake than she realized.

So intent was she on Clay and their discussion, she failed to realize a summer storm was fast approaching. She started with surprise as the first raindrops pelted against her bare arms.

Clay glanced up and saw the dark thundercloud rapidly moving over them. Grabbing her hand, he rushed them to the car. They climbed inside just as the first torrent of raindrops assaulted them.

The rain was intermixed with a barrage of hailstones, followed quickly by blinding flashes of lightning and resounding thunder. Katie flinched, pulling her legs up to rest her feet on the car seat and wrapping her arms tightly around her upraised knees. She buried her face against her knees, her body shaking. Often these storms were fast moving and brief, and she prayerfully hoped this was one of those times. Being safe inside the El Tovar was far different from being stranded here in the open with the elements raging around them, protected only by a flimsy sheet of metal.

Clay's hand against her shoulder made her jerk in surprise. She glanced over at him, teeth chattering, and found him watching her with understanding.

"You're really scared, aren't you?"

She could barely hear him above the sound of the rain pounding against the tin roof. He had to be joking!

"This doesn't scare you?"

He studied her several moments. Through the gloom she could see his eyes narrow. There was no sign of uncertainty in his visage at all. She wondered if anything frightened him.

Reaching across the seat, he pulled her across and into his arms, wrapping her securely in his embrace. He allowed her to bury her face against his chest as time after time the lightning flashed around them.

Storms had always frightened her, but more so since the night she had fled her husband. It had been storming that night, too. With each crack of thunder another blow had rained down upon her, just like the pounding of the rain outside. With each flash of lightning, she could see Darius's face as he moved closer and closer. Suddenly the arms holding her were a threat. Forgetting where she was, she screamed and tried to push out of Clay's arms. His hold only tightened, and she began pummeling him with her fists.

"Katie!"

"Let me go! If you fear God, Darius, please let me go!"

Clay shook her until her head snapped back and she could see his distressed face. Slowly recognition returned, and she realized it was not Darius who held her. Whimpering, she once again buried her head against his chest. The thunder of his heartbeat drummed against her fist where it clutched at the material of his shirt.

"What has he done to you?" The hoarseness of his voice whispering against her ear blended with the retreating sound of the rain.

"Nothing!" she cried. "I'm sorry. It's just the storm!"

She knew he didn't believe her, but he allowed the subject to drop. She could feel the tension in his arms as they once again securely wrapped around her, and she knew it was only by a tight rein on his will that he allowed her to say no more. Once before he had held her thus, at her parents' funeral. Whereas her husband should have been the one giving her comfort, Clay was the one who had stayed by her side through the tortuous ordeal. Clay had held her securely while she cried her heart out. She had turned to him as the strong brother she had never had, and he had responded with gentle kindness. She had felt sheltered. Protected. Much like she felt now. But the feelings he evoked in her were not sisterly, and if she was honest with herself, she would admit they hadn't been at the funeral, either.

When his voice broke the silence, it was not with words she expected him to say. "Do you remember the verses from the Bible you used to quote me?" he asked huskily.

Pulling her bottom lip between her teeth, she thought of all the times she had shared verses from Psalm 139 with him. He had such wanderlust, and every time he'd come home, within weeks he would be off on another jaunt. Each time she had reminded him of the verses.

" '*Whither shall I go from thy spirit?*' " she began hesitantly, her voice growing stronger as the words began to penetrate. " '*Or whither shall I flee from thy presence? If I ascend up into heaven, thou art there: if I make my bed in hell, behold, thou art there.*' " As she continued reciting, she felt the power of the words seep into her soul and soothe the feelings of terror the storm had engendered. God had been with her then, and He was still with her now. She shyly glanced up at Clay, and he gave her a slow, heart-stopping smile.

"Feel better now?" Although his voice was quiet, she could see the anger still darkening his eyes. Paradoxically, she was unafraid, realizing the anger was not directed at her.

She nodded, thanking him with her eyes. Not only had the fear subsided, but the storm had subsided, as well. As quickly as it had come, it had passed. The tension eased from her body, leaving her exhausted.

Clay continued to stare at her, the smile slowly fading from his lips as she continued to stare back. In one quick movement, he pushed her back to her own side of the car. Without another word, he started the engine, revving it with unnecessary violence. Slamming the car into gear, he returned them to the El Tovar.

❧

"I'm truly sorry, Cleo. I forgot all about our trip to Flagstaff."

Cleo grinned mischievously at Katie while she continued to set the table for dinner that evening. "I can't say I'm surprised.

Why should you remember little ole me when you were spending the day with that handsome hunk of manhood?"

Katie flushed with embarrassment. There was no way she could explain the real state of things to Cleo. While it was true Clay was a handsome man, he treated her more like a sister than anything else. They had been neighbors from the time she had been an adolescent twelve-year-old. It was true that at one time she believed herself madly in love with him. It was hard to believe that it had been almost twelve years ago. Half of her lifetime.

Katie stared around her helplessly. "I feel like I should be doing something other than just standing here."

Cleo shook her head firmly. "Dinah gave you the day off. The *whole* day off. Go have fun!"

Fun! Being interrogated by Clay could hardly be considered *fun*. She was so afraid she would give something away without meaning to that, when he was near, she felt as if she were on pins and needles.

"Katie."

As though her thoughts had conjured him, he stood in the doorway to the dining room.

"I need to talk to you a minute," he told her.

Sighing, Katie crossed the room and stopped in front of him. Only hours before he had seemed so angry; now his voice was quiescent. His calmness bothered her, because that was how Darius was right before a storm.

He led her away from the dining room and outside, crossing to the Hopi House where the nightly dances were just beginning. They seated themselves away from the fire, and as usual, Katie became entranced by the sound of the drums and the movement of the dancers.

Her thoughts were jerked back to the present at Clay's next words.

"I'm leaving on the evening train. I'll be going home to see Darius and have a talk with him. Find out what he wants to do." He looked at her seriously. "I already know what you say you want, but I need to make sure."

"I'm not going back," she told him quietly.

"And if Darius wants to come to you and apologize? Ask forgiveness?"

The thought made Katie go cold all over. She bit her bottom lip in agitation. It took several tries before she could make her voice sound louder than a squeak.

"Please, Clay. Don't tell him where I am. Please."

"Katie. . ."

She turned, clutching the front of his shirt with both fists. *"Please!"*

His hands curled warmly over hers, his face a mask of confusion. Her desperation must have finally gotten through to him. He opened his mouth to speak several times, but the only thing he finally said was, "I'll make no promises."

With that, she had to be satisfied. By mutual consent, they turned to watch the dancers together, both busy with their own thoughts.

When the train was finally ready to leave, Katie walked with him to the small station. As a last gesture, he bought her an ice cream from the boy at the stand.

Clay gently rubbed the knuckles of his hand down her cheek.

She had never seen him looking so serious, his eyes darkened to the color of the evergreens on the sides of the canyon.

"Take care," he told her. "I'll be back in a few days."

There was nothing she could say. She wanted to beg him not to betray her whereabouts to Darius, but she held herself in check. Her throat tightened with tears. She had always been fond of Clay, and now he was walking out of her life again. She didn't really believe him when he said he would return.

Darius would want a divorce and claim her property as his own, and then Clay would be off on one of his jaunts again.

As though he could read her thoughts, he cupped her face in his palm. "I'm coming back," he reiterated, and then the whistle blew, the conductor shouted for all to board, and Katie watched as the train began its trek south to Williams.

She returned to the hotel to try to find Dinah. She needed to work, and they needed the help. No one knew that better than she did.

Everyone was busy about her duties, all except Dinah. She was nowhere to be found.

"Cleo," Katie asked, "have you seen Dinah?"

Cleo stopped pulling the tablecloths off her tables and gave Katie a puzzled look.

"You know, it's the funniest thing. This man came into the hotel, and Dinah turned three shades of white. She told me to keep working, and she headed for the kitchen."

"That's odd," Katie agreed, but her mind wasn't entirely on what was being said. She was wondering if Clay would tell Darius where she was, and if Darius would care. "I'll look for her in the kitchen, then."

When she finally found the manager, Dinah was hovering near the back door of the kitchen. She turned to Katie, and Katie privately thought she had never seen the woman look so plain. She forgot her own problems in the face of Dinah's distress.

"Miss Weston, are you all right?"

"I'm fine, Katie. What did you need?"

But Katie knew she wasn't fine. Her voice was strained, lacking its normally authoritative tone.

"I'd like to help with the cleaning in the dining room."

"Fine," she answered distractedly.

Katie hesitated, wanting to say more, but Dinah's problem was really none of her business. They made a fine pair, Dinah and herself. It would be hard to say which one was more disturbed.

Katie finally left the manager to her own thoughts and tried to purge her own with hard work. It was hours later before she realized the only thing the hard work had accomplished was to make her tired.

Chapter 4

Clay hunched down in the seat of the train, listening to the clacking of the wheels as the distance increased between him and the woman he loved.

How long had he been in love with her? He wasn't quite certain, having always considered her a pest with her adolescent crush, always following him around. By the time he realized what was happening to him, it was too late. She was already betrothed to his brother at their parents' instigation and their intense satisfaction.

It was his reason for what Katie called his "wanderlust." Every time he thought he had his feelings under control, he'd come home to find out he'd only been deluding himself. He would be home a short time before he knew he had to get away again, that or do something that would affect everyone's lives.

This last time he had gone to Washington State to work in a lumber camp. His skills as a doctor had really been put to the test there. He had been relatively happy and content—that is, until he received the telegram two months ago telling him Katie had disappeared.

No one would ever know the thoughts and feelings that had beset him at the news. His first thought was that she had been kidnapped, his blood turned to ice at that notion. She was, after all, the heiress to a large fortune. No one could have convinced him she would leave of her own volition.

He had gone home to help look for her. While searching her room, he found a newspaper ad for Harvey Girls tucked beneath the clothes in her drawer. That discovery had been his first clue that she had indeed left on her own.

When appealing to the Harvey hiring center in Kansas, he was told there was no Katie O'Neil working for the Harvey establishment. It had never occurred to him she would be using her maiden name. For the last two months, he had been traveling the Santa Fe rail system and visiting every Harvey House along the way. The El Tovar had been the last, and his hope of finding her had been almost obliterated. He had been unprepared for the feelings that flashed through him at the sight of her tired face, and even more unprepared when she had crumpled to the floor in a dead faint. Even now his heart pounded at the memory.

He sighed, rubbing his forehead tiredly. The main crux of his dilemma had been all the deceit. All the lies Katie had told did not fit in with the picture he had formed of her in his mind. She had always been so adamantly truthful, sometimes without realizing the pain she was inflicting on others. He, for one. And she had always been a Christian light, shining in the otherwise dark world of his universe. She was forever spouting Bible verses at him. If only she knew how those verses had stayed with him wherever he had gone. Often they had kept him from succumbing to temptations he otherwise might have given in to.

It rattled him to find that Katie would have no compunction about lying. Something just wasn't right here. He could still see the panic in her eyes when he had lost his temper. It wasn't just fear. It was absolute, unmitigated terror. And the storm! What on earth had happened to her to put that look on her face? He wouldn't be able to erase that picture from his mind in a thousand lifetimes!

Though he hated to admit it to himself, he knew the answer to his questions rested with Darius. Anger burned within him at the thought his brother might be responsible for that look on Katie's face. He wasn't certain he really wanted to find out the truth, because he was afraid of what he might do. Still, he had to know. Had his brother changed so much in the time he had been away? When he thought about it, he remembered little incidents in the past he had ignored, but maybe they had been clues to something Clay just hadn't recognized at the time.

When he finally arrived back in Philadelphia, he was tired and dispirited. The cab left him at the door to the O'Neil mansion, and he wearily climbed the steps, using his key to open the door without bothering the servants.

His mother was just crossing the hall when he entered. Her face lit up at the sight of him.

"Clay!" she exclaimed.

"Hello, Mother."

"Well," she replied, her look curious, "come inside and tell me where you've been."

Sighing, Clay placed an arm around her shoulders and

walked back with her to the parlor. "I'll tell you about things later, Mother. Right now I am badly in need of a bath and some sleep." He glanced around the room. "Where is Darius?"

His mother seated herself next to the ornate fireplace that was kept lit even in warm weather—for ambience, his mother would say. The patio doors stood open, a slightly cooling breeze ruffling the curtains. Clay seated himself on the sofa across from her.

"Darius and your father have gone to the solicitors to see what needs to be done about Katie's business."

Clay froze. "What do you mean?"

"Well, Darius is thinking of filing for divorce on grounds of desertion."

Before he could answer, they heard the front door open and men's voices in the hall. Clay rose to his feet just as the parlor door opened.

"Clay!" His father hurried across the room and gave him a brief bear hug. "Where in the name of heaven have you been?"

Clay looked past his father's shoulder to Darius standing behind him. The smile Darius gave him was strained. Clay held out his hand while searching his brother's face for some sign of the younger brother he remembered. This Darius was cold, his face a closed mask.

"Well, if it isn't my long-lost brother. Where have you been off roaming this time?"

"I was looking for Katie."

The room went so silent it was possible to hear the snaps from the logs in the fireplace. Both men seated themselves, staring up at Clay wordlessly.

"Did you find her?" Darius finally asked.

"I found her."

Clay heard his mother's sharp intake of breath, but his eyes were fixed on Darius. He didn't miss the small start and the look of consternation that quickly passed over his brother's face.

"Alive?"

He turned to his father. "Yes, alive."

His father closed his eyes, his face going pale. "Thank God!"

Clay didn't like Darius's stillness or the blank look in his eyes. Darius always looked like that when he was hiding something.

"Where is she?" Darius asked.

"She's asked me not to tell you."

"What!" The simultaneous reaction from his parents and brother was pretty much what Clay had expected, but whereas his parents were obviously distressed, Darius was downright angry. Clay glanced at each person in turn.

"She has her reasons, and for the time being I intend to respect that." He fixed a steely glare on his brother. "But I need to talk to Darius alone."

Discomfited, Darius shrugged his shoulders. "Whatever for?"

"You would rather discuss this in front of Father and Mother?"

His voice held a soft threat that brought an instant reaction from his father.

"Now wait just a minute, Clay!"

Darius motioned him to calm down. "It's all right, Dad. I think I know what he wants to talk about."

His mother had been silent after that first outburst; now

she spoke up. "Can't it wait until later, Clay? You're dead on your feet."

Clay knew she was right. His brain was not functioning at full capacity, and he would need all his wits about him when he finally faced his brother.

"You're right. It can wait. I'm sure both Father and Darius are longing for a drink and maybe something to eat. It is past dinnertime."

The two men seemed less than satisfied with his words, but they put an end to further discussion. Clay gave a slight bow and left the room.

Clay waited until the next morning when his parents had left the house before confronting his brother. Darius was the first to speak.

"So you found Katie. And what wild story did she tell you to explain her disappearing act?"

Once again seated across from his brother in the parlor, Clay wondered how his brother could look so cool and calm about the whole thing.

"She didn't tell me anything, except that she isn't coming back."

Darius looked smug. "Well then, I can go ahead and file for divorce on grounds of desertion."

Clay felt his anger growing. "I'm more concerned with why Katie looked so terrified when I lost my temper. She looked as though I was about to beat her."

Grinning, Darius looked him over from head to foot. "So you lost your temper, huh? I can see why that would terrify such a small thing. You *have*—what's the word I'm looking for?—*developed* a bit over the last few months."

"Keep that in mind, Darius," Clay warned, "because I want the truth."

Darius didn't miss the threat. The smug look on his face was replaced with a wary one.

"Just exactly what does this have to do with you?" he asked belligerently.

Trying to hang on to his composure, Clay told him, "She's family, Darius. And I want to know what happened. What did you do that made her run away like that?"

Darius jumped up from his seat and went to the French doors opening onto the patio. He stared moodily out at the garden that was fast drying in the warm July temperatures. He glanced over his shoulder at Clay, his look one of extreme guilt. Clay squirmed in his seat, afraid of what was coming next.

"I didn't mean to hurt her," Darius told him calmly, "but I had had too much to drink."

Clay's stomach tightened. Liquor was illegal in the United States; that meant only one thing. His brother had become involved with something he probably couldn't control. He crossed one leg over the other nonchalantly, but even Darius wasn't fooled by his relaxed attitude. Darius studied him as though he were a cobra about to strike.

"Go on," Clay encouraged softly.

"I wanted an heir," he said, watching Clay cautiously. "She was a little, let us say, reluctant about giving me one."

Clay felt the color drain from his face, his body frozen into immobility. "Are you saying. . . ?

"I'm saying," Darius interrupted, his voice hostile, his look one of extreme guilt, "Katie refused to fulfill her role as wife, so I took what was owing to me."

Clay was across the room so fast his brother had no hope of evading him. Clay lifted the younger man by the front of his shirt, his fist reared back to strike.

"Clay!"

His father's commanding voice scarcely stopped the forward thrust that would have sent his brother flying through the doors to the patio beyond.

"What's going on here?"

Breathing hard, Clay slowly released his grip and allowed Darius to slip from his grasp. When he turned to his father, he barely had himself under control.

Darius shook out his clothing, straightening his tie at the same time. "Clay objected to something I said, that's all."

Their father looked from one to the other, his brows meeting together in a frown. "Then it's a good thing your mother forgot her purse, isn't it." He glowered at Clay. "There will be no violence in my home, do you understand? If need be, your mother can suspend her trip, and we will remain at home. Whatever you have to say about Katie can just be discussed with us present."

It was obvious the idea held no appeal for Darius, and Clay had no intention of bringing his parents into this sordid conversation he fully intended to finish.

"Now, Father," Darius lied smoothly, "this has nothing to do with Katie. Just a disagreement between brothers. Clay was a little disturbed I talked you into selling our interests in the mine in California."

Clay's father leveled a severe glare at him. "The mine has nothing to do with you. You haven't been here for us to discuss business with, and decisions needed to made. If you want some say-so in how things are run, then stay around and contribute."

It took several minutes for Clay to get his breathing under control enough to give his father an answer.

"I understand," Clay agreed, impaling his brother with a look that promised retribution.

His father contemplated them both suspiciously. "If I leave with your mother as arranged, can I be assured there will be no more threats of violence?"

"Of course," Darius assured him.

"Clay?"

Clay glared at his brother. He wasn't one to give his word lightly, and right now he wasn't certain he could keep to such a promise. Darius's smug look didn't help the situation.

"Clay?" his father repeated.

Clay nodded, his hands tightening into fists at his side.

They could hear the door open and close, and then Clay's mother was in the room.

"James? Are we going or not?" Her eyebrows lifted slightly as she recognized the tension in the air.

James stared at each son in turn before, satisfied, he nodded his head. "Just coming, my dear." He picked up her purse from the table and handed it to her. He turned back to Clay, scowling a warning. "Remember."

After they had gone, Clay spun toward his brother. "Right now, I want nothing more than to rip you apart."

"I know, and I don't blame you."

The words suggested understanding, and Clay directed a surprised look at his brother. "What's gotten into you, anyway? Cheating on Katie, lying to Dad—you're not the man I seem to remember. And where the dickens did you get the alcohol? Have you been frequenting a speakeasy?"

Darius's face colored. "You needn't sound so self-righteous," he snapped, ignoring the latter questions. "I already told you I didn't mean for it to happen. It's just. . ."

"Just what?" Clay regarded his brother warily, struggling to be objective. Something was seriously wrong with Darius, something that was making him almost desperate. He could see it in the coiled tension of his body.

"Did you know Katie's father left his money in trust to Katie?"

Clay frowned. "No, but it doesn't surprise me. Lots of fathers do the same. So what?"

Darius smiled without humor. Clay didn't like the look on his face.

"When Katie has our child, the money will be placed in *my* hands as trustee. I need that money, Clay."

Clay slowly rose to his feet, the feelings rushing through him begging for release. "That's what this is about? You would hurt your own wife over *money*? What kind of animal are you?"

Darius studied him with growing comprehension, a look of amazement crossing his features. "You're in love with my wife! That's it, isn't it?"

Clay could neither confirm nor deny it. He dropped back into the chair, restlessly brushing his hand through his hair.

"Well, well, well, who would have thought?" Darius relaxed

back against the cushions, recognizing the power he now held over Clay. Clay could see it in his face. "What on earth do you see in the girl?" he asked curiously. "She's one of the drabbest women of my acquaintance."

Clay settled a fierce glare on him. "She's not drab at all," he denied hotly, ready to forget the promise he had made just moments ago to his father. "She may not be a beauty, but she's certainly not drab. I thought you liked Katie. I even thought you were beginning to love her. You didn't need her fortune. We have enough money of our own."

Darius shook his head, clicking his tongue. "Clay, Clay, you are so naive. Don't you know, there's *never* enough money. Besides, *we* don't have the money; Father does. I want control of my own money."

Clay could hear the desperation in his brother's voice once again, and he stood up and began pacing the floor to relieve himself of some of his pent-up anger. If he couldn't calm himself, he wasn't sure what he might do. "Then why Katie? Why not one of the other wealthy women of our acquaintance? You certainly had enough of them in love with you."

Smiling with satisfaction at the statement, Darius plucked a loose thread from his black double-breasted suit. He negligently flipped it on the floor.

"True, but Father and Mother had settled on Katie." He glanced up at Clay, his expression suddenly vicious. "Where is she, Clay?"

Clay stopped pacing, feet spread apart, arms folded across his chest, eyes sparkling dangerously. "As though I would tell you. And don't try to divorce her for desertion to get her money, or so help me, I'll bring every one your seamy affairs into the light. I don't know why you need this money so badly, but I intend to find out," he threatened.

Chapter 5

Katie, hurry up, or we'll be late!"

Picking up her hat, Katie hurried from the room to join Cleo for their journey to the bottom of the canyon on mule. She had been here almost three months and had yet to make the trek, and she was looking forward to it, if a little apprehensively.

When she saw Cleo in her split skirt and boots, she was thankful she had bought the same in Flagstaff. Many women came here unprepared for the trip, so El Tovar kept a supply of the skirts and boots on hand, but Katie had decided to purchase her own. Besides, she thought they looked rather chic and intended to wear hers often.

When they reached the spot where the mules were waiting, Katie stopped suddenly. There, standing talking to Barton, the mule skinner, was Clay. He had left two weeks ago, and now he was back. Her heart started pounding with trepidation. She hadn't seen him come in on the evening train. How long had he been back? He turned and saw her standing there. Excusing himself to Barton, he came to her, taking his Stetson from his head and twirling it in his hands. If he had looked handsome in his suit, he was quite something in his jeans and blue cotton shirt. He looked just like one of the cowhands who often frequented El Tovar. The jeans looked as if they had seen a lot of wear, and she wondered again where his travels had taken him.

His look quickly passed over her, and when his eyes met hers, she found her mouth suddenly dry.

"You look well," he told her.

That was it? That was all he had to say? She wanted to bombard him with questions, but the only thing she could think of to say was, "You wanted to see me?"

His slow smile had her heart turning a somersault and righting itself again. She thought she had gotten over her childish crush on him, but that look still made her heart do flip-flops.

"I'm taking the mule trip to the bottom of the canyon. I heard you were, too."

She frowned. "Clay. . . ?"

He hushed her with a finger on her lips. "Don't worry about it. We'll discuss things later. Right now, let's just have some fun, okay?"

She would have argued, but just then Cleo joined them. She quirked an eyebrow at Katie, and Katie rolled her eyes at Cleo's knowing look.

"Hello, Dr. O'Neil," Cleo said, giving Clay one of her best smiles. "Back again?"

Clay's narrow-eyed appraisal touched first on Katie and then on Cleo. "I had some business to attend to back home. I thought I would return and take the mule trip I've heard so much about. Have you been before?"

"Once. It's not for the fainthearted, I can tell you that."

Clay's skeptical look returned to Katie, and she lifted her chin. "I've been looking forward to this since I got here."

Barton called out for everyone to mount up, effectively ending their conversation. The mule skinner moved up and down the column, checking cinches and straps. Satisfied, he mounted up himself, and they prepared to head out.

Clay positioned himself behind Katie. Katie wasn't certain she liked the idea of having his eyes always on her back. She suddenly felt like a child standing before her teacher and having to perform some feat she was unsure of.

As they began their descent, the rocks misplaced by the mules' hooves scattered and tumbled over the path's edge to the chasm below.

They hadn't gone very far before Katie felt her stomach start to rebel at all the jostling. She struggled against the encroaching nausea, her breathing coming more rapidly as she tried to hold back the bile rising to her throat.

The canyon walls seemed to twist and turn in a gyrating pattern of reds, browns, and yellows. She didn't realize she was swaying in the saddle until she heard Clay's panicked yell from behind.

As though from a far distance, she heard him stop his mule. Her brow furrowed in confusion. It was forbidden to stop the animals without the mule skinner's instructions. What did Clay think he was doing?

She felt firm hands gripping her waist just seconds before she tumbled into darkness.

Clay watched with his heart in his throat as Katie stirred, her eyelids fluttering open and her gaze fixing on him with a look of total stupefaction. He leaned back on the bed, watching her come to full wakefulness.

"Why didn't you tell someone you were pregnant?" he demanded, his fury charged by his fear. "You never should have been on that mule!"

She turned her head away, her throat contracting as she swallowed hard.

"Katie!" He cupped her chin, forcing her to look his way. Her blue eyes darkened with a fleeting emotion as they met his. Her chin began to quiver, and he choked back his anger and frustration. He slowly slid his fingers down the side of her cheek, reluctantly dropping his hand to his side.

"I didn't know," she snapped.

He stared at her in amazement. "How could you not know?"

Her face turned red with embarrassment. "This is a not a proper discussion to be having."

Sighing with exasperation, he shook his head. "I'm a doctor, for heaven's sake. I ask you again, how could you not know? Surely you suspected."

She pushed herself upright, leaning her back against the iron headboard. Brushing her hand through her already disheveled hair, she looked everywhere but at him. She plucked at the quilt nervously with shaking fingers, and Clay covered her hand with his own to still it. He remembered she'd always had this nervous habit of fidgeting with her hands.

When she spoke, her voice was barely a whisper. "My monthly times have never been regular. I suspected when I was experiencing sickness in the morning; but then it went away, and I thought it was only the heat."

Clay didn't know what to say. He realized he would have to tread carefully. Katie was already in a charged emotional state, and with good reason, but the hormones raging through her body would make the situation more volatile. He didn't want her to disappear again.

He rose from the bed, fixing her with an authoritative look. "You cannot continue to work here. I won't permit it."

She flashed him an angry glare. "What do you mean you won't permit it?"

He took several calming breaths to still his own turbulent emotions. "Katie, be reasonable. This is no kind of work for an expecting mother."

Scrambling from the bed, she faced him with arms akimbo, her eyes shooting dangerous sparks. He didn't think he had ever seen her so angry.

"If you're telling me I have to go back to Philadelphia, then you can just forget it. Things have changed. Other Harvey Girls have been married and had children and continued to work. I can do the same."

"Over my dead body. I'll go to Miss Weston if I have to."

His very stillness and the quiet of his voice caused her eyes to widen with obvious apprehension. She knew he wasn't joking and that he would not compromise.

"Don't threaten me, Clay. If you tell Dinah, then I'll tell her why I'm here. I think she would be on my side."

"Do you really want to find out?" he asked quietly. There was power behind the O'Neil name, and she knew he wouldn't hesitate to use that power if necessary to get what he wanted.

She paused so long, he thought she wasn't going to answer. When she finally did, his heart twisted at her look of defeat.

"What do you want me to do?" she finally whispered.

He sighed heavily. "For one thing, don't look at me like that!"

"Like what?" she returned angrily.

"Like I'm about to beat you or something. For crying out loud, Katie. Be reasonable. I only want what's best for you *and* the baby."

"As do I," she told him and realized it was true. Although she had hoped and prayed she was not with child, God had His own plans for her life, and she found herself oddly excited at the thought of the child she finally conceded was growing within her.

"And do you really think this is best?" he demanded. "You could lose the baby, you know."

She paled at the statement. Clay was a doctor, so surely he knew what he was talking about. She rubbed her forehead tiredly. "I need to think."

He looked as though he was about to object but then thought better of it. He went to the window and stared out, unthinkingly tapping his stethoscope against his leg. There were times when he wished he had the same kind of faith Katie had. Right now was one of those times. He had no clue what to do about this situation except maybe offer up a prayer or two. Frankly, he could empathize with Katie's desire not to return to his brother. Still, this was no place to raise a child. He sighed again, telling her over his shoulder, "All right. If you're careful, you're early enough in your pregnancy that some work should be no problem."

She smiled with relief, but it was short-lived.

"However," he continued, "if I see you overburdened, I won't hesitate to step in. Do you understand me?"

She stared at him in surprise. "You're staying?"

"I'm giving you a week to think things over," he stated unequivocally. "At the end of that time, I expect you to have come to your senses."

Katie went down to work that evening, her heart and mind full of confusion. She had been praying all afternoon God would show her what to do, but her mind seemed closed to the answer that kept repeating itself over and over in her head. This was no place to raise a child.

Oh, God, she prayed yet again, *what am I to do?*

As she rounded the corner of the dining room, she came upon Dinah and the stranger Cleo had pointed out to her before. They were deep in discussion. The man was handsome and well dressed, his dark hair touched with gray highlights. Dinah seemed afraid, probably because of the man's obvious anger. His dark eyes flashed with it.

Katie recoiled from the anger she sensed, yet at the same time it sent her hurrying forward to Dinah's defense. Before she reached them, however, she couldn't help overhearing the man's declaration of love, and she stopped, suddenly not wanting to intrude.

The man gripped Dinah by her upper arms and pulled her forward. "You have got to believe me! Hang it all, Dinah, I've been searching for you for years. I'm not about to just walk away now."

Dinah pushed ineffectively against his chest with her flat palms, her head shaking slowly from side to side. "How can you say you loved me? You never gave me any indication!" Tears pooled in her eyes. "Marcie told me what you said. She told me you said I was homely!"

The stranger looked pained. "Dinah," he remonstrated softly, "Marcie *lied*."

Katie tried to pull back without being seen, but she couldn't stop the conversation from reaching her ears.

"Why would Marcie lie? She was my best friend!" Dinah told him.

The stranger's voice was soft when he spoke, but his words were distinct. "She lied because she knew I loved you and that I didn't want *her*."

Dinah suddenly pushed out of his hold, her eyes blazing angrily. "I don't believe you!"

She turned to run, stopping when she saw Katie. The stranger had started after her, but he stopped, too.

Katie felt her face flame. "I'm sorry. I didn't mean to eavesdrop," she said, glancing apprehensively from one to the other.

Dinah took a deep breath, brushing shaking hands down her white dress. She visibly tried to get herself under control. "Did you need something, Katie?"

Katie shook her head, impressed with Dinah's professionalism. "No. I was just headed to work."

Dinah glanced back at the stranger before moving forward and taking Katie by the arm. "I'll go with you."

The man's voice followed them as they crossed the room.

"Dinah Weston, we're going to finish this conversation sometime."

The manager's lips compressed, her color rising high. Katie wisely remained silent. When they reached the dining room, Dinah released Katie's arm.

"How much did you hear?" she asked quietly.

"How much did you want me to hear?" Katie returned, concerned about Dinah's white face.

"I would like you to forget you ever heard any of it," she replied, meeting Katie's eyes with ones filled with doubt and regret.

Something about her hopeless look spurred Katie on to say, "He sounded sincere to me."

Dinah flashed her an angry glare. "Get to work, Katie."

"Yes, ma'am," she agreed, accepting the rebuff without offense. It really was no concern of hers.

The El Tovar was more crowded than usual, and Katie was nearly run off her feet. Clay had settled himself in the corner of the dining room, and it unnerved her to know he was watching her every move.

When some miners from the Orphan Mine began to make a nuisance of themselves, Clay appeared by her side. The fierceness of his look affected more than Katie. The three miners hurriedly apologized and then retreated out the door after leaving her a hefty tip.

Clay's lifted eyebrows spoke more eloquently than any words

he could have spoken, and Katie sighed with irritation.

"Don't say it," she warned.

He crossed his arms over his chest, a scowl marring his normally handsome features. "I don't need to, do I?"

Katie wasn't sure she could handle several more days of his continued presence. He was going to make her a nervous wreck before the week was out.

Pressing her lips tightly together to check the words she wanted to emit, she whirled around and stalked away.

Two days later the telegram arrived.

Chapter 6

Clay stood at the canyon's edge, staring into the yawning chasm. The vast space was filled with emptiness, much like his own life. How had things gone so wrong? If he had stayed around, could he have helped his brother? He snorted softly. How could he help his brother when he couldn't even help himself? For several years now he had been fighting a battle with himself over whether to give his life to Christ. Wherever he had gone, Katie's scriptures and admonitions had followed him. His pride had kept him from admitting he needed a savior in his life. Now, the thought of his own brother's death and his spending an eternity in hell was the catalyst that made Clay realize he didn't want that same fate for himself. Maybe if he had given in sooner, he could have saved his brother from that horrible fate. The guilt weighed heavily on his heart. He knew what he needed to do, but he wasn't quite certain he deserved the grace God was willing to give him. He stared up at the heavens. *God, if You're there, show me the way.*

"Clay?"

He turned at the sound of Katie's voice. He stared at her quietly, wondering what she was thinking. She had taken the news of Darius's death well. Too well. The only word he could use to describe her reaction when he told her the news was *relief.*

She placed a hand against his sleeve, and he tensed.

"I'm sorry about Darius. I really am."

She sounded sincere. He wasn't about to tell her the details of his brother's death. He had kept his promise not to tell his family where Katie was, but he had left the address with his lawyer. McQuinn needed him to come home to help settle Darius's estate, as well as Katie's.

"We have to go back to Philadelphia," he told her.

Startled, she stepped back, her eyes going wide. She shook her head, and he sighed heavily.

"You have to, Katie. There's paperwork to attend to." He smiled wryly. "You're a very wealthy woman now."

"I don't want to go back."

Anger sliced through him. "For crying out loud, think of someone else for a change. My parents need to have this settled!"

He felt like a heel at the hurt that flashed through her eyes. He hadn't meant to strike out at her, but she was the only one handy. He turned his gaze back to the canyon. They stood in silence for some time, and he could feel her sympathy reaching out to him through the fog of his grief.

"Have you seen the movie *Faust*?" he asked her.

Her forehead crinkled at the odd question. She hesitated before answering. "No, but I've heard of it. Isn't it about a young man who sells his soul to the Devil in exchange for youth and earthly pleasures?"

He nodded, seeing again the emptiness of the canyon before him. Darius and Faust had much in common. Darius had indeed sold his soul when he became involved with organized crime. Although Chicago was the heart of it, he had found out Philadelphia had its fair share. And his brother had been entrenched for some time.

"When do we need to leave?"

Her question surprised him. He turned to her, lifting one brow in query. She smiled without humor.

"I'll go back and help you get things taken care of, then I'm coming back here."

"There's no need," he argued.

"There's nothing for me in Philadelphia, Clay. I'm happy here. For the first time in several years, I feel content."

He couldn't argue with her there. He had felt the peace and serenity of the desert seeping into his own soul. Still, there was the baby to think of. He reached out and traced the blue shadows under her eyes with his finger.

"Katie," he remonstrated softly, "you can't go on working like this. You're going to wind up hurting yourself or the baby."

She pulled away from his touch. "I already know that. I intend to quit."

His heart jumped in his chest. "Then you will come back with me?"

"Not to stay. I'll go for as long as it takes to get legal matters out of the way."

He pressed his lips tightly together, turning back to the changing view of the canyon. "And then what?"

"And then," she told him, "I intend to buy some land and

have a house built near here."

He wasn't surprised. "And has it ever occurred to you that my parents might like to see their grandchild?"

She turned to him in surprise, her mouth parted slightly. "That had never occurred to me. That's true. This child will be your parents' first grandchild."

"First and only," he told her bitterly.

She looked at him with sadness. "There's always you, Clay. Someday you might get enough of wandering around and want to settle down."

She had absolutely no clue. "Katie. . ."

"Dr. O'Neil! Dr. O'Neil!"

Both Katie and Clay turned at the excited voice. Cleo came running up, struggling to get breath to speak.

"I've been looking everywhere for you," she panted. "Come quickly! Albert has cut himself badly with a knife. There's blood everywhere!"

Clay started toward the hotel at a run, and Katie took Cleo by the shoulders, trying to get her to catch her breath. "Calm down, Cleo. Get your breath."

Cleo took in several deep gulps of air. "Thank the good Lord Dr. O'Neil was still here," she panted, her face whiter than Katie had ever seen it.

"How bad is it?"

"I don't know, but like I said, there's blood everywhere."

Katie sent a prayer heavenward for Albert as they hurried back to the El Tovar. He was one of the nicest men she had ever met. He reminded her much of her own father, and he treated her with the same consideration.

Cleo parted from Katie at the door of the dining hall while Katie went to find Dinah Weston and let her know she would need some time off to go to a funeral. She knew she would have to tell the manager the truth eventually, but she dreaded doing so. Her lies would leave Dinah wondering about Katie's testimony of Christianity. She had let her Lord down badly, both in her lies and in her desertion of her husband. She had allowed fear to compromise her principles. Still, she was reluctant to burn her bridges behind her. There would be time enough to straighten everything out when she returned from Philadelphia.

Dinah was sympathetic. She allowed Katie the time, asking her to return as soon as possible and telling her that she would be missed. Katie didn't miss the sparkle in the woman's eyes or the flush in her cheeks.

"Are you all right, Miss Weston?"

Dinah's mouth spread into a broad smile. "I'm getting married, Katie!"

Katie's mouth dropped open, and Dinah giggled at her surprise. It took several seconds for Katie to get over the shock.

"Congratulations!"

"I haven't told anyone else yet. I'll be quitting my job and moving back to Kansas."

Katie tried to marshal her thoughts into some sort of order. "To Mr. Peterson?" Katie had learned a few days ago the name of the gentleman with whom Dinah had been arguing.

Dinah's smile lit her face and made her almost pretty. "That's right. He. . . We used to know each other a long time ago."

Katie didn't know what to say. Dinah lifted a brow in her direction.

"I was going to suggest you apply for the position of manager here. I would have given you a good recommendation, Katie. You are such a hard worker, and it's obvious you love this place."

Katie didn't miss the past tense. The question must have registered in her eyes, because Dinah smiled and shook her head.

"I don't think you're going to be here much longer, either," she told Katie, smiling. "It's plain to see Dr. O'Neil is in love with you, and you with him."

If Katie had been stunned before, she was shocked almost senseless with that pronouncement. Surely Dinah had to be joking. Probably the woman was so happy herself, she was beginning to see romance everywhere. It couldn't possibly be true. She didn't bother to comment, asking instead, "When will you be leaving?"

"The end of August. I've given a month's notice, so I will still be here when you return from Philadelphia." She smiled slyly. "*If* you return from Philadelphia."

For a moment, Katie was tempted to blurt out the whole sordid story to the manager, but she stifled the impulse. Dinah would be leaving. There would be no need to involve her in her own problems.

"I'm really happy for you, Dinah. I hope your life will be truly blessed."

"It already has been," she responded. "I have made so many friends and seen so much of the country. It will be hard to leave here. You all seem like family."

Katie didn't miss the tears in Dinah's eyes and had to

blink away her own. She knew exactly what Dinah was talking about.

"I'll see you when I get back, then," Katie told her. "I don't know how long I will be, but it shouldn't take more than a week."

The other woman nodded, dismissing her to return to her duties.

As Katie passed the music room, she heard the Victrola spinning out one of the new songs that had become so popular. The plaintive melody of Vaughn DeLeath's "Are You Lonesome Tonight?" spoke to her, and she hesitated in the doorway.

Clay was standing at the Victrola, staring down at the spinning record. Katie froze at the sight of him. Sensing a presence, he glanced up, straightening to his full height when he noticed her. The look she saw in Clay's eyes made her heart start pounding against her ribs. Her lips parted slightly in surprise.

Could it be true what Dinah had said? Old feelings rushed over her in a wave. She had only been deluding herself all these years. It was Clay she loved. Always had. She had tried so hard to purge him from her thoughts, but he had always remained there in the back of her mind, like a lingering presence.

Knowing Clay had seen her as nothing but an adolescent with an embarrassing crush, she had allowed her father to talk her into marrying Darius, knowing at least she would always be close to Clay. How could she have been so foolish? It only proved Clay had been right. She had been nothing but an immature child. Dear heavens, what had she done?

"Katie. . ."

Clay started across the room, but Katie couldn't face him

right now. Too many thoughts were racing through her mind. She needed to find somewhere quiet where she could pour out her heart in sorrow and repentance to her Lord. Turning, she fled.

❧

Katie was staring out the window of the train at the passing scenery. Clay watched her for several minutes before taking a deep breath and asking her, "Katie, do you remember when you were twelve, and you fell through the thin ice on the pond behind our house?"

She continued to look out the window, but he could see her mouth tip into a wry smile. "I remember," she said softly.

"What do you remember?" he asked, watching her carefully.

She turned to him then, frowning at the question. "You pulled me out."

His eyes narrowed. "I couldn't have done it alone."

Her frown increased. "What are you saying?"

Clay sighed. "Think back, Katie. Tell me what you remember."

"Why?"

He quelled his rising irritation. "Just please do it."

Confusion crowded her features, but shrugging her shoulders, she told him, "You, Darius, and I went skating. You warned me not to go beyond the thin ice markers, but I saw something shiny on the ice."

She stopped, casting him a questioning glance.

"Go on," he encouraged.

Her face took on a faraway expression, and he could tell that in her mind she had gone back to that time.

"I went to see what was on the ice. You yelled at me to stop, but I didn't. I realized that what I saw was only a reflection from a thin ice spot. I turned to go back, but the ice started cracking beneath my feet. I remember the horrified look on your face."

She stopped again, smiling at the memory. Her eyes met his.

"I remember," he told her softly, a catch in his throat. "Then what happened?"

"I don't remember much after that. Things happened so fast. The water was so very cold. I know you pulled me out."

"Do you remember what happened to Darius?"

She bit her lip, thinking hard. "Yes, I remember now. Darius jumped in the water and held me up until you could get a rope to pull me out."

The expression on her face told him that drawing forth such memories was having the effect he hoped to achieve. Her features softened.

"Darius caught a bad cold and had to stay in bed for a week," he reminded her.

She shook her head slowly, a dazed look on her face. She met his eyes again. "And you were so angry with me," she stated softly.

"Of course I was angry. Both of you could have died!"

She turned away, sliding a white gloved finger slowly back and forth over the glass of the window. "Why did you bring this up now?"

"Before I answer, I want you to remember another time."

"I don't see the point," she told him, anger lacing her words.

"So humor me, okay?"

He knew her irritation was increasing by the way she was

beginning to twist her fingers in the folds of her rust-colored crepe silk dress. Her fidgeting was always a sign she was disturbed.

"Remember when your father bought you that little pug dog?"

She turned, anger changing her eyes to a cobalt blue. "Clay. . ."

"Remember when the dog got into some rat poison and became sick and died? Because he knew how sad you were, Darius brought you a stray he had found down by the railroad tracks."

She stared down at her hands. "Father wouldn't let me keep it because he said it was diseased and filthy," she said quietly.

"And Darius took it home, cleaned it up, and brought it back, convincing your father to let you keep it."

"I loved that dog," she said, a catch in her voice. Clay was afraid she was about to burst into tears. She glared at him. "Why are you doing this?"

He took a quick breath. "Because, Katie, we are about to go home to my brother's funeral. I think the only memory you have of him is that last night with him. I wanted you to remember what he was like before."

A tear slid down her cheek. "That doesn't change what he did."

"No, honey, but I wanted you to think of him the way he was before. He's dead, Katie. You need to forgive him."

She threw him an appalled look. "How can you say that?"

He reached to take her hand, but she jerked it away. "I've done a lot of thinking. You have told me for years Jesus wanted a relationship with me. You promised He would forgive my sins and take away all my pain. Didn't you?"

He pulled a slim Bible from his pocket that he had only recently purchased and opened to the book of Matthew. She watched him turning the pages until he found the verse he wanted.

" 'For if ye forgive men their trespasses, your heavenly Father will also forgive you: but if ye forgive not men their trespasses, neither will your Father forgive your trespasses.' "

The look she gave him nearly broke his heart. The steady clacking of the wheels of the train penetrated the silence that suddenly settled around them. She began digging through her purse, and he handed her his own white handkerchief.

"For your sake, Katie," he told her solemnly, "you need to forgive him. Remember he wasn't always the way he was at the end. It's what I've tried to do."

"What happened, Clay? What happened to change him so much?" she questioned huskily, the tears coming in an unending stream.

"I'm afraid he fell under the spell of alcohol and easy money. I've seen it so many times. Alcohol can make a man, or woman for that matter, do things they would never normally do." He tilted her face until he could look into her swimming eyes. "I'm not excusing it, Katie, just trying to explain it to you."

When she sucked in her bottom lip, she looked so much like a lost child that he wrapped her in his arms and held her close. The tears turned into heartbreaking sobs, and Clay closed his eyes, understanding her pain.

Now was not the time to tell her he loved her. But soon.

Chapter 7

Katie placed her palms flat against the cool windowpanes of her Philadelphia hotel room, staring down at the people scurrying to get out of the rain. With her finger, she slowly traced the path of a raindrop sliding down the glass.

How apropos that it should be raining today, the day of Darius's funeral. The dismal weather suited her mood. She tugged in her bottom lip between her teeth, trying to stem the tears that threatened again.

Clay's words kept circling round in her mind. She had to forgive to be forgiven. Darius had hurt her by his actions, but she had also hurt God by her own. Why was it that people always managed to see in others what they never saw in themselves?

Ever since Clay had started her remembering, the memories had been flooding her mind in waves. Darius had been good to her for most of the three years she had been married. He had been considerate and thoughtful, if not loving.

Less than a year ago he had started changing. She had never spoken to anyone of the times he came home drunk and would fly into a rage at the least provocation; then, taking his anger out on her, he would disappear into the night, not to return until the early hours of the morning.

Before those turbulent times, they had attended concerts together, gone on cruises, and attended soirees, among a myriad of other things. He had been a good friend, and she had naively thought she could learn to love Darius in place of his brother. It shouldn't have been so hard.

Now she knew she had only been fooling herself. It was Clay she loved. Clay's shadow had stood between them even then, but only her heart had recognized it. Perhaps if Darius had shown her any emotion, she might have been able to turn her heart toward him, but he had always kept her at a distance. Always a friend, never a lover, and she had been content to leave it that way.

One thought persistently haunted her. If she had tried harder to win Darius to the Lord rather than going her own separate way, could she have somehow prevented all of this from happening? Could she have made the first move to a more familiar relationship? She thought that question would stay with her for the rest of her life. Although he hadn't loved her as a man should love a woman, in his own way, Darius had still loved her. She could see that now.

She felt her child move within her, the soft butterfly movements still catching her by surprise. She laid a hand against her stomach, a soft smile touching her mouth. Regardless of the past with Darius, he had left her something beautiful to cherish and love. She would try to think only of that from now on.

A knock on the door interrupted her thoughts. She turned from the window, straightening her black silk Canton crepe dress. The color did nothing to improve her wan looks, but right now she didn't care.

"Come in," she called, knowing it would be Clay.

He opened the door, his black worsted wool suit making him look distinguished despite the sorrow she could see in his eyes. Katie caught her breath at the sight of him. He was so very handsome. The double-breasted jacket hugged his body like a glove, revealing more than concealing his powerfully broad shoulders. His tailored black pants ended in cuffs just above his highly polished black leather shoes.

"Are you ready?"

Katie nodded, picking up her black wool topcoat to protect her from the rain. Clay took the coat from her and held it out so she could slide her arms into the sleeves. He pressed her shoulders lightly, offering comfort that Katie gladly would have accepted. Instead, she stepped out of his reach, turning to study him more thoroughly. What was going through his mind right now? Was he thinking the same thoughts she had been? Did he think she was partly responsible for Darius's death? She had been afraid his parents would think so and had been unable to face them when they arrived.

"Are your parents upset I didn't stay with them last night?"

He smiled slightly, shaking his head. "No. I think they understand more than I realized."

Katie panicked at the thought. Seeing her look, he hastily assured her, "No, not that. I mean about the women and the drinking."

Relaxing slightly, Katie tried to smile, but it fell short of its mark. "They must be glad to have you home."

His serious blue eyes delved deeply into hers. "It's a hard time for all of us, Katie."

Her lashes fluttered down to hide what she knew would be revealed in her eyes. "I know," she whispered.

He said no more, taking her arm and leading her from the room to the waiting car outside. Clay handed her into the backseat of the new Franklin, climbing in beside her. The chauffeur gave Clay a quick glance to see they were settled, then headed out into the traffic of a city trying to avoid the torrential downpour.

"I don't remember your father having this car," Katie told him, trying to break a lengthy silence that was becoming increasingly uncomfortable.

"The Franklins are new," he told her absently, his mind obviously on something else. "Father decided to buy one because of its air-cooling system."

Silence fell between them again, remaining until they arrived in sight of the churchyard. Katie stared out at the sodden landscape in surprise.

"But where is everyone?" Katie asked in disbelief. Surely a little rain wouldn't keep people from coming to pay their respects. The O'Neils were well thought of in Philadelphia and throughout the whole Northeast.

Clay climbed from the vehicle, his lips pressed tightly together. Only two other cars were visible.

"Father thought it best to have a private ceremony."

Katie glanced at him sharply. Something was not right

here. "What aren't you telling me, Clay?"

He took her by the arm and started toward the people waiting under the awning over the grave site. "Let's leave it until later, all right?"

She really had no option, but she intended to find out what would cause her father-in-law to do something so out of character.

She studied James O'Neil as they approached and noted the tired lines on his face. He had aged in the few months she had been gone. She felt a pang of regret. She had always loved her father-in-law, though at times he could seem a tyrant.

It was obvious her mother-in-law was faring no better. Norma had always been an immaculate dresser with constant attention to the details of her appearance. Now her dress hung on her from obvious weight loss. She was oblivious to the rain that periodically blew toward her, dampening her clothes.

The only other person in attendance was Mr. McQuinn, the family lawyer. Although Katie had rarely seen the man smile, today he looked positively grim.

All three looked up as they approached. A brief smile touched Norma's mouth before she once again cast her gaze back to the coffin resting in the ground. James continued to study Katie, making her increasingly uncomfortable. Mr. McQuinn merely gave them a brief nod.

Clay took Katie by the arm and led her to the opposite side of where his parents stood. He nodded at his father and settled into respectful silence.

Moments later the minister could be seen crossing the grounds from the chapel. When he approached, Katie sighed with relief. The man was new to her, but sympathy shone out of his eyes. He looked like a man one could trust with the truths of heaven. Clay introduced him as Adam Thomas, the new minister of the church where they attended.

The service was brief but sincere. Adam reminded them all of the boy Darius had once been, highlighting the good things he had done and even mentioning some of the more humorous episodes of his childhood. Once again memories came flooding back to Katie, and a tight smile touched her lips. Darius had been a real scamp as a child. She wondered how the minister knew the things he was saying. James or Norma must have spent considerable time with the man.

The prayer the man led did not make false promises of heaven but rather asked for peace and blessings on those who remained behind. Katie grew even more impressed with the man. When the service was over, the others turned to leave, but Katie hesitated. Clay glanced at her in question. She stepped toward the flowers resting at the head of the grave and pulled a rose from one of the arrangements. She knelt by the grave and touched the rose briefly to her lips.

Closing her eyes, she lifted up a heartfelt prayer of forgiveness for Darius and asked the same for herself. When she opened her eyes, Clay was standing close by, his face creased in concern. Katie gave him a brief smile before tossing the rose into the open grave. With that flower, she symbolically threw away all the hurt and anger she had been feeling for months.

"I forgive you, Darius," she whispered.

She hadn't realized the others had stopped to watch until

she heard Norma burst into tears.

"Oh, Katie. . ." she cried before turning and burying her face in her husband's coat. James held her close, his eyes meeting Katie's. She saw him swallow hard before, nodding, he turned and moved away, still holding Norma close to his side.

Katie glanced at Clay and noticed the relief he didn't bother to hide. Something else lurked behind the sadness in his telling eyes, but Katie was too tired to try to figure out what it was. She had not slept the night before, and now her nerves and adrenaline were failing her as the pressures of the last days finally subsided.

Clay helped her to her feet, wrapped an arm around her shoulder, and started walking them toward the car. "McQuinn will be waiting at the house. Are you up to this?"

She nodded. "Let's just get this over with."

When they arrived, the others had already gathered in the parlor. Clay seated Katie on the sofa next to the fireplace, and Katie was grateful for its warmth. Her tiredness and nerves and the chill of the rain had converged to make her feel cold both inside and out. Clay seated himself next to her, his attention focused on the attorney.

"Go ahead, McQuinn."

When all was said and done, Katie sat in stunned amazement. Her father's money that had been put in trust for her was still intact, but everything else would have to be sold to pay Darius's debts. For herself, Katie didn't mind, but for her in-laws who were so proud of their family name, she knew the news had to be devastating.

Norma had to be taken from the room, so distraught was

she. James was solicitous toward her, his love evident in his desire to protect her.

Katie looked at Clay. "You knew, didn't you?"

He turned away from her, nodding his head. "There's more to it, but my father and I want neither you nor Mother involved. It's being taken care of."

Katie thought of pressing the issue, but she didn't really want to know. What they were talking about was not a part of her life. It was something Darius had chosen for himself.

"Is there anything I can do to help your parents?"

He sighed heavily. "You can tell them about the baby."

Katie was about to protest, but Clay forestalled her. "It will give them something good to think about."

She knew that was true, but she was also afraid they would try to keep her here, or maybe take the baby away from her. They had that kind of power.

Reading her look, Clay took her by the shoulders and pulled her close. Their eyes met in silent communication.

"Listen to me, Katie. No one will ever hurt you again, do you understand me? I won't let that happen. Not again."

She wasn't certain what he meant. "What are you saying, Clay?"

"I'm telling you I won't allow anyone to hurt you or the baby. I will never again allow things to be unclear between us. I'm putting my cards on the table. I love you, Katie, and I think you love me."

She frowned, and he went on. "I know this is neither the time nor the place, but I won't allow you to disappear again and not understand how I feel about you. How I have felt about you for years. It's why I always went away after being around you for even a short time. So many times I almost blurted it out, but I thought Darius really cared for you, and I couldn't hurt him."

Katie stared at him in surprise. Then it was true. She had read it in his eyes before, but she had been afraid to believe it.

"Oh, Clay." It was all she could say. So much was left unsaid, but in truth, it needed to remain unsaid. The past was the past.

"If you go to Arizona," he continued, "I will be going, too. If you stay here, I will stay, too. Whatever you decide, I want to be with you."

She opened her mouth to speak, but he placed his fingers across her lips. "No. Not now. Let's not say anything more right now. As I said, this is neither the time nor the place. Just answer me one question. Do you love me?"

She nodded, pressing her lips against his fingers in a kiss. He sucked in a breath, his eyes turning a molten blue. He replaced his fingers with his lips and allowed his kiss to tell her everything she needed to know. She reveled in the security she felt in his arms, the warmth that filled her as his kiss deepened. When he finally released her, they both were breathing hard.

"I have always loved you, Clay," she whispered. "I just never allowed myself to admit it. I was always faithful to Darius, even in my thoughts."

He kissed her again, this time taking his time about it. When he finally released her, Katie knew she would never doubt his love again.

James came back into the room, and Katie took a step away

from Clay, but he wrapped an arm tightly around her shoulders and pulled her back to his side. He set his chin firmly and turned them both to face his father.

"Father, there is something we have to tell you."

Epilogue

Katie was breathing hard, sweat beading her brow despite the cold December temperatures.

"Clay," she admonished, "you've delivered babies before."

He glared at her from a pasty white face. "Not my own!"

Katie hid her smile. The man was in a positive panic. Even so, his words touched her heart. This was *his* child. He had accepted that fact even before they were married. She loved him even more for that.

She lay in the bed of their new home, preparing to deliver a child who had decided to come into the world a few weeks early. Not far in the distance was the Grand Canyon, an easy day's car ride from where they had decided to build.

"We could call a midwife," she suggested, garnering her a black look from her husband.

"There's no time. Listen to me, sweetheart. When I tell you to push, you've got to push."

Katie felt the first stirrings of real fear. Something in Clay's voice told her all was not right.

"Clay?"

A spasm wrenched the words from her mouth, and she cried out in pain.

"Now, Katie!"

She pushed until she thought she could push no more. Finally, she could hear the wail of a baby as Clay spanked its backside.

"It's a boy," Clay cried, excitement evident in his voice. He quickly cleaned the infant and wrapped him, laying him in the cradle instead of handing him to Katie.

Sighing, she lay back against their bed.

"No, honey," Clay told her. "There's no time to rest. We've still got work to do."

Startled, she opened her mouth to speak, only to have the words choked off as another contraction seized her. So *this* was what had her husband so concerned. Twins. At another time she might have felt the amazement, but right now all she could think of was the pain lancing through her body.

Wearied already, she still managed to gather enough strength to continue pushing until she felt the final rush as her other child entered the world.

"It's a girl," Clay told her, this time his voice soft with feeling.

Katie lay back exhausted until he placed her son against her breast. She smiled at the wrinkled little face of her son while Clay tended to their daughter.

After he had their daughter clean and wrapped, he came and sat next to Katie on the bed. He noticed the tears in Katie's eyes and smiled with understanding.

Bending forward, he kissed her gently. His professional

look scanned her from head to toe. "How are you feeling?"

Katie was having a hard time keeping her eyes open. "Tired," she murmured, and he smiled.

"That's to be expected. Rest now, sweetheart. I have our babies safe."

She closed her eyes as lethargy overtook her. Sighing, she drifted off to sleep.

❧

Clay watched his wife sleeping and felt such an overwhelming surge of love that he could barely breathe. He turned to look at the infant sleeping peacefully in her arms, then he glanced down at the infant sleeping in his own arms. Two. How could he not have known?

The little tykes looked cherubic as they slept the sleep of exhaustion after birth, but he knew they would awaken soon and demand to be fed. He smiled at the thought. His life had certainly changed over the last few months and, it appeared, was about to change even more.

Katie's face, too, looked peaceful as she slept, and he thought she had never looked more beautiful.

He tugged the crocheted blanket Dinah had sent them closer to his daughter. From her letter, it appeared that Miss Weston—now Mrs. Peterson—was going to have her own bundle of joy in a few months. Katie was thrilled.

He touched his daughter's cheek with a finger. "Well, little Sarah, it's a good thing your mama had a boy's *and* a girl's name picked out."

Clay continued his watch over his family until the room began to darken from the sun's descent. He got up to light the lamp sitting by the bed. Soon they would have electricity, but for now they would have to make do with the oil lamps.

"I love you."

The quiet voice startled him. He turned to find Katie regarding him with eyes glowing with love. His heart turned over at her look. How had he managed to be so blessed?

"I didn't know you were awake," he told her softly, coming to give her a kiss.

"I love you," she repeated.

"I love you, too."

She began humming the Irving Berlin tune "Blue Skies." As she studied their sleeping son, little Adam's mouth puckered in his sleep as though he would add his own voice to the happy melody. Clay smiled, recognizing the joyful lilt in Katie's voice for what it was. Indeed, as far as he was concerned there was nothing ahead but blue skies. Time and love had healed old wounds. As Katie was so fond of saying, today was the first day of the rest of their lives.

DARLENE MINDRUP

Darlene Mindrup lives with her husband in Goodyear, Arizona. She has raised two children, a daughter, Dena, and son, Devon. Having served in the air force herself, Darlene is proud of her two children, one who has married a marine and the other who is now proudly serving in the air force. After nineteen books with Barbour, Darlene still finds her most rewarding heroines to be those who are unconventionally lacking in beauty. As she has always said, "Romance is not just for the young and beautiful." Nowadays, Darlene spends a good portion of her time being the church secretary for the West Olive Church of Christ.

A Letter to Our Readers

Dear Readers:

In order that we might better contribute to your reading enjoyment, we would appreciate your taking a few minutes to respond to the following questions. When completed, please return to the following: Fiction Editor, Barbour Publishing, Inc., P.O. Box 719, Uhrichsville, OH 44683.

1. Did you enjoy reading *Grand Canyon Brides*?
   ❑ Very much—I would like to see more books like this.
   ❑ Moderately—I would have enjoyed it more if ______________

____

____

2. What influenced your decision to purchase this book?
   (Check those that apply.)
   ❑ Cover ❑ Back cover copy ❑ Title ❑ Price
   ❑ Friends ❑ Publicity ❑ Other

3. Which story was your favorite?
   ❑ *From Famine to Feast* ❑ *The Richest Knight*
   ❑ *Armed and Dangerous* ❑ *Shelter from the Storm*

4. Please check your age range:
   ❑ Under 18 ❑ 18–24 ❑ 25–34
   ❑ 35–45 ❑ 46–55 ❑ Over 55

5. How many hours per week do you read? ______________

Name ______________________________________

Occupation __________________________________

Address ____________________________________

City__________________ State__________ Zip__________

E-mail______________________________________